Praise for Virginia Macgregor

'Undobutedly a future classic' *(Clare Mackintosh, author of* Sunday Times *Top Ten bestselling* I Let You Go*)*

'A life-affirming read... Warm, wise and insightful' *(Good Housekeeping)*

'Sharp, funny and hugely moving, this is a must read' *(Fabulous)*

'It is impossible not to fall in love with nine-year-old Milo in this touching novel' *(Stylist)*

'The characterisation and dialogue make it easy to feel empathy for the family and readers will cheer Milo on to achieve his goal' *(Sun)*

'[An] understated and likeable tale that just might restore your faith in human nature' *(Bella)*

Virginia Macgregor is the author of *What Milo Saw*, *The Return of Norah Wells*, *Before I Was Yours* and, most recently, the young adult novel *Wishbones*. Her work has been translated into over a dozen languages. After graduating from Oxford University, she worked as a teacher of English and Housemistress in three major British boarding schools. She holds an MA in Creative Writing, and was, for several years, Head of Creative Writing at Wellington College. She is married to Hugh and they live with their daughter, Tennessee Skye, in Concord, New Hampshire.

Wishbones

VIRGINIA MACGREGOR

ONE PLACE. MANY STORIES

HQ
An imprint of HarperCollinsPublishers Ltd.
1 London Bridge Street
London SE1 9GF

This paperback edition 2017
17 18 19 20 LSCC 10 9 8 7 6 5 4 3 2 1

First published in Great Britain by
HQ, an imprint of HarperCollinsPublishers Ltd. 2017

ISBN: 978-0-00-821729-7

Printed and bound in the United States of America by
LSC Communications.

For my darling Hugh and my dearest little Tennessee Skye: thank you for teaching me, each day, what it means to be truly beautiful – and truly lucky.

Hope is the thing with feathers
That perches in the soul
And sings the tune without words
And never stops at all.

Emily Dickinson

I was born seven weeks premature. An incubator baby. Tubes stuffed up my nose, eyes screwed shut, looked like a tiny wrinkly vole.

I wasn't meant to survive.

When the nurse put me into Dad's arms for the first time, he said: *She's light as a feather*. That's how I got my name.

Kids at school think it's funny, the boys especially.

Featherweight champ, they say.

Quack quack, they chant, waddling with their feet turned out.

Tweet tweet, they chirp, flapping their arms.

I was so small that doctors came up from London and peered at me through the incubator walls and journalists sneaked onto the ward to ask questions and take photos.

I wonder whether that was what made Mum hospital-phobic – the scare she got from me being so small. And then I think about her other phobias too and where they came from, like her leaving-the-house phobia and her swimming phobia and her running-out-of-food phobia.

You were the tiniest baby Willingdon had ever seen, Dad's

told me more times than I can remember, like I'd won a prize. Anyway, it's all turned out to be what Miss Pierce, my History teacher, calls *ironic*, because people say the same thing of Mum now – except the opposite: that she's *The Biggest Woman Willingdon Has Ever Seen*. People sometimes ask me if I'm adopted. I know what they're thinking: how can someone so small belong to someone who takes up as much space as Mum?

People are still really interested in Mum and her weight and the fact that she hasn't come out of the house in years. Last summer, I found Allen, a reporter from the *Newton News*, hiding behind our hedge with his camera angled at Mum's bedroom window. He said he'd give me twenty quid if I let him take a photo. I told him to get lost, obviously.

Anyway, Mum's been chubby ever since I've known her, it's just the way she is. What's more important for you to know is that she's the best mum in the world. A mum who's funny and clever and always has time to listen and doesn't obsess about stuff like homework and being tidy – or eating vegetables. And although she's a little on the large side, she's beautiful, like proper, old-fashioned movie-star beautiful: long, thick, wavy hair, a wide, dimply smile and big soulful eyes that change colour in different lights – sometimes they're blue and sometimes they're green and sometimes they're a brown so light it's like they're filled with flecks of gold.

Whenever I think about Mum and how awesome she is and how close we are, I realise that there can't be many daughters out there as lucky as me.

So Mum being overweight has never mattered to me.

As far as I'm concerned, there are a million worse things a mum can be.

That is, it never mattered until last night, New Year's Eve, when everything went wrong. Really, horribly wrong.

New Year's Eve

1

'You sure you don't want to come out?' Jake asks. 'Rock the town together?'

Jake's the only guy I know who can be cool and geeky at the same time. We've been best friends since we were a week old. My mum and Jake's mum were pregnant with us at the same time and they went to this baby group, so we were destined to be together. Mum and Steph are really close too. Or they were until this Christmas when they had a blazing row. Now, Mum doesn't want Steph coming round any more.

'Rock the town in *Willingdon*?' I ask.

Willingdon is the smallest village in England. Population 351 – blink and you'll miss it. Jake and I are the only kids here.

Jake laughs. 'Well, rock the *village* then.'

It's 11.30pm, New Year's Eve, and we're lying on Jake's bedroom floor, staring at the glow stars on his ceiling and listening to one of his Macklemore albums. Before his parents got divorced, Jake used to listen to hip-hop with his dad. He doesn't really see his dad now so I guess listening to those albums is a way for Jake to feel like they're still close.

'I've got to get back to Mum.' I get up and brush bits of popcorn off my jeans. Popcorn was the only thing that kept me going through Jake's zombie invasion film.

Jake rolls over. 'So you're letting me go out all on my own?'

'Why don't you call Amy?' I ask.

He shakes his head. Amy's meant to be Jake's girlfriend but he seems to spend more time avoiding her than actually going out with her.

At New Year, most people prefer to be in crowds: everyone pressing in, counting down, filling up their champagne flutes, music blaring. I like it quiet, just me and the person I love most in the whole world: Mum. I love Dad too, but he's so busy zooming around on emergency plumbing jobs that he doesn't have time to talk. Even on New Year's, he's out repairing people's blocked loos and leaky drains and frozen pipes. So Mum and I see the New Year in together. In those last few seconds before the clock ticks over, we hold our hands and our breaths and send wishes out to the New Year.

I love it. The magic of it. The stillness. The feeling that anything could happen.

'I'll call you,' I say to Jake.

'At 12:01,' he throws back.

That's a tradition too, my 12:01 post-New Years Eve phone call to Jake.

'12:01. I promise.' I lean over and kiss his cheek – a bit too close to his mouth, which makes us both jolt back and stare in opposite directions. 'You can tell me all about your resolutions,' I say quickly.

Jake raises his eyebrows. 'I'm not perfect already?'

'Perfect's overrated.'

He smiles.

The thing is, beside his bad taste in films, Jake's as close to perfect as it gets. Next to Mum and Dad, he's the best thing in my life.

There are loads of people out on Willingdon Green, standing on their front lawns with plastic champagne flutes looking at the sky. Behind the fireworks, droopy Christmas decorations hang from people's houses and the shops on the parade, which makes the village look tired.

When I get to our cottage, which sits bang opposite St Mary's Church, it's the same as always. Dad's Emergency Plumbing Van is missing from the drive and a blue light flickers through the lounge windows. It's been Mum's room ever since she got too large to manage the stairs. And to share a bed with Dad.

We've had to build ramps everywhere and to make all the doors bigger so that she can fit through them. Including the front door. Which is all a bit pointless because Mum hasn't left the house in thirteen years.

So, the lounge is basically Mum's world.

I've thought about ways to get her out of the house or to help her with a diet, but whenever I suggest going for a walk, she finds an excuse not to move from her armchair, which has the telly dead in front of it and the window that looks out to The Green to the right of it, so she can alternate between looking at a made-up world and a real world she's left behind.

I suppose she's happy enough. And if you love someone, you have to accept them how they are, right?

Alongside the extra-wide doors, Dad ordered Mum a supersize wheelchair. It came in a container ship from America and I sometimes take Mum for rides around the ground floor of the house in it. The wheelchair is so wide it nearly touches the walls. *Mum's* so wide she nearly touches the walls.

If Willingdon is the smallest village in the UK, then our cottage must be the smallest house in the UK. When I was five, Steph, Jake's mum, gave me this pop-up *Alice in Wonderland* book. One of the pop-ups is of Alice when she's eaten the cake and got really, really big: her legs and arms and head stick out of the doors and windows and it looks like any moment now, her house is going to burst open. I've still got that book and every time I look at it, I think of Mum and how big she is and how little our cottage is and how maybe, one day, the walls and doors and windows will fly off and there'll be nothing left but Mum sitting in her chair in the middle of Willingdon watching a re-run of *Strictly Come Dancing*.

On the way up the drive, I see Houdini, our pet goat, straining on his lead. He's come out of the kennel Dad made for him, and he's staring up at Mum's window – and he's screaming his head off.

'It's okay,' I say, patting his belly. 'The fireworks will stop soon.'

Houdini's a local celebrity: people from the village come and rub his horns for luck. The vet reckons he's about seventy years old but we can't be sure. A few years before I was born, Dad found him wandering by the motorway that runs just outside Willingdon and brought him home and he's been living in our front garden ever since.

'It's going to be the best year ever,' I whisper into Houdini's ear.

Houdini stops bleating, but he doesn't take his eyes off Mum's window.

'You want to come in?'

He bows his head like he's nodding.

'Okay, just don't chew anything.'

Houdini and Mum have one big thing in common: they're always hungry. I reckon that if Mum ran out of food, she'd start chewing flowers and inanimate objects too.

I kiss the top of Houdini's head, untie his lead from the post Dad drilled into the floor of his kennel, and take him inside.

He lets out a croaky bleat and his bell tinkles. It's a huge cow-bell Dad ordered from Switzerland to help us find Houdini when he goes missing. Which happens about once a week. We usually find him in Rev Cootes's garden or at the empty Lido in Willingdon Park.

I open the front door.

'Mum!' I call out.

No answer. Which is weird. Mum always answers. She's got one of those deep, rich voices that make people stop and listen.

'Mum!' I push Houdini into the kitchen. 'Stay there – and don't eat anything.' I close the kitchen door and go to the lounge. 'Five minutes till midnight, Mum!'

I hear a groan.

I run to the door and throw it open.

'Mum!'

And then I see her – lying on the carpet, packets of prawn cocktail crisps and Galaxy chocolate wrappers and sticky tins of pineapple strewn around her.

When I look closer, I see that her mouth is foaming and that her eyes are rolling behind their flickering lids.

You know that expression? *The bottom fell out from under me?* Well, I get it now, how, in a second, your whole life, everything you thought was safe and solid, just disappears and leaves you grasping at thin air.

I kneel down beside Mum's body, shaking.

Mum's re-run of *Strictly Come Dancing* is playing on the TV. A long-legged blonde and an old, squat, B-list celebrity are waltzing around the dance floor – they're spinning and spinning and spinning under the glare of the studio lights, their mouths stretched into those manic smiles people put on for TV.

My attention shifts back to Mum. Apart from the fact that she's massive, the woman lying in front of me doesn't look anything like Mum. She's one of those bodies the camera pans over after an invasion in Jake's zombie movies: her limbs are sticking out at weird angles and her mouth is slack and her skin pale. When I touch her brow it's sweaty but her skin feels cold.

Come on Feather, think.

I did a life-saving course at the pool, though most of the stuff was linked to pulling people out of the water.

Before I can do anything, I have to clear a whole load of *Max's Marvellous Adventures* books that have fallen around Mum. She must have been reaching for one before she collapsed. They're these old-fashioned, American stories about a boy who walks around in a red superhero outfit with a goat as his sidekick. I reckon that it's a sign – that Houdini stepped right out of one of those books and started wandering alongside the motorway outside Willingdon because he was meant to be with us. Anyway, Mum loves those stories.

I snap back into the present.

Mum's wheelchair is lying on its side.

Yanking Mum onto her back takes all the strength I've got. I have to use the weight of her body to get some leverage. I feel a thump in my chest when her back hits the carpet and I worry I've winded her.

For a second she opens her eyes.

'Mum!'

She's still there. Thank God.

She stretches out her hand. I grip it and hold it to my chest.

'You're going to be okay, Mum,' I say. 'Everything's going to be okay.'

But her eyelids drop closed again and her hand goes limp.

'Mum… please – wake up!'

Outside, the fireworks bang. It feels like explosions detonating in my skull.

I tilt Mum's head and check her airway.

This isn't happening. That's all I keep thinking. *This can't be happening.*

I put my ear to her mouth, but my blood's pounding so loud I can't hear anything.

Leaning in closer to her mouth, I wait to feel her breath against my cheek, but there's nothing.

I get out my mobile and speed dial Dad. It goes straight to answerphone.

'Dad – you have to come home. It's Mum.'

As I hang up, I realise I'm on my own. And if I don't save Mum, it'll be my fault.

I put one hand on top of the other, splay my fingers and place them on her sternum. I don't even know whether this is what I should be doing and Mum's so big I can't tell whether I've found the right place, but I have to do something.

I push my hands up and down: *one two three*… I breathe into her mouth… *one two three*…

This is hopeless.

I grab my phone again to dial 999.

And then I pause.

Mum would hate it: the ambulance pulling up outside our house, everyone from the village staring at her being carried out on a stretcher. That is, if the stretcher will even hold her.

I don't want to be gawped at, Mum says whenever I suggest we go out to the cinema or to the shops or for a walk in Willingdon Park. She won't even come to watch me in my swimming galas. I tell her it doesn't matter what people think, that she's way prettier and cleverer and funnier than any of the stupid people who make comments. But I get why she finds it hard – when you're as large as Mum, people can be mean. Really mean.

And then there's her whole hospital-phobia thing.

But she's dying. She's actually dying. Why am I even considering not calling an ambulance?

I dial.

'I have to do this Mum,' I whisper. 'I'm sorry.'

'We're going to have to call the Fire and Rescue Service,' says one of the paramedics.

I was right about the stretcher. There was no chance Mum was going to fit on it.

I look over the paramedic's shoulder. Everyone on The Green has forgotten all about New Year's Eve and the fireworks: they're huddled in clumps staring at the ambulance with its flashing lights.

'They'll have better equipment to get her out,' he adds.

I wish Dad would come home.

And I wish they'd hurry up and get Mum to hospital. The paramedic said she's stable but he won't explain why she's not waking up.

Plus, I'm angry that the 999 woman didn't listen when I told her that they'd need extra manpower, that Mum wasn't like a normal emergency patient. And because she didn't listen, only two paramedics turned up. So they had to get help from Mr Ding, the owner of the Lucky Lantern Takeaway Van, and this other guy I don't know who's recently moved into the cottage next door. And even then they couldn't lift Mum.

Dad's plumbing van hurtles along The Green. He jumps out.

'Feather!'

'It's Mum—' I start but he's already running inside.

By the time the fire engine turns up, Dad's standing next to me on the pavement with a zoned-out look. He couldn't cope with anything happening to Mum any more than I could. His hair's sticking up and I notice that his faded blue overalls are hanging off him. He's been losing weight just about as fast as Mum's been putting it on.

And the number of people standing on The Green now, staring at us, has doubled.

I know Mum's unconscious, so it's not like she's going to remember this, but I still feel bad. Really bad. Because I can see it. All of it. And I know she'd hate it:

The neighbours staring at her and cupping their hands over their mouths and whispering;

The police car plonked in the middle of the road, its blue lights flashing;

The fire engine parked right up to the front of the house with a mobile crane-like attachment sticking out the top.

After they take the lounge window out, I stand there watching, like everyone else, as a crane lifts Mum out of the cottage. Only it doesn't look like Mum. It looks like a massive unconscious woman I've never seen before, a woman trapped in a huge net that's being hauled out of our cottage like an enormous bloated, human fish.

And it's true. Dangling unconscious in that net, Mum looks more like a wounded animal, a beached whale or a bear that's been shot down, than a person. And you know what the worst bit is? As the crane lowers Mum onto the front lawn and as the firemen open the net, it's like I'm seeing her for the first time – in 3D, HD, Technicolor:

The grease stains on the front of her sweatshirt.

The smears of chocolate on her sleeves.

The sticky splodges of pineapple syrup on her tracksuit bottoms.

Her stomach hanging over the waistband where her T-shirt has rucked up.

And her messed-up hair, matted and knotty. If there's one thing Mum's proud of, it's her hair. That's why, every night, I wash it for her in a bowl of hot water I bring in from the kitchen, and, every morning, before I go to school, I make sure it's brushed. It doesn't matter that no one will ever see it – it matters to her. And anything that matters to Mum matters to me.

I feel guilty for feeling embarrassed, and for letting the firemen haul Mum out here for everyone to gawp at.

As I watch the firemen and the paramedics lever Mum into the ambulance on this inflatable stretcher thing they call an Ice Path because it's used for rescuing groups of people who get trapped in ice, or water or in mud, I realise that I've betrayed the most important person in my life.

I should have found another way to get her help.

Dad turns to me. 'What happened, Feather?'

He doesn't mean to, but the way it comes out, it sounds like it's my fault.

'I found Mum lying on the floor,' I say. 'I came back from Jake's just before midnight...'

I look at the ambulance and think of Mum in there, all alone.

'She wouldn't breathe,' I say, my voice shaky. 'They think she's had some kind of fit.'

Dad's got bags under his eyes and he's got that pale, shell-shocked look the soldiers have in the pictures Miss Pierce showed us at school.

'I should have been with her. I shouldn't have gone out.'

'Feather... come on...'

Dad puts his arm around me but I push him away.

'It's true Dad. If she hadn't tried to get up on her own...'

My hands are shaking. I wish I could turn back time, just by a few minutes, then I could have prevented this from happening.

Dad steps forward again and folds me into his arms and this time I don't fight back.

He kisses my forehead and says: 'It'll be okay, Feather.'

I nod, because I want to believe him. Only right now my world feels a zillion miles from *okay*.

Dad tells the paramedics that we'll follow in the car, which is his way of saving them from having to point out the obvious: that there's no room for us in the back of the ambulance.

As we watch the ambulance turn out of The Green, followed by the fire engine and the police car, I realise that it's already 1am. I've missed the New Year coming in.

And then I see Jake running across The Green, and I realise that I haven't kept our 12:01 promise and that makes me feel worse.

'I was worried...' Jake says. 'When you didn't call. And then you didn't answer your phone.' He looks over at the people gathered on The Green, at our open front door and at the lounge window sitting on the drive. 'What happened?'

I shake my head and then lean into his chest. He holds me and for a while, we just stay there, not saying anything.

Then Jake takes my hand and we go back into the house. When we get to the kitchen, we find Houdini standing with his front hooves up on the windowsill, his big bell clanging against his chest. He's got the same zoned-out look as Dad did earlier, which makes me think that he must have known that something was up with Mum before anyone else did. Maybe Dad's right. Maybe Houdini is a magic goat.

As the three of us stand watching the last of the fireworks petering out in the dark sky, I make the most important resolution of my life:

If Mum wakes up, I say to myself, to the sky and the stars and anything out there that might be listening, *if she lives, I'm going to look after her better. I'm going to make her well again – for good.*

January

2

I stand at the door and look at all these grown-up people sitting on tiddly chairs in the Year 4 classroom of Newton Primary.

'I'm sorry we have to be in here.' I recognise the man at the microphone. He helped the paramedics with the stretcher. He's doing up Cuckoo Cottage next door.

Taped to the wall behind him, there's a poster of a woman in a red dress with curly writing running up her body: *Slim Skills: The Key to a Whole New You.*

I've been reading up about being overweight on the NHS website and it said that joining a weight-loss group was a good first step, so I found the one closest to Willingdon and this is it: my first Slim Skills meeting.

I look around for Jake – he's meant to be here for moral support – but there's no sign of him.

'There was a booking clash with the assembly hall,' the man goes on. 'I'll make sure it's sorted for next week.' He spots me and juts out his chin. 'It's Feather, isn't it?' he asks.

Everyone turns to look at me.

There are a whole load of people from Newton that look vaguely familiar and then I notice Mr Ding, the owner of the Lucky Lantern Takeaway Van, which sits in the middle of Willingdon Green. He smiles at me and wobbles on his tiny Year 4 chair.

I'd never thought of Mr Ding as needing to lose weight. I mean, you'd be suspicious of someone in the Chinese-takeaway business being skinny, right?

A couple of places along from him sits Allen, the reporter from the *Newton News* who I found in our back garden a while back.

'Are you lost?' asks the microphone guy.

'No…' I begin.

I know what they're thinking: what's a scrawny kid doing at weight-loss meeting?

Be brave, I tell myself. *If you're going to take this resolution seriously, if you're going to have everything in place for when Mum wakes up, you have to be proactive.*

I take a breath. 'No, I'm not lost.'

A door bangs somewhere in the corridor. A few seconds later, Jake rushes in. He smells of fresh air and Amy's perfume.

'Sorry… got caught up,' Jake says, breathless.

Which means that Amy wouldn't let him go.

Jake and I go and sign the register at the back of the room and then we sit down. I can feel people looking at me and I know it's because they've heard about Mum. The day after she got taken to the hospital, there was an article in the *Newton News* with a fuzzy picture someone must have taken on their phone: it looks a polar bear under a green sheet is being stuffed into the back of the ambulance. I bet Allen took that photo.

Anyway, Jake does the paper round so he nicked all the copies he could get his hands on and we made a bonfire in the back garden.

'You bearing up?' Jake asks.

'I'm fine.' I squeeze his hand. 'Now you're here.'

The guy at the front clears his throat. 'As I was saying.' He smiles out at the room. 'I'm Mitch Banks, your Slim Skills Counsellor. And I'll be with you every step of the way.'

What if she can't take steps yet? I think.

He walks away from the microphone, grabs a pair of scales off the floor and holds them above his head.

'At the heart of every meeting is the weigh-in.' He bangs the scales. 'They're our nemesis, right?' He pauses for dramatic effect and then leans forward and eyeballs us. 'Our truth teller?'

Half of the people in the room nod. The other half look like they've been asked to take their clothes off and run around Newton naked.

'Well, these scales are about to become your best friend.'

'Mum won't fit on those in a million years,' I whisper to Jake. Even if she did manage to get both feet on the standing bit, the digital numbers would go berserk. Mum's in a whole other league.

'We'll work it out,' Jake says.

That's another reason I love Jake: he's fixes stuff.

Mitch goes on. 'So we start from where we are.' He thumps the scales with his left hand. The numbers flash. 'We'll make a note of our weight in our personal journals. Charting our progress is a key part of the Slim Skills method.'

I've already made a weight chart: it's on my bedroom wall. I'm aiming for Mum to lose twenty pounds a month. The point isn't to get her all gaunt looking – I still want her to look like Mum. I just have to make sure she gets better. Once she wakes up, that is. Which she will.

The room's so silent you can hear the Year 4 chairs creaking under all those grown-up bums.

'So, who's going first?' Mitch scans the room.

Everyone stares at their feet, like we do at school when we don't want to answer a question. I'm no expert but this guy doesn't seem to be going about things quite the right way. I mean, if it took guts for me to come here, and I'm not here for me, think about how all the overweight people are feeling.

'I'll go,' Mr Ding says, which I think is really brave.

'I hope this doesn't mean he'll stop making those amazing spring rolls,' Jake whispers.

People come all the way from Newton for Mr Ding's spring rolls. Dad gets them for us as a treat when he's had a long day and is too busy to cook.

Mitch stands up and walks to the front and, one by one, Mr Ding and the other people from Newton heave themselves out of their Year 4 chairs and go and queue for their weigh-in.

'So, what are your names?' Mitch Banks stands over me and Jake, holding up a Sharpie and a white sticker.

'Feather,' I say, 'Feather Grace Tucker.'

Mitch writes FEATHER in big capitals. 'That's a nice name.'

I shrug.

He turns to Jake.

'And you?'

'Jake.'

Mitch hands us our name stickers.

'So, why are you here?'

'You know why I'm here,' I say.

'I do?'

'You helped Mum – on New Year's.' My cheeks are burning up.

'Oh… yes.'

'You live next door to us.'

'Right.' He scrunches up his brow. 'Forgive me, but I still don't understand.'

'We need to get help for Feather's mum,' Jake says. 'We thought you could help.'

'She's in a diabetic coma,' I add.

It's better to say things straight, that's what Mum's taught me. What she means is – it's better *not* to be like Dad. Dad thinks that dodging things or joking about them will make them go away. Like Mum being overweight – and look how that worked out.

'Oh… I'm sorry,' Mitch says.

'That's why she went to the hospital. She had a fit. But it's okay, she's going to wake up,' I add. 'Isn't she, Jake?'

Jake nods. 'Of course she is. Mrs Tucker is the toughest woman I know.'

Mum and Jake get on really well. She sees him as the son she never had.

'I'm glad to hear it.' Mitch scratches his forehead. I guess his Slim Skills manual didn't prepare him for this kind of situation.

'And when she does, I'm going to help her lose weight. That's why I'm here,' I say.

'That's a kind thing to do, Feather,' Mitch says. I can hear the *but* sitting on his lips. 'A *very* kind thing indeed.' He smiles. 'Do you think she might need a bit more help… I mean, medical help?'

'You get people to lose weight, right?' Jake blurts out.

Jake feels just as strongly as I do about Mum getting better.

'We help people help themselves, but Feather's mum...' Mitch says.

'You're discriminating against Mum because she's *too* big?' I ask.

'No... not at all...'

'She hates doctors and hospitals. When she wakes up, she's going to freak out,' I say.

He nods. 'Well, maybe, once she's back home and feeling stronger, you could come with her and then we can have a chat.'

'She won't be able to do that. Not at first, anyway.'

'She won't?'

'Mum doesn't leave the house.'

'Oh—'

'I thought I could learn stuff and tell her about it. And that maybe it would help her to know that other people are struggling too.' I take a breath. 'I'm coming here on her behalf. And Jake's my best friend, so he's going to help me.'

My plan was to pick out a few people who Mum might like and then invite them over to the cottage to show her that there are people who understand how she feels and can help her as she tries to get to a healthier weight.

Besides me and Dad and Jake and Jake's mum, Mum hasn't had a visitor in thirteen years. But if I'm going to keep to my resolution of helping her get well again, that's going to have to change.

Mitch lets out a sigh and sits on one of the low tables next to the little chairs.

'Even if Slim Skills can help your mother... she's going to have to do this for herself.'

Mum can't do anything for herself. She can't get out of her chair or put on her clothes or clean her face or walk. Dad and I work on a rota to make sure she has everything she needs. Which was what led to her not being able to get any help the other night when she collapsed on the carpet. No, Mum needs someone to help her take the first steps.

'The philosophy of the Slim Skills programme states that a person has to want to get better.' Mitch smiles like he's on a TV ad.

I brush my fringe out of my eyes. I'm beginning to feel that coming here was a mistake. Mitch doesn't understand. But it's okay – Jake and me have got a whole list of other things to try.

'I think we'll go,' I say.

'Feather…' Jake starts. 'We're here now, let's see how it goes…'

'It's not working!' I snap.

Mitch stands up and says, 'Feather—'

'If you can't help Mum, I'll find someone else. Someone who understands.'

'I do understand, Feather. I was just trying to make clear that it's your mother's journey—'

'She's not on a journey. She's in hospital, in a coma – and it's our job to help her.'

Mitch definitely doesn't get it. He's probably just doing this because he can't get a proper job. What kind of guy runs a weight-loss group anyway?

I peel off my name sticker, hand it to him and head out of the door. Jake runs after me.

'Hey, what happened in there?' he asks.

I keep walking down the corridor.

'We'll try something else…' I say.

'I think you should give Mitch a chance.'

I ignore Jake. It's one of the ways we're different: when things aren't going well, he thinks it's worth waiting things out, whereas I just cut loose. Take Amy, for example: I think he should have dumped her ages ago.

As we walk past the assembly hall, I stop and stare at a poster by the swing doors:

THE WILLINGDON WALTZ, SUNDAY 1ST OF JUNE.

June 1 is Willingdon Day and the waltz competition is like the icing on the cake. Willingdon Day isn't that big any more but everyone still looks forward to it. It's my birthday too.

'Hey, it's Mrs Zas,' Jake says. 'Cool.'

Everyone calls her Mrs Zas because her real name is too long for anyone to remember. She's only been in the village for a couple of months. She set up Bewitched, the fancy dress shop next to the church. Apparently, when I was too small to remember, there was this amazing dance teacher who more or less taught the whole village to dance, only she got ill and so had to stop working. There weren't any dance classes for years and years and then Mrs Zas stepped in. People in the village are still adjusting. Willingdon is kind of old-fashioned and Mrs Zas goes around in these loud wooden clogs and brightly coloured headscarves – and she's always in costume, which is a good form of publicity for her shop, but still a bit out there. Today, she's got a black-and-red dress on with a million frilly bits and she has castanets tied to her wrists and she's darting around the dance floor, straightening people's backs and arms and giving them instructions in her gravelly Russian voice.

'You must flow… *floooow*…' Jake imitates her, sweeping his arms through the air like he's painting on a gigantic canvas.

We watch Mrs Zas clip-clopping around in her clogs.

Dad said the Willingdon Waltz used to be so big that, one year, the BBC came to film it for a documentary. *You were too young to remember*, Dad said. It's not really fair how all the good things seem to have happened when I was *too young to remember*.

'Maybe your mum will come out and watch this year…' Jake says. 'If she's feeling better.'

'Maybe…'

Mum loves watching *Strictly* so much, you'd think she'd be really keen to see the Willingdon Waltz, especially as she's got the best view of the Green from the lounge window. But it's like she's got a thing against Willingdon Day as a whole. Every year, when it comes round, she gets antsy and tells me to draw the curtains and to turn up the TV and, once we've had some birthday cake and I've opened my presents, she goes to bed early.

I take the flier and put it into the back pocket of my jeans.

'Let's get out of here,' I say.

3

They put Mum in a single room and pressed two beds together so she'd fit. Dad's asleep in the seat next to her, wrapped up in one of those white, holey hospital blankets. While I've been staying at Jake's, Dad hasn't left Mum's side, which is a good thing. If Mum's going to get better she needs to see how much Dad loves her. And how we couldn't live without her.

'She looks so peaceful,' Jake whispers.

Steph dropped us off. She's waiting in the car park. I told her to come in, that after everything that's happened Mum will have forgotten all about the row they had at Christmas, but Steph said it was best not to crowd Mum.

I'm glad I've got Jake with me at least.

As I look at Mum's sleeping face, I imagine what it must be like to lie there, my heart beating, my blood pumping, my brain sending its Morse code messages from synapse to unconscious synapse, and yet to be unconscious – being there and not there. Being both at once.

Jake's right. She does look peaceful. Though, with her hospital-phobia thing, she's going to be anything but peaceful when she wakes up.

'I wish someone would tell me what's going on,' I say.

I asked the doctor to explain and he said I should ask Dad and Dad said that it was complicated, which basically means he thinks I'm too young to handle it. If Mum weren't in a coma, she would have stood up for me. She says I'm more mature than most of the grown-ups she's met.

So, I grab the clipboard at the end of Mum's bed and flip through the notes.

'Feather...' Jake starts. 'I don't think that's a good idea.'

'If I'm going to help Mum, I've got to have the facts.'

I scan down the page. It's mostly random scribbles from the doctors and nurses who've been doing her obs, notes on medication and blood pressure and temperature and stuff. And then I see it.

Weight: 37st 2lb.

'What is it?' Jake leans in.

I drop the clipboard. It clatters to the floor.

Dad stirs in his sleep.

Jake picks up the chart and puts it back in its holder.

'Feather?'

'We've never weighed Mum,' I say to him. 'I mean, I knew she was big, but thirty-seven stone? Can anyone even get that heavy?'

No wonder she got sick.

I look at Mum. It's like she's floated away in that big body of hers and I worry that maybe she won't ever find her way back to me.

I go over and kiss her cheek and feel relieved: it's warm and soft and alive.

'We're going to get you better, Mum, I promise,' I whisper by her ear.

And then I put my arms around Mum's body and give her

a hug, because that's what she always does to me when I'm feeling tired or sad or ill. Mum's hugs are the best: her arms are so big they fold you up and make you feel like you're in the safest place in the world. I've often thought how rubbish it would be to have to hug one of those bony, skinny mums I see sitting in their cars outside Newton Academy.

'Here,' says Jake, handing me the photo frame we picked up from home.

It's basically the only photograph in the whole house. Mum hates photos just about as much as she hates water and hospitals and running out of food. She says that we should remember the past in our heads and in our hearts, rather than being frozen into bits of shiny paper or screens. She doesn't seem to mind this one though. It's of me sitting in the middle of The Green, hugging Houdini. I'm about ten and I'm wearing a pair of faded dungarees and I've got loads of freckles and Pippi Longstocking plaits and I'm grinning from ear to ear.

It was Jake's idea to bring it. He said that even though Mum was unconscious and even though her eyes are screwed shut and her brain's far away, it's important to surround her with things she loves.

As I place the photograph on the bedside table, I hope that maybe in middle of the night, when none of us are here to notice, her eyelids will flicker open and, if they do, she'll see my grinning, freckled face looking back at her and it might help her remember I'm here and that I want her to come back to me.

Before Jake and I leave the room, I take Mum's brush and run it through her hair. I'm relieved to see that the nurses washed it. Like Mum's eyes, Mum's hair is beautiful. It's a goldy-blonde and smooth and shiny and, when she lets it down, it goes all the way down her back. In all the time I've known her, Mum hasn't had a single haircut. When I was little, it made me think of Rapunzel and I got this picture of Mum hanging her hair out of the lounge window and Dad dressed up as a prince scaling the side of the house to save her.

My hair's like Dad's: brown and straggly.

For a few minutes I get lost in brushing Mum's hair. I think of all the times I've brushed it back home, mostly late at night, before I go to sleep, while I tell her about my day. One of the good things about having a mum who doesn't ever leave the house and doesn't have a job or anything to do except watch re-runs of *Strictly* is that she always has time to listen.

'I love you, Mum,' I whisper, and put the brush down.

'We'd better go,' says Jake, 'Mum's waiting.'

I nod. Though, if I could choose I would curl up next to Mum on the bed and stay with her until she wakes up. I want to be the first person she sees when she opens her eyes.

As Jake holds open the door for me, I hear a couple of nurses chatting in the corridor. We saw them on our way in, an old one with a square jaw and a young one with a sharp black bob. They were sitting at the nurses' station drinking their tea and filling in their charts and listening to slushy stuff on the radio. I should lend them Jake's Macklemore albums.

'Done her meds?' the old one says.

A rustle of paper.

'Yeah. Crazy doses,' the young one says.

Ever since Mum got to be the size she is now, she's had to take triple-strength medicines: her body's so big and it's got so much blood in it that she has to overdose on paracetamols just to make a dent in her headaches.

'Ever seen one this big?' the young nurse says.

I hear Jake gasp beside me.

Blood rushes to my cheeks. Nurses shouldn't be allowed to talk about patients like that. *No one* should be allowed to talk about *anyone* like that.

'Come on, Feather, let's go.' Jake takes my arm.

I shake him off and yank open the door. I'm standing in the middle of the corridor now. The nurses don't notice that I'm staring right at them and that I can hear every word they're saying.

'How long do you reckon she has?' the younger nurse adds. 'I mean, when she wakes up?'

My body freezes.

'Feather...' Jake says.

'Shhh!'

'Six months – if she's lucky,' the older nurse says. 'I mean, at that size, any number of things could get her.'

'Don't listen to them, Feather. They don't know what they're talking about.'

'They're nurses, Jake,' I hiss. 'They know *exactly* what they're talking about.'

I charge to the nurses' station and stand in front of them, my hands on my hips. Jake hangs back.

'What did you say?' I look from one nurse to the other.

'Oh!' The younger nurse steps back like I've trodden on her toes.

The older nurse shoots her a glance. Then she turns to me. 'Nothing, my dear.'

'It didn't sound like nothing.'

'Sorry we disturbed you,' the older nurse says.

'You didn't disturb me. You were saying, about Mum—'

'Feather, let's go,' I hear Jake say from behind me.

'I'm not going anywhere,' I say. 'I want you to explain why you said those things about Mum.'

'It's okay, dear,' the older nurse says, smiling one of those fake, *there, there, dear* smiles. I'm beginning to realise why Mum hates hospitals so much.

'No. It's not okay. You said...'

The older nurse looks down at me. 'You look tired, dear.'

'I'm not tired. I want to know about Mum not making it.'

The young nurse goes red.

The older nurse puts her hand on my arm.

Jake's standing beside me now.

'Maybe you should talk to your dad.'

And then a call bell buzzes from one of the other rooms and the older nurse says, 'Excuse me', and then the younger one says, 'Sorry' and walks back to the nurses' station and I'm left standing there.

I feel Jake taking my hand. 'Come on, Feather, let's get out of here. Like they said, you can talk to your dad. We'll come back tomorrow morning.'

But I don't need to talk to Dad. I know what they meant: that it's lose–lose. That even if Mum wakes up from her coma, she's going to die anyway. And that, if we don't do anything about it, and fast, she'll be gone in six months.

4

After swim practice, I go to the Willingdon Mobile Library to use the internet. The day after Mum went into hospital, I ripped the Wi-Fi router out of the wall in the lounge and hid her laptop in the garage. Stopping her from being able to do online food deliveries is the first stage of my get-Mum-well plan.

I scan through the NHS website looking for articles on gastric bands. I'm worried Mum's got too big for them to even be an option. Apparently the NHS pays for dangerously overweight patients to have bands fitted around their stomachs so they feel full and stop eating as much. Only Mum's never wanted to see a doctor about her weight so we didn't even get that choice and now I'm worried it's too late.

My phone buzzes. It's one of those cheap ones that only calls and texts.

'Mum's woken up.' Dad's voice is all choked up.

Steph's at work and Jake's with Amy, so I get the first bus to Newton Hospital. I run into Mum's room and throw my arms around her and hold her so tight she gasps.

'Steady on, Feather, or you'll send me into another

coma…' She gives me a tired laugh. I can tell she's trying to hold it in, how freaked out she is by being in hospital.

Dad sits on the other side of the bed, grinning.

'We missed you, Josie,' he says.

Mum's eyes dart around the room. The drips. The white walls. The heater hissing under the window. I can feel her nerves fizzing.

'It's okay, Mum,' I say and lean over and kiss her cheek.

Mum's eyes focus on me and she seems to calm down a bit. 'It's good to see you, My Little Feather.'

Dad and I spend ages sitting on Mum's bed holding her hands and stroking her hair and giving her hugs. I know Dad's thinking the same as me: that this time we're going to be more careful; that we're going to grasp onto her so tight that she never slips away again.

'What was it like?' I ask. 'Being in a coma?'

Mum smiles. 'I don't really remember much, Feather. But it felt quite nice actually – floating around in this nowhere, no-time place.'

I guess that for someone as big as Mum, feeling floaty must be quite cool.

'I heard you calling me, Feather,' she adds. 'And when I woke up, I saw your photo.' She shifts her head to the picture of me on her bedside table.

'So you're glad you're back?' I ask.

'I'll be glad when I'm home.' Mum yawns. 'I'm really tired.'

I want to make a comment about the fact that she's been sleeping for days but maybe sleeping isn't the same as being in a coma.

'Come on, let's leave Mum to have a rest,' Dad says.

I give Mum a kiss, jump off the bed and then Dad and

I head to the hospital canteen for a hot chocolate and a sandwich.

'We've got to make some changes,' I say to Dad.

He rubs his eyes. 'Let's take a day at a time, Feather.'

I shake my head. 'We can't afford to take a day at a time. Mum's really sick.'

Dad pokes at a bit of gherkin in his sandwich and then puts it down. He hasn't eaten properly in months.

'I know that,' he says.

I take a breath.

'It was our fault, Dad.'

He doesn't answer.

'Dad?'

He pushes his sandwich back into its packet and scrunches it up.

'Let's not talk about this now, Feather.'

'You can't bury your head in the sand about this, Dad.'

It's the first time I've been this blunt with him but I have to keep going, otherwise I'll lose my nerve.

'It's our fault that Mum got sick.'

He goes quiet again.

'Did you think we were helping her, Dad? Making her fry-ups, letting her guzzle tins of pineapple syrup, bulk-buying Galaxy bars and crisps…?'

'It's not just about food, Feather.'

'Of course it's about food, Dad. Haven't you noticed how much she eats? That's why she's got so big. That's why she's sick.'

Dad stands up. 'Come on, Feather, let's go home and get things ready for Mum.'

I grab his arm and yank him back down into his chair. 'No, Dad, you have to listen—'

He sits down slowly.

'Everything we do for your mum is because we love her.'

'Love her?' I clench my jaw. 'Feeding Mum rubbish wasn't kind or generous – or *loving*: it made her sick.'

From the way people are looking over at us, I realise I've been shouting. But I don't care. All that matters is Mum. We've got six months and I'm not going to waste a minute of it.

Dad hangs his head and looks into his calloused palms. After a long silence he says:

'I understand what you're saying, Feather. And I know you mean well...'

'It's not about meaning well, Dad—'

Dad looks up, leans forward and puts his hands over mine. He's done this since I was little: wrapped my little fists in his big palms. Usually, it's the best feeling in the world – like nothing can ever be wrong with the world when Dad's holding me. But it doesn't feel like that today.

'This is something even you can't fix, Feather.'

I take a breath and say:

'We made her ill, Dad. And now it's our job to make her better.'

Dad pulls his hands away from mine.

I grab his hands again, pull them towards me and squeeze them tight. 'I can't do this on my own, Dad. You have to help me.'

He doesn't answer.

'Dad?'

Dad stares blankly at my hands, gripping his. Very slowly, he nods. But I'm not sure it's gone in. Not properly.

5

I settle Mum into her armchair. And that's when she notices.

'Where's the TV?'

If the lounge is Mum's world, the TV is her sun. A fifty-inch, flat-screen, HD, surround-sound sun which Dad got Mum for her fortieth birthday two years ago.

Steph and Jake helped me carry the TV to the garage. Jake said he'd put it on eBay, which will help my get-Mum-healthy fund.

I kiss the top of Mum's head. 'We thought you could have a break from it.'

Mum stares into the space where the TV used to be.

I feel kind of bad. Mum's been looking forward to coming home and I know part of what she's looked forward to is going back to the things that have filled her days up to now, which are basically food and TV. And me.

'We'll find other things to do, Mum.'

Mum closes her eyes. She looks knackered. The trip back from the hospital took ages and the nurse with the square jaw made Mum walk from her hospital bed to the ambulance – because she wouldn't fit on the front bench of Dad's van. Anyway, it's the furthest Mum's walked in years.

Plus, she hadn't been eating much in hospital because the doctor's put her on a diet, so she's feeling a bit wobbly. But it's a good thing because it means she's lost weight. I saw on the notes in her medical chart that she'd lost one stone. Now I need to make sure the weight keeps going down.

Mum coughs. And then she stares up at the wall.

'And what happened to our router? And where's my laptop?'

'You shouldn't have to worry about doing the shopping. Dad and I are going to do it from now on.'

She looks at me and blinks and then goes back to scanning the room for all the changes.

'And why's Dad's bed in my room?'

I thought that if it was just a matter of not having space for both of them in Mum's bed, then we could bring Dad's bed down too. They could be together again, like old times.

Mum keeps scanning the room – frowning. She looks at the two beds pressed up against each other and her wheelchair and her armchair and her medical equipment.

'There's no room to swing a cat in here,' Mum says.

Steph warned me that the beds might be taking it a bit far but I told her it would be fine, that Mum would get used to it.

As we pushed Mum's wheelchair out of Newton Hospital, the young nurse (the one who said Mum was going to die) ran after us and gave Mum a pile of leaflets on how to get healthy. Mum dumped them in the car park bin muttering:

'Waste of trees.'

I wish she hadn't done that. But I agree with her to this extent: it's going to take more than a bunch of leaflets to stop her eating so much. It's going to take someone who loves her and won't give up on her, even when things get really hard. In other words, it's going to take me. And getting rid of the TV and putting Dad's bed in the lounge is the first step.

'Where's my bed?' Dad calls down from the landing.

I go out to the hallway and look up at him. He's got bags under his eyes that make him look one of those droopy-faced dogs.

'I thought it would be nice for you guys to be together. After everything.'

It took Steph, Jake and me ages to get the bed down, but it'll be worth it. When I drew up a timeline of when things started getting really bad with Mum, I worked out that Mum coming to live in the lounge downstairs four years ago made both of them go sad. I mean, Dad still does everything for Mum and you can tell that he totally adores her, but that's not the same as being happy or loving each other romantically. I thought that maybe if I could bring them closer again, then Mum would get better faster.

'This isn't your business, Feather,' Dad shouts down the stairs.

'It's completely my business!' I yell back.

It's the second time in twenty-four hours that I've shouted at Dad. But then Dad never shouts at me either. I guess we're both a bit stressed out.

I keep going:

'You're my parents. And Mum nearly died. I had to do something.'

It feels weird, standing there in the hall between Mum, sitting in her chair in the lounge, and Dad upstairs.

'There's no room in the lounge,' Dad says.

'There's plenty of room,' I lie.

Because Mum and Dad being squished up together in the lounge is the plan. It's what will make them close again.

This is how I see it:

Mum + Dad happy together = Mum happy.

Mum happy = Mum motivated to get healthy.

Mum motivated to get healthy = Mum stays alive.

We hear the creaking sound Mum makes when she heaves her legs up onto the footrest that goes with the armchair. Dad got the chair and footrest for her at the same time as the TV. Officially, it's a love seat, which means it's meant to hold two people, but Mum hardly fits all by herself. It's the ugliest chair you've ever seen. Think of a gigantic, padded purple cabbage – with a slightly smaller padded purple cabbage for your feet.

My phone goes and I slip into the kitchen. It's Steph.

'How's it all going?' she asks. 'How's Jo taking the changes?'

Like I said earlier, Mum and Steph had a barney at Christmas and since then Mum's been ignoring her. They won't tell me what it's about. Mum + Steph being friends is another plan I need to put into action if I'm going to get Mum happy again and motivated to lose weight.

'Not well,' I say.

I hear Dad close the door to his room upstairs.

'And I think we should have told Dad. About the bed.' I sigh. 'I wish you and Jake were here. I'm not sure I can cope with being in the house alone with Mum and Dad.'

There's a pause. Which makes me feel guilty because I know that it's probably Mum's fault that she and Steph fell out and that Steph's really cut up about it and that she's still been doing all this stuff to help Mum. Plus, Steph is divorced so she doesn't even have the option of sharing a room with her husband.

'I'll be fine,' I say to Steph. 'I'll be fine.'

'I'll send Jake over when he gets back.'

'He's with Amy?'

'Yeah.'

Jake's basically had a girlfriend since we were in nursery. He's one of those guys that girls fancy: floppy, sandy hair that he has to keep flicking out of his blue eyes; dimples; a big smile. And for some reason, he seems to go along with it, picking up a new girl as soon as an old girlfriend gets bored or angry because he doesn't give her more attention.

None of those girls looked right with Jake. You know how, when you see a couple that are meant to be together, their edges go blurry and they kind of meld together and become more like one person than two? Well, Jake's never had the blurry-edged thing: he and his girlfriends always looked like two people.

Steph once told me: *Jake needs to have a girl around…* And when I asked her, *What about me, aren't I a girl?* Steph had laughed and given me a hug and said, *You're different, Feather.* Which made me feel kind of hurt and happy at the same time.

Anyway, Steph and I are on the same page about Amy. I think she secretly hopes Jake and me will get together and get married and have loads of grandchildren she can coo over, which is kind of embarrassing but it's nice to know that she'd want me as part of her family.

'Hope everything works out,' Steph says.

'Thanks, Steph.'

I go back out into the hall. It's really quiet. I imagine

Dad sitting in the middle of his bedroom floor in the place where the bed used to be.

'Dinner's in half an hour,' I call out to them both.

I borrowed *Cook. Eat. Live.* from the mobile library and Steph took me shopping for ingredients. I'm going to make Mum the best salad in the world.

As I go back into the kitchen and pull out the chopping board and get the vegetables out of the fridge, I tell myself: *It's going to be okay. It's all going to be okay.* And I say it over and over until it begins to sound a bit true.

6

'Mum?' I knock on the lounge door.

She's lying in bed, staring at a damp patch on the ceiling that Dad's been going on about fixing for years. Dad must have helped her out of her armchair.

When she sees me, she smiles, which makes me think that maybe she's forgiven me for taking out the TV.

'It's good to have you home, Mum.'

'Why don't you put that down and come and have a chat.' Mum smiles and pats her armrest.

Our chats are the best things in my day. *You two could natter for England*, Dad says. And it's true. There's nothing we don't talk about. But right now, getting Mum healthy is more important.

I carry over the tray with the massive salad I've made: a big pile of lettuce and peppers and cucumber.

'That plate's so green it's giving me a headache,' Mum says.

'You'll love it, Mum. It's called The Green Goddess Salad.'

'Quite a grand name for a few salad leaves, don't you think?' Mum stares at the plate and then she shakes her head. 'I'm sorry, lovely, I'm not hungry.'

Mum's always hungry.

I put the tray on her bedside table and then notice a scrunched-up packet of prawn cocktail crisps on the floor. I dig my nails into my palms. I did a sweep of the whole house. Dad must have given it to her.

'I read on the internet that it takes twenty-eight days to break a habit,' I say as I pick up the crisp packets and put them in the bin. 'Twenty-eight days is not even a month. You can do it, Mum.'

I've put targets on the six-month timeline in my room. Those nurses said that if Mum doesn't get to a healthier weight, she'll die in six months – well, I'm going to make sure that, by the end of every month, she's lost a whole load of weight.

'Twenty-eight days to do what, my love?' Mum asks.

Mum's slouched right down in her bed so I grab her elbow, help her to sit up and wedge a pillow in her back.

I perch beside her on the edge of the bed.

'To get you well again,' I say.

Mum leans forward and brushes my fringe out of my eyes.

'I am well, my love. I've got you, and Dad; that's all the good health I need.'

I shake off Mum's hand and tuck a napkin into her sweatshirt.

'You need to get your body healthy, Mum.'

Mum grabs at her napkin and throws it onto the bed sheets.

'What I *need*, is the TV back.'

I stand up. Mum never talks to me like that.

'We could do fun things instead,' I say. 'We could go on walks. Little ones at first…'

'You know I don't like walking.'

By that, Mum means she doesn't like walking outside, where there are people.

Mum stretches her arm out. I let her take my hand. 'Why do we need to go out, Feather?' She glances at the slit in the curtains, which is just wide enough to let her see out and just small enough to make sure no one can look in, not unless they're standing right under it. 'We've got everything we need right here,' Mum adds.

I take my hand out of Mum's and lift the tray onto her lap.

'I just thought that a few changes might do you some good.' I pick up the fork and the plate. 'The salad's organic. It's full of good vitamins and nutrients. The book says...'

'The book?'

'*Cook. Eat. Live*. I borrowed it from the library. It's not about dieting, it's about eating food that's good for you, that makes you healthy and happy.' I pause. 'I've told Dad I'm doing the cooking from now on.'

Dad has always done the cooking. It's Tucker legend that when Mum first tasted Dad's roast chicken, she decided he was the man she was going to marry.

Mum smiles. 'You can't boil an egg, love.'

'Well, I'm going to learn. And I've already made a start – with this salad.' I spear a bit of lettuce onto the fork.

Beads of sweat have gathered along Mum's hairline. Her body's like an old heater – either stone cold or scalding hot and nothing in between.

I hold the fork closer to Mum's mouth, which makes me think about the stories Mum told me about when I was little and hated eating. I'd throw things off the side of the high chair and laugh.

Mum pushes the salad away. 'I'm groggy from the hospital, Feather. I'm sure my appetite will come back later.'

I hold the fork closer to Mum's mouth. 'I'm not going until you've had a bite.'

'Please, Feather, I just need a bit of a rest.'

When I was little, I didn't see Mum locking herself indoors as unusual. Staying inside was just what Mum did. And then, when I got older and kids at school made comments, I always defended Mum. I said that it was Mum's choice and that it was just as good a choice as going out and that, anyway, she was perfectly happy and busy doing things inside.

But over the years, she started eating more and more. And she got bigger. Much bigger. By the time I was in secondary school, Mum couldn't fit through the front door any more and she'd stopped going upstairs to sleep: her legs were too weak to carry her body. And then she stopped walking altogether.

The funny thing is that Dad and me just went with it. To us, Mum was Mum: funny and kind and always there for us and beautiful too, with her long hair and her soft skin and her big, sparkly eyes. It's only now, after Mum nearly died, that I realise that she wasn't okay at all, and that she must have known it, and if she knew it, I want to know why she let herself get so sick.

'You won't be all right,' I say. 'Not if you don't get to a healthy weight.'

'I lost two stone while I was in hospital.' Mum pats her belly and smiles. 'It's a start, Feather.'

I smile back at Mum because I don't want to rain on her parade, but two stone is a drop in the ocean when you're Mum's size.

'Nurse Heidi's coming to weigh you tomorrow,' I say. 'So you've got to keep making an effort.'

Nurse Heidi is the community nurse. She works with the GP in Newton and she popped in earlier when I was sorting out the house with Steph and Jake.

'I don't need to be weighed,' Mum says.

'Losing weight at home is going to be harder than losing weight in hospital, Mum. Mitch said it has to be your journey.'

'Who's Mitch?'

I feel my cheeks flushing. 'He lives next door. He helped—' I stop. Mum doesn't know about what happened on New Year's Eve. 'He runs this club.'

'What club?'

'A support group for people who want to get healthy.'

Mum's smile drops.

I know Mum would find it hard to sit with a bunch of strangers talking about being overweight. I mean, she won't even talk to *me* about being overweight.

'Why don't I get Dad and we could all eat the salad together.'

'Your dad needs to eat more than a salad. He's fading away.'

Mum looks out through the slit in the curtains again. Dad's giving Houdini his tea. I take advantage of her being distracted by lifting the fork back to her lips.

She snaps her head back and knocks the fork out of my hand. A piece of lettuce catapults over Mum's duvet and lands on the floor.

My eyes sting.

'Darling.' Mum touches my hand. 'I know you mean well...'

I pull my hand away. She doesn't get it, how serious her condition is.

'It'll all be fine,' Mum says. 'I'm fine.'

'You're not fine. You're sick. Really sick. And if you don't get healthy…' I gulp.

They haven't told her. Just like they tried to keep it from me. That if she doesn't do something to get to a healthy weight, she's going to die.

I take a breath. 'If you don't make an effort, you'll have to go back to hospital, Mum.'

I know it's mean to say that, with her hating hospitals, but she has to understand how serious this is.

I put the plate of salad back on the tray and walk to the door.

'Feather…'

I look back at her.

'You have to try.' My voice trembles. 'We need you – I do and so does Dad and Steph and all the friends you haven't seen in years. We all want you to be well again.' I pause. 'It's not fair, Mum.'

It's the first time I feel like one of those teenage girls who yell at their mums. It's never been like that between us. We're friends, best friends. We understand each other. But it's not fair, is it? To keep eating crisps, to pretend everything's going to be okay.

I have to get through to her: if she doesn't make changes right now, I'm going to lose the person I love more than anyone in the whole world.

I slam the door and walk out.

7

I find Dad outside scraping some earth out of one of Houdini's hooves. Sometimes I think he loves Houdini more than he loves anyone, including me and Mum.

'Here, Houdini may as well have this,' I say, handing him the plate of salad I made for Mum.

Dad lets go of Houdini's leg and Houdini hoovers up the lettuce and the bits of tomato and pepper. His bell rings out through the village.

'Mum didn't want it?' Dad asks.

I shake my head.

'Give her time, love,' Dad says.

I ignore his comment and take a piece of paper out of my pocket. 'I've made a list, Dad.' I hold it out to him. 'Things I think we should do to help Mum.'

Dad pulls his reading glasses out of his overall pocket and holds the paper up to the light above the front door.

I watch him scan down the items:

1. *Go to Slim Skills and get tips for making Mum healthy.*
2. *Get Mum to go to Slim Skills.*
3. *Get Mum and Dad to be happy with each other again.*

I notice Dad pause after this one.

4. *Get Mum and Steph to make up.*
5. *Take Mum for a walk around The Green every day, even if it's only a few steps.*
6. *Look into alternative weight-loss programmes: hypnosis, acupuncture, Chinese medicine, diet pills, reflexology and gastric bands.*

Dad hands the piece of paper back to me.

'We should leave it to the doctors, Feather.'

'The doctors aren't going to do anything. They just gave her a bunch of leaflets. Leaflets won't help. *We* have to help her, Dad.'

'It's complicated with your mum, Feather.'

I'm sick of hearing that word: *complicated*. And I'm sick of what it implies: that because something's hard, we shouldn't do anything about it. Or that because something's difficult to understand, I won't get it.

Dad takes off his glasses and puts them away.

'And they're expensive, Feather. Those things you wrote down.'

'I've got some money saved up. And I'll get a job. Plus, you've got so many call-outs at the moment, you must be making some money.'

'I know you mean well, Feather…'

'Of course I *mean well*,' I say, 'I want to help Mum. Don't you?'

I want to shake him. Doesn't he realise that Mum nearly died? That she might still die?

'You're acting like none of this has happened, Dad. Don't you remember what it felt like to sit next to Mum while she was in a coma, not knowing whether she was going to wake up? I thought that if anyone would understand…'

He gives Houdini a pat and starts to walk up the ramp to the front door.

'Do you love Mum?' I ask Dad.

He looks up at me, his eyes dark and shiny. Houdini head-butts my shins like he's trying to tell me something. His bell tinkles.

'Of course I love her, Feather.' His Adam's apple slides up and down his throat. 'Of course I do.'

And then I don't say anything because I know that if I do I'll regret it. I just get up and go back into the house.

Jake swipes the screen. His face glows.

We're sitting on my bedroom floor using his mobile to surf the Internet. His dad gave it to him to make up for never being around.

'It says you need to work out your BMI,' he reads from the obesity section of the NHS website.

'What's that?'

'Body Mass Index.' He taps the screen. 'Here, there's a calculator. Your mum's forty, right?'

'Forty-two.'

'And she's what, five foot two?'

'Yeah, roughly that.' We've never measured Mum but she's a bit taller than me and I'm five feet.

'And her chart at the hospital said she was thirty-seven stone?'

I nod. My stomach churns. I'm not sure I'm ready to have a calculator tell me how overweight Mum is. Though I guess I've heard the worst of it from the nurses already.

Jake shakes his head. 'Wow.'

'What?'

'She's 97.2.'

'What does that mean?'

'Well, put it like this: if your BMI is over 40, you're classified as obese.'

'Mum's not obese.' I'd seen pictures of women who were obese when I was doing research on the Internet the other day. Obese people have massive rolls of fat that hang over each other and tummies that swung between their legs and they have ten thousand wobbling chins and they can't go on airplanes because they wouldn't be able to fit on the seats. Mum isn't like them.

'I think she is, Feather.'

'Let me see that.' I snatch his phone and scroll down. And then I see a paragraph that makes me freeze:

An individual is considered morbidly obese if he or she is 7 stone over his/her ideal body weight, has a BMI of 40 or more, or 35 or more, and experiencing obesity-related health conditions, such as high blood pressure or diabetes.

'Morbidly...' I say under my breath. 'That means dead, right?'

Jake doesn't answer.

'Maybe it's not a good idea to read too much of this stuff,' Jake says, holding out his hand for his phone.

I grip the phone harder. 'It means dead – dead-like?'

'Yeah, but your mum's going to be fine. We'll make sure of it.'

I keep looking down the article...

Symptoms of morbid obesity:

- *osteoarthritis*
- *heart disease*
- *stroke*
- *diabetes*
- *sleep apnea (when you periodically stop breathing during sleep)*

The list goes on and on.

Jake grabs his phone back and switches it off.

'We'll work it out, Feather.'

There's a creaking on the stairs. We look towards the door.

'Your dad?' Jake asks.

I nod. Dad's been hiding away in his bedroom all evening. The fact that he's going downstairs can mean only one thing: he's given in and decided to spend the night in his bed in the lounge next to Mum. My heart does a little jump. Maybe he's beginning to realise that he has to help her. Maybe he does still love her.

The lounge is just under my bedroom, so I can hear everything that goes on in there. Including Mum's snoring and, until we put the TV in the garage, her re-runs of *Strictly*.

I close my eyes and imagine Dad getting into his stripy PJs and slipping into his bed pressed up against Mum's double bed. I even imagine him curling up to Mum, putting his arm across her – even if he can't quite reach all the way round.

The backs of my eyes go hot and prickly: he *does* still love her, I know he does.

A few moments later, I hear banging.

'What was that?'

We stand up and go to the landing.

More banging comes from the lounge.

I shake my head. 'I'm an idiot. Dad hasn't gone to join Mum, he's gone downstairs to get his bed.'

'You can't be sure…' Jake says.

'I'm sure.'

The banging goes on for a while and then, when Jake and I go back to my bedroom and squeeze onto my bed and stare up at the ceiling, we hear Dad stomping up and down the stairs as he carries the bed back upstairs, a plank at a time.

And you know the worst of it? He and Mum don't say a word to each other. Our cottage is so small you can hear everything. And I know it's not because Mum's asleep because she doesn't sleep at night: she has naps in the day in front of the telly. Or she did when she had the telly. And anyway, she'd have been woken up by all his banging.

No, they don't exchange a single word.

'Your parents are made for each other,' Jake says. 'They'll work it out.'

I shake my head. 'Dad's not going to help me. After everything that's happened in the last few days, he's not even going to make an effort to get closer to Mum.'

I don't know how I'm going to help Mum get better on my own. Even Steph, who usually always makes things better, can't help because Mum's blanking her. And Mum won't help herself because she doesn't get it, how sick she is.

'I'm here, Feather,' Jake says.

I turn to face him. His eyes look glassy in the blue shadows of my bedroom.

'I'm not going to sit back and risk losing Mum,' I say.

'I know. We're going to work on this together. We'll do whatever it takes.'

'You really mean that?'

He nods. 'I really mean that. It's going to be okay, Feather. It's all going to be okay.'

I lean my head on his shoulder and close my eyes and my heartbeat slows and I try really hard to believe him.

8

On Saturday morning my alarm goes off at 5.30am. It's dark outside and the cars along The Green look like white ice-lollies. There's ice on the inside of my window too. I asked Dad, once, why we couldn't have the windows replaced, and he said the same old thing that he says to any of my suggestions about fixing things or replacing things or buying new things to make the cottage nicer: *We're a mend-and-make-do kind of family, Feather.* Well, sometimes, mending and making do doesn't cut it. I'm freezing.

I get into my tracksuit and grab my swim bag. If we don't go early, the pool gets too full to practise properly.

There's no sound coming from the lounge, which feels weird. I'm used to hearing the buzz of Mum's cookery programmes or the music from her re-runs of *Strictly*.

I think about popping my head round the door to say *Hi*, like I usually do before my swim practice, but I've had this hollow feeling in my stomach since the salad incident last night. Mum should be the one to say sorry, otherwise she'll think I'm not serious about getting her to lose weight.

I walk past Dad's open door and my heart sinks. I really

thought he might give it a go, sleeping downstairs with Mum.

Dad and I take it in turns to do mornings. When he's got an early plumbing job, he helps Mum get ready and when he needs a lie-in because he's been out on a late job, I do it.

Everyone in Willingdon knows Dad's white van with GEORGE AND JO'S EMERGENCY PLUMBING written in red letters along the side. Dad told me that before Mum stopped leaving the house, she was his PA. She did all the accounting and the paperwork and the advertising and telephone calls. She was good at keeping people happy and had all these creative ideas for how to get new customers. Mum's got a clever reading and writing brain. She trained to be a lawyer but then decided she wanted to be a full-time mum and ended up helping Dad with the business instead. Dad and I have the non-writing and reading brains. We're better at fixing things than reading things.

Without your mum, I'd have gone out of business years ago, Dad says. *She's the magic-maker*. He used to say that all the time, that she was the magic-maker. And she was. Steph told me that, as well as helping Dad and looking after me, she did bits and bobs around the village, like first aid training. She ran weekly workshops in Newton Primary.

When I was little, Dad joked that Mum had magical powers. He told me about how she was always in the right place at the right time when someone needed her, like when one of the fryers exploded in Mr Ding's restaurant and burnt his arms and when Steph got stung by a bee and went into anaphylactic shock and when some random guy visiting the village had a heart attack right in the middle of The Green. Mum was better than a magic-maker: she brought people back to life. I wish I'd been a bit older when Mum still walked around the village, so I could have seen her doing all those cool things.

She stopped doing Dad's paperwork about five years ago, said it made her tired. I sometimes wonder how Dad's been coping all this time without her. I went into his room once and there was paperwork lying everywhere; most of the envelopes looked like bills and some of them had words like *URGENT* and *LAST REMINDER* stamped across the top. But I knew Dad would take care of it. He might not be the best at admin, but he works harder than anyone I know. This last year he's been doing call-outs every hour of the night and day. So the business must be doing okay.

'Hi, Houdini,' I say as I walk down the front steps. He steps out of his kennel and gives me a bleat. Dad's put a yellow woolly coat on him because of the cold weather, which makes him look like a fuzzy egg yolk. Houdini nudges my swim bag.

When I give his beard a stroke, Houdini looks up and holds my gaze for a moment. I reckon that animals have life more sussed than we do: I bet he'd think of a good plan to get Mum healthy.

As I look across The Green to the rectory, I notice a suitcase sitting on Rev Cootes's front doorstep. Rev Cootes is really old and wrinkly and lives alone and never has any visitors; and he doesn't have family either, or any family that drop by anyway. And no one really goes to his services, except Steph, who started going after the divorce. So, basically, Rev Cootes is weird. And not cool-weird: he's scary-weird. I wouldn't ever go to see Rev Cootes alone. He's probably got those children from the kids' bit of the cemetery chopped up and pickled in jars in his basement.

I check to make sure he's not crouching behind one of the

gravestones and then walk across The Green to the vicarage until I'm close enough to get a good look at the suitcase. It's got an American Airlines tag on it and an I LOVE NYC sticker on the side. Rev Cootes knowing someone from New York is about as likely as Mum coming out to do pirouettes in the middle of The Green.

The front door flies open. Rev Cootes stands in the doorway, holding his watering can, glaring at me. It's the same glare he uses whenever we have to come over and get Houdini from his front garden. No matter what system Dad puts in place to keep Houdini fenced in, he finds a way to wriggle out of his collar and climb out of our garden and scamper over to nibble on his graveyard flowers. Rev Cootes treats the St Mary's Cemetery like it's an exhibit in the Chelsea Flower Show. Which means he hates Houdini. And you know the crazy thing? Houdini *loves* Rev Cootes. I've told Houdini about my theory that Rev Cootes is an axe-murderer or a child-abductor, but Houdini doesn't listen, he just goes up to him and head-butts his shins and tries to nuzzle his hand. It's properly weird.

I turn to go but before I do, I look past Rev Cootes into the vicarage. There's someone standing behind him. I see a shimmer of short blond hair under the hall lamp.

The regional swim heats are coming up soon and what with Mum being in a coma and all the plans I've been making to get her healthy, I neglected my training. Swimming hasn't seemed very important next to keeping Mum alive. But I know I shouldn't throw away all the work I've put into making the team and I've got this secret hope that if I make it to the regionals, Mum will be so proud of me that she'll come and watch. I think she'd be proud of how fast I've got with my butterfly. But whenever I talk about swimming, she goes quiet and then she changes the subject.

Steph's my swim coach and she and Jake come along to support me at all my races, which makes up a bit for Mum not being there. I know Steph will be waiting for me this morning, but I take the long way to her house because I want to drop off some notes in the shops on Willingdon Green.

The notes read:

Feather Tucker
Looking for work as a part-time Sales Assistant.
Hard-working. Shows initiative. Good at counting.
Salary negotiable.
Mobile: 07598 223456

If I'm going to save up for Mum's gastric band and her personal trainer, I'm going to have to start earning some serious money.

When I get to Bewitched, Mrs Zas is kneeling in her front window with a pile of clothes and three naked mannequins. She's puffing on an electric cigarette and between the puffs she's humming. Her door sign is flipped to OPEN, which is weird – I can't imagine anyone wanting to rent a fancy-dress costume at six in the morning. Anyway, I decide it can't hurt to pop in.

'Good to see you, Feather,' Mrs Zas says. She puts down her cigarette and pulls a nun outfit over the plastic boobs of one of her mannequins.

Mrs Zas is wearing a black headscarf and a hoopy gold earring and a pirate outfit, which she's kind of bursting out of. She's in bare feet, her clogs tossed behind her.

I hand her one of my leaflets. She takes her purple-rimmed plastic glasses off from the top of her head and peers at my note.

'I thought you might need some help,' I explain.

People come from all over to rent Mrs Zas's fancy dress costumes, plus she has a big rack of ballroom dancing outfits that people use for The Willingdon Waltz competition. And she never seems to have anyone else working in the shop.

Mrs Zas gets up and slips into her heels. 'I'll give it some thought.'

'When do you think you'll know?'

Mrs Zas raises her eyebrows. 'You're – what do they call it in England? *Dogged?*'

I'm not sure it's a compliment so I don't answer.

'I like it,' she says, and smiles. 'You need to take life by the throat.' She puts her fingers around the neck of a mannequin and shakes it dramatically to make the point. She drops her hands from the mannequin and smiles with her big, red lipsticked mouth. 'I'll give it some thought, Feather.' She taps a bit of forehead through her headscarf.

I wonder why she always wears headscarves – and what her hair's like underneath. I can picture it being really long and black and shiny, like a witch's.

'If you do think of something, I'm afraid I'll have to be paid,' I say. I know it's a bit rude but the whole point of getting a job is earning money and, despite the shop being busy a lot of the time, Mrs Zas always looks strapped for cash. I mean, otherwise she'd buy her own clothes, right?

Mrs Zas nods. 'Of course.'

I sometimes wonder why, of all the villages in England, Mrs Zas ended up in Willingdon, the place where nothing ever happens. And from all the evidence I've seen, she lives alone, which must get pretty lonely. So maybe it will be nice having me around.

'Thank you for considering giving me a job.'

I head to the door.

Mrs Zas smiles and nods, goes back to putting a Frankenstein's monster outfit on the mannequin she throttled and starts humming again, mumbling a few words between her hums: *turn... turn... turn...*

By the time I get to Jake's house, he and Steph are already by the car. I want to hug them both. They feel more like family than Mum and Dad right now. Jake says he likes being an only child but I wish I had brothers and sisters. It gets lonely being stuck between Mum and Dad. I mean, I love them, but I wish that there were someone to share stuff with, especially the bad stuff. I once asked Mum why she didn't have any more kids and she went quiet and then she kissed me and gave me one of her big, warm hugs and said: *I have my Feather – and she's worth a million children* – which I didn't think was a proper answer, but it made me feel good anyway.

'Sorry I'm late,' I say.

I'm late for most things. By my reasoning, late people get more out of life because they squeeze extra things in. Anyway, Steph usually has a go at me, because she's an on-time kind of person, but this time she just gives me a hug. I know she feels sorry for me after everything that's happened with Mum. I think I'd rather have been told off.

'Ready to beat your PB?' Jake asks. He's Steph's assistant coach and my timekeeper.

'I'll try,' I say. I'm going to do this for Mum.

I jump into the back.

It was through Steph that I got into swimming. When Mum and Dad were busy with the plumbing business, she'd take Jake and me to the pool on Saturday mornings and she got so into it that she did a coaching qualification and started coaching the Newton team. Jake and I would come and watch her training the older children and then, one summer, Mum and I spent weeks doing nothing but watching the Olympics on TV and, when I saw those amazing swimmers doing butterfly stroke, I knew that I wanted to swim like them. So I asked Steph if I could try out for the team.

They're holding the Junior UK Championships at the Newton pool this summer and if I make it through the regionals, I'll be there competing with the best Junior Fly swimmers in the UK.

'Go! Go! Go!' I hear Jake's voice above me as I turn and kick off the end of the pool. 'Faster!'

My arms and legs feel like they're pinned to the bottom of the pool by lead weights. If I'm going to make it through the regional heats in March, I'll have to get a whole lot faster.

'Focus!' Steph yells as I push my arms over my head. 'Arms out… kick harder…'

Usually, swimming's the only thing guaranteed to get me out of my head. As I pull myself in and out of the water and propel my arms over my head and feel the rush of water along my body, my breath syncs into some weird energy and I disappear into another place, a place where it's just me and the water. And the more I let myself go to that somewhere place, the better I swim. It's the best feeling in the world.

But today, all I can think about is Mum.

When I finish, I can tell from Jake's face that I'm closer to my Personal Worst than my Personal Best. I don't even ask him to give me my time.

In the changing room, I turn to Steph.

'What did you and Mum fight about? At Christmas, I mean?'

As usual, she doesn't answer.

'Can't you patch things up?' I ask.

Steph fiddles with the locker key. 'Damn thing.'

'Steph?'

She looks at me. 'It's complicated, Feather.'

'She needs you. Like, *really* needs you. Now more than ever.'

'She'll let me know when she's ready.'

'Ready for what?' I ask.

'Ow!'

I notice a small droplet of blood on Steph's thumb. She's jabbed herself with the safety pin.

'It's about something that happened a long time ago.' Steph's voice is all jagged.

'Well, if it happened so long ago,' I say, 'it can't be that important any more, can it?'

'Just talk to your mum, Feather. It's not for me to say.'

'Not for you to say what?'

She shakes her head.

'Mum won't talk, Steph. You know she won't. Not about anything except who's doing what on *Strictly*, which is like the least important thing in the world – and now that we've taken her TV away, she won't even talk about that.'

'It's not up to you to fix your mum,' Steph says.

And that's the end of our conversation.

If Steph won't tell me what happened, I'll have to find out some other way. And then I'll figure out a way to get them to be friends again. If I'm going to get Mum better, I'm going to need all the help I can get.

9

I push through the front door, drop my swim bag in the entrance and run down the hall.

As I stand in the kitchen doorway, my hair dripping down my shoulders, I can't believe what I'm seeing: Mitch is sitting at the kitchen table next to Mum, who's sitting in her wheelchair.

'You opened the door, Mum?'

Mum laughs. 'You're looking at me like I let in an axe-murderer.'

'But you *never* answer the door.' I pause. 'Ever.'

The last time we had guests in the house was four years ago, for my birthday. And it didn't end well. One of the boys took pictures of Mum on his mobile and sent them to my class. When I worked out what he'd done I punched him on the nose, grabbed his phone, dropped it into his glass of Coke and told him to leave. He ran home and told his parents and, within half an hour, all the kids at my party had been picked up.

Apart from Jake, I haven't had any friends round since. I don't really mind – in some ways it's easier, it means I don't have to keep explaining about Mum or worrying how people will react. And anyway, I feel about Jake a bit like Mum feels about me: he's worth a million friends.

'It took a while for me to get to the front door,' Mum says. 'Mitch was already halfway down the drive. But I made it.' Mum winks at me. 'I thought you'd approve.'

Every muscle in my body relaxes. So Mum's finally decided to make an effort. Me ignoring her this morning and showing her that I'm not going to back down must have worked.

I spin round to face Mitch.

'So why did you come over?'

'Feather, love, be polite. Mitch is our neighbour. He's doing up Cuckoo Cottage.'

'I know.'

People from London and other posh places have been buying up the cottages on The Green as holiday houses. It's pushed lots of the locals out of their homes and businesses. It's why Mr Ding had to sell his restaurant space and get a takeaway van. Sometimes, I have dreams about how no one lives on The Green any more except for us, that it's like a ghost town or a place after there's been some kind of natural disaster and everyone's moved out. Our cottage is too small for rich people to be interested in. And anyway, Dad wouldn't sell, not in a million years.

'I thought it couldn't hurt to pop by and see how your mother was doing,' Mitch says.

'Mitch was telling me about the meeting you went to.'

She's going to kill me.

'Mum, I'm sorry,' I blurt out. 'I didn't mean to. Not without asking you first. I thought I'd just go and check it out—'

Mum holds out her hand and I come over and kneel next to her chair on the kitchen tiles.

'It's okay, my darling, I know you meant well.' Mum turns to Mitch Banks. 'The group sounds interesting.'

I feel my eyebrows shoot up. 'It does?'

I still can't quite believe that Mum's going along with all this. All Mum's been talking about since she got back from hospital is that she wants things to go back to normal. And what she means by normal is before New Year's Eve, when she would spend her days eating and watching TV.

Sometimes I have the same wish: I love how easy things used to be, how we'd spend hours laughing and talking, snuggled up watching TV and eating Chunky Monkey ice cream straight from the tub, as if the rest of the world didn't exist.

Only I'm determined that Mum won't slip back into the habits that made her sick.

'So you don't mind, Mum?'

'No, I don't mind.'

Mum threads her fingers through my wet hair. She's told me that when I was born my hair was blonde, not brown, and that when she held me in her arms for the first time, stroking my downy hair, she thought: *Light as a feather with hair like washed-out sunshine.*

Mum leans over and kisses the top of my head.

Mitch Banks clears his throat. 'When you walked in, I was inviting your mother to join the group.' He beams.

'Seriously?' I jump up and skip around the table. '*Really*, Mum?'

Mum nods again.

'We can go together. Steph could drive you—'

'Let's not bother Steph,' Mum says.

The only other option is Dad's van, except Mum wouldn't fit on the front bench. I get this picture of Mum sitting in the back, surrounded by sinks and toilet bowls and pipes and screws, the van leaning to one side, one of its tyres hissing because it's collapsed from carrying so much weight.

'Or you could walk,' I suggest. 'We could take it really slow.'

It took hours for the swelling in Mum's ankles to go down after the walk from the car to the lounge on the day she came home from hospital. Her feet had bulged out of her slippers, her tracksuits was drenched in sweat. But that just proved that she had to do it more, didn't it?

'We'll see, my darling.'

'Did you eat my bran muffins, Mum? Nurse Heidi said you have to eat regularly. Healthy things. Low GI. Slow-burning.'

Mum licks her lips, in the way she does when she's just had a packet of crisps. I really hope Dad hasn't been feeding her again.

'I did. They tasted like upholstery.' Mum laughs.

'Hey!'

'I'm just saying it like it is, love. And anyway, Houdini enjoyed the leftovers.'

Mum feeds Houdini things through the lounge window. 'He didn't look too impressed either.' Mum turns to Mitch. 'Is there anything I can eat that tastes like proper food?'

'There sure is,' says Mitch. 'I'll drop in some recipes.'

My heart's going to explode I'm so happy at how positive Mum's being.

Mitch stands up. 'I'd better get going.' He holds out his hand to Mum. 'I'll be in touch.'

I get up too. 'I'm sorry I was rude. We'll see you on Tuesday, won't we, Mum?'

I put my arms around Mum's neck and give her a hug.

'We're all going to help you get better.'

And then I squeeze Mum tight and close my eyes and feel so grateful that she's making an effort.

Only, just as I'm holding her close, my face close up to hers, I can smell prawn cocktail crisps on her breath.

10

Although it's the first day of school after the holidays and although I know that everyone's going to be talking about New Year's Eve and Mum being carried out of the house like a beached whale, I woke up feeling springy. Mum's agreed to take part in a Slim Skills meeting and that's a first step, right? And maybe, by the meeting on Tuesday, I'll have found a way to get Mum and Steph to talk and then Steph can come too, for moral support. And maybe I'll be able to persuade Mum to walk there, or at least walk part of the way, which would be a humungous step.

I knock on Mum's door.

'Mum? It's me.'

When she doesn't answer, I go in. I find her asleep, her feet poking out of the end of her duvet. Knots of spider veins circle her ankles and her toes are swollen like pale cocktail sausages. And she's snoring.

I go and kiss Mum's cheek and whisper in her ear: 'I've made you a yummy breakfast, Mum.'

She stirs but doesn't wake up, so I run downstairs to get the Bircher muesli I put together last night. I found the recipe in *Cook. Eat. Live.* It's this gloopy mix of yoghurt and nuts and dried fruit and oats and grated apple that melds together overnight. Swiss people eat it before they go zooming up mountains and it keeps them going for ages. My plan is to fill Mum up with food that keeps her going for longer, that way she won't stuff herself with prawn cocktail crisps and Galaxy bars and pineapple syrup.

Except, when I get to the kitchen, I smell frying.

And then I see Dad emptying a pan of greasy sausages and buttery mushrooms and fried eggs onto a plate.

'Dad!'

He jumps. A mushroom slips off the side of the dish; it looks like a slug lying there on the kitchen tiles.

'You scared the life out of me, Feather.'

'I've made Mum's breakfast already,' I say.

I go to the fridge and take out the muesli.

'Your mum's not going to eat that.' Dad puts the serving dish on Mum's tray. Then he tucks a wad of kitchen paper under the plate.

'And she *is* going to eat crisps, right?'

'Sorry?'

'I know you gave her crisps, Dad. You can't keep doing this.'

'We'll put your breakfast on the tray too,' Dad says. 'Then she can choose.'

I shake my head.

'No, Dad. If you give Mum a choice, you know what she's going to pick.' I take a breath. 'We have to make sure that Mum doesn't take in more calories than she burns.'

'It's going to take more than salad and muesli to get your mum well, Feather.'

'I know, Dad. But we have to start somewhere.' I must

be the only teenager on the planet who's trying to convince her parents to eat healthily.

Dad nods like he always does when he disagrees but doesn't want a fight. I look at his tufty hair and at the wrinkles on his forehead and at the puffy baggy bits under his eyes because he's been out on so many night shifts. And, for a second, I think he's going to give in. But then he just comes over and takes my bowl of muesli and puts it on the tray and goes to Mum's room.

That's another classic Dad move: when he doesn't want to fight back, he goes quiet and does what he wants anyway.

'It's not right, Dad!' I yell after him.

But he doesn't turn round.

Maybe I can get Mitch to talk to Dad. Or Nurse Heidi. He needs facts and statistics, hard evidence. Like the fact that when people as big as Mum don't get to a healthy weight, they could die.

As I walk past the vicarage, I notice that the suitcase has disappeared from Rev Cootes's front steps. I go and stand by the school minibus stop; it's next to the row of graves where the little kids are buried. Rev Cootes fusses more over the flowers on those graves than over the old people ones. In the summer, they're so full of roses and pansies and dahlias that you can hardly read the inscriptions any more.

Looming over the children's graves stands the stone statue of an angel with droopy wings and an inscription that reads:

Our Little Angels. You'll always be with us.

A few of the gravestones have photographs of the children tucked behind glass frames, but mostly, there are just names and dates, especially on the really old ones. Some of the graves date back hundreds of years. Miss Pierce, my History teacher, explained that in the old days kids got more diseases than they do now and that it was harder to save them because medical science wasn't as advanced.

Although I've stood next to those small graves a million times waiting for the school minibus, the tight feeling across my chest never goes away. There's something wrong about kids dying before they've had the chance to do anything with their lives. Plus, looking at the graves makes me think about Mum and how she nearly died, and that makes me even more determined to get her better – and to make sure Dad stops feeding her rubbish.

'Morning, Feather!'

I look up. It's Mrs Zas standing on the doorstep of her fancy-dress shop, waving at me.

I wave back.

'Morning, Reverend Cootes!' Mrs Zas says. She rolls her *R*s like she's about to burst into song.

Reverend Cootes bows his head over one of the kids' graves, pretending he hasn't heard. I bet he disapproves of Mrs Zas, because she's the exact opposite of him in her bright colours and noisy high heels and loud voice, but also because of the costumes in her shop. Mum told me that religious people believe witches and ghosts and monsters and werewolves are evil.

The funny thing is that Rev Cootes ignoring Mrs Zas never stops Mrs Zas from being nice to him.

'I think I might have a job for you, Feather,' she calls over. 'Come and see me soon.'

'Thank you!' I call back.

A moment later, Jake's at my side. He puts down his school bag and punches me on the arm. 'Hey, Feather!'

I give him a massive hug and hold onto him for a bit longer than usual. Jake's the one constant, happy thing in my life right now.

'I need you to help me get your mum and my mum back together,' I whisper, still holding on.

He stands back and holds up his hands.

'I don't get involved in girl stuff.'

'It's not girl stuff. It's Mum needing her best friend because getting better's going to be really hard.'

The school minibus rattles down the road. It's white and rusty and the N from NEWTON ACADEMY has faded away.

'You have to find out what they rowed about and then we have to sort it out.'

'You can't solve the world's problems, Feather.'

'I'm not trying to solve the world's problems. I'm trying to help my mum. And I need some support from you.'

'Okay, okay. I'll see what I can find out.'

Jake looks past me – his eyes are so wide, I wonder whether a UFO has just landed in the middle of St Mary's Cemetery.

'Who's *that*?' Jake asks.

I spin round.

There's a guy stomping through the cemetery. He's got headphones, which makes him look like he's lost in some other world, and his hair's really light and even at this distance he looks so thin you wonder how his body stays pinned to the ground.

Jake and I are the only teenagers in Willingdon: the school bus does a detour especially for us. Whoever this guy is, he's not from around here. But this is the really weird thing: he looks as though he's meant to be here; when I look at him I feel like I'm meant to know him.

Just as the bus pulls in, the guy jumps on, gives the driver a note, then goes to sit at the back and takes out an old battered paperback. No one's ever read a book on the school bus before, not unless it's cramming before an exam.

Everyone else on the bus fixes their eyes on him, like Jake and I did, but he doesn't seem to notice – or to care. He just sinks into his seat and stares at his paperback.

I keep wondering whether maybe he came here one summer with his parents, whether maybe they're one of the rich families from London who bought a cottage on The Green and now leave it empty for most of the year.

The guy looks a couple of years older than Jake and me. He's so thin that his collarbones stick out. In fact, the whole of him looks hollow, like there's something missing. I'm almost grateful that Mum's the weight she is, it would be worse to have her look like this – like a ghost.

'Weird, hey?' I whisper. 'Do you think he's sick?'

Jake shrugs.

'He looks interesting though,' I add.

'Interesting?' Jake pokes me in the ribs.

I blush. 'Not like that, I just mean that there's something about him – he looks kind of familiar, don't you think?'

'I hope you're not going to feed him that line,' Jake grins.

'What line?'

'*Haven't we met before?*' Jake says in a voice that's obviously meant to be mine but that sounds totally lame.

'Just forget it.'

Jake leans over and gives me a loud kiss on the cheek. 'Just teasing, Feather.'

Sometimes it totally feels like Jake's my brother.

There's another thing that's different between me and Jake: I can't ever remember him not being in a relationship; I've never even been out on a date. Or kissed anyone. Or received a Valentine's card. On my birthday a year ago I asked Jake whether he would kiss me just so that I could stop worrying about it, but he got all embarrassed and then refused and said, *It's meant to be special*. He paused. *Plus, I'd be cheating on Amy*. And I know he's right, but it would still make me feel like less of freak to know that I've at least kissed one boy before I die.

We have made a pact though: if we're still living in Willingdon when we're fifty (and if Jake hasn't been an idiot and married someone like Amy), we're going to buy a house and live there together and get old and wrinkly together. It's kind of a relief to know that when Mum and Dad aren't around any more, I'll always have Jake.

Jake looks back at the guy. 'I know what you mean. He's cool.'

By which, Jake means that the guy's way *too* cool to be seen hanging around with us. Or rather me. Which kind of sucks, because he does look interesting – more interesting than any other guy that's stepped onto the Newton Academy minibus.

It's the longest Monday ever. I find it hard to concentrate in lessons because my brain keeps buzzing all over the place: I make up healthy recipes for Mum and think about the Slim Skills meeting on Tuesday and how Mum's actually coming and about how Jake's promised to sort things out between our mums and about how I have to work out a way to get Dad on board. Anyway, thinking about Mum makes quadratic equations and Mount Vesuvius and iambic pentameter seem pretty pointless. The only lesson that I feel remotely interested in is Miss Pierce's History class.

'I thought we'd do some poetry today,' Miss Pierce says.

The class groans.

'Aren't poems for English?' Jake calls out.

That's another reason girls like Jake: he makes them laugh and he's not afraid to stand up to teachers. Take Amy: for a second, she's stopped drawing hearts on the back of her file and is looking at Jake like he's some kind of hero.

Sometimes I worry that if I wasn't the only person Jake's age living in the village, if our mums hadn't brought us together when we were babies, he wouldn't even notice me.

'Poems are for every occasion Jake,' Miss Pierce looks straight at him with her sharp, blue eyes. 'And in the case of the First World War, poetry was one of the only ways that the men could truly express what they were going through.'

Jake has some teachers totally wound round his little finger, but Miss Pierce wins every time. And Jake doesn't mind because he likes her just as much as I do. She's one of those teachers who cares more about pupils than about impressing the Head or his millions of deputies, which means she actually talks to us like she's interested in hearing what we have to say rather than waiting for us to come up with the right answer.

'Don't we have textbooks for that?' Jake asks.

'Textbooks tell us facts, Jake, poems tell us the truth. And they bring us together: they teach us about our common humanity, about how the past and the present are connected, about how a man sitting in a trench a hundred years ago writing a love letter to his girlfriend back home might feel the very same thing as you feel when you pass notes to Amy under the desk.'

The class erupts in laughter.

That's another thing about Miss Pierce: she always knows exactly what's going on.

Jake blushes and stares down at his desk.

Amy grins stupidly because she's got attention, even though she probably doesn't understand what she got attention for.

'These two men have given us the greatest treasures from the First World War,' Miss Pierce says, switching on the projector. The black and white faces of two young men flash onto the whiteboard. 'Wilfred Owen and Siegfried Sassoon.'

'Didn't they meet in a loony bin?' Matt calls out from the back of the class.

'They met at Craiglockhart Hospital, Matt, where soldiers were recovering from shell-shock.'

I've heard that term before but I've never really got my head round it. I put my hand up.

'Yes, Feather?'

'What's shell-shock?'

Matt laughs from the back of the class. 'It's when you get shocked by a shell falling on your head!'

'Shut up!' Jake calls back.

Miss Pierce doesn't tell Jake to mind his language, like other teachers would. It's her opinion that there are times when colourful language is necessary and, obviously, telling Matt to get lost is the perfect occasion.

'It's a good question, Feather, and something that psychiatrists are still trying to understand today. Matt is right in so far as there's an initial shock, when a soldier experiences the devastating effects of a bomb or, more likely, days and days of bombardment in the trenches. But it's more than that. It's the way that bomb echoes through a person's mind days and weeks and months and sometimes years after the trauma.' Miss Pierce looks up at the faces of the two young men on the projector and her eyes go sad. 'We carry the past with us, and sometimes that past is so very, very sad that it haunts us and damages us.'

The class goes really quiet and then Miss Pierce hands out the poems and for a whole half-hour I get lost in Miss Pierce's words and the words from the poems and thoughts about the past and how we 'carry it with us'.

Miss Pierce's lessons are the one thing that make going to school bearable. She's the only teacher who gets it, about me finding it hard to read rather than just not wanting to read. *There are lots of ways to learn about the world besides reading books*, she said to me once, and I try to remember that whenever I get down about not being very good at school.

By the time the last bell goes, I'm bursting to leave. I head straight down the corridor to the main doors but then something catches my peripheral vision. It's the guy from this morning – he's heading into the counsellor's office. And I get that same warm feeling I got this morning, like I've known him my whole life. Maybe that soul-mate thing is true, that there are people walking around in the world that you're just meant to meet.

I look back at the counsellor's office. No one goes to see Miss Tippet, not voluntarily. She has coffee breath and BO and makes you draw pictures of your feelings like you're a four-year-old. Jake got sent to Coffee Breath when his parents divorced and he stopped working.

I reckon that if I wait out here for the guy to come out, I can think of an excuse to start a conversation. I try not to stand too close to the door in case he comes out and thinks I'm eavesdropping. The doors at the Academy are paper-thin, probably because the government ran out of money at the end of the building project. All the trimmings are cheap: door handles keep falling off and light fixtures hang off the ceiling because they won't stick to the plasterboard ceiling and the tables and chairs are wobbly.

Out of the corner of my eye I notice Jake and Amy coming down the corridor arm in arm.

'See you later,' Amy says, kissing Jake's cheek but looking at me the whole time.

She always finds excuses to leave when she bumps into me. I think she's worried that because I'm friends with Jake my lack of coolness will seep through him and taint her shiny image. I bet she wishes that someone would drop a bomb on me and that I'd just disappear out of Jake's life.

I wait for Amy to join her friends at the other end of the corridor and then I turn to Jake and say:

'He's in there.'

'Who?'

'The guy from this morning, on the bus.'

'He's with *Miss Tippet*?'

'Yep.'

'Wow, what did he do to deserve that?'

A second later the door flies open and the guy comes out. He can't have been in there for more than a few minutes – maybe he took one sniff of Miss Tippet and decided against the counselling session.

'Hi,' I say. It comes out lame-sounding.

He nods and heads down the corridor.

'You just started at Newton Academy?' Jake calls after him.

The guy stops and turns round. 'Yeah.'

Yeah. An American accent. And then my brain pings: the cases on Rev Cootes's step with the American Airlines labels. This guy is staying with Rev Cootes? No way.

'Want to go to get a coffee?' I ask him.

Jake shoots me a glance, which says: *Since when did you start drinking coffee?*

'Maybe another time,' the guy says.

'You live in Willingdon?' I burst out, desperate to get some information out of him before he goes. I need to know whether I've seen him before or whether I'm being totally delusional.

'Yeah. For now.' He looks at his watch. His wrists are so thin you can see all the bones.

Maybe he's got some kind of cancer, that's what makes people really thin, isn't it? But then, if he had cancer, why would he have moved in with Rev Cootes and started school at Newton Academy?

'I really have to go,' he says.

I wonder why he's in such a hurry; it can't be to go and spend time with Rev Cootes.

'See you around then,' I say.

We watch him walk away.

Jake smiles and shakes his head.

'What?'

'You'll scare him away.'

'I only asked him if he wanted a coffee.'

'You made it sound like a marriage proposal.'

'I did not.'

Jake rolls his eyes. 'I'm just saying, you've got to chill a bit.'

I look back down the corridor.

'It'll be nice to have someone else around, that's all,' I say. 'Besides us, I mean.'

Jake furrows his brow and I can tell he's a bit offended. Which is kind of off considering he's always leaving me to be with Amy. But Amy aside, we've always agreed that it being the two of us is just fine, that we don't need anyone else. But we both know that Willingdon can get lonely – and boring.

Willingdon is famous for four things, (none of which makes life any more interesting for Jake and me:)

1. Being the smallest village in Britain.
2. Hosting the Willingdon Waltz.
3. Having a Lido (that closed down years and years ago).
4. Mum. Mum's size.

'I reckon he's in Year 12,' Jake says. 'I saw him going into a Year 12 Form Room earlier today. I don't think he'll be interested in hanging around with us.'

'Well, as long as he's not middle-aged or pushing a Zimmer frame, I don't care,' I say.

I watch the guy disappearing through the front doors at the end of the corridor. I can feel Jake watching him too.

Miss Tippet waddles out of her office holding a manila file. I crane my neck to see the label: CLAY COOTES.

Jake must see it too because he whispers: '*Cootes?* Wow, poor guy. He definitely needs saving.'

Maybe, if he's related to Rev Cootes, we have met before.

'Hi, Miss Tippet.' I smile at her because I feel sorry

for her, even if she's smelly and hasn't got a clue about teenagers.

A mix of sticky deodorant and sweaty armpit wafts off Miss Tippet.

'You're seeing Clay Cootes?' Jake asks her.

If there's one thing Jake and me have in common it's this: we pick at things until we get to the truth.

Miss Tippet squishes the files she's carrying up against her boobs, which makes me want to look away.

'You know my client details are confidential.' She sounds like she's reading from a manual.

'Well, we're his friends,' I say, 'we look out for him.'

She raises her eyebrows. 'You do?'

'Yes,' I say, 'we hang out with him all the time.'

Miss Tippet raises her bushy eyebrows. 'Clay has only just arrived.'

So I was right, that was his suitcase.

'Yeah, well, since he's arrived, we've been spending time together. He's our new best friend,' Jake says. He's joining in to make me feel better about liking Clay, which makes me remember why I love him so much. He beams at Miss Tippet in his usual charming, handsome way. I sometimes wonder whether it's weird, that I find Jake handsome when I don't fancy him; when he's basically my brother.

The counsellor drops her shoulders. 'Well, I must say I'm relieved to hear that. I was worried Clay might be a bit alone, you know, living with his grandfather, being new to the school. Though I imagine his mother still has contacts in Willingdon.'

His mother lived in Willingdon? That means Mum and Dad and Steph must know her. That means my gut feeling might be right after all.

I tilt my head to one side. 'Yes, must be hard for him.' And then I take a gamble, hoping I got the accent right. 'America is so different...'

She nods. 'New York is another world. Poor Clay is a long way from home.'

I hear Jake take in a sharp breath. He loves New York. He wants to do make-up for those zombie-invasion films he loves and there's a school in New York where they teach it. He'd have to get a scholarship though because Steph couldn't afford the fees, not in a million years.

'You'd think his parents would have found him some help out there, don't you?' Miss Tippet goes on.

Counsellors are meant to let you do the talking, right? Well, once Miss Tippet gets going, it's like one of those taps Dad gets called out to fix: drip, drip, drip... until you think your head's going to implode.

She adjusts her bra strap under her nylon jumper. 'I mean, therapists are as common as dentists out there.'

'Yes, they are.' Jake nods earnestly.

'We help him,' I say to Miss Tippet. 'With his... you know...'

'Oh, I'm so glad.' Miss Tippet puts her hand to her chest. So he is sick. Though he looks more like he'd need a doctor than a counsellor kind of sick.

Miss Tippet leans in. Sweat. Coffee breath.

'I don't imagine his grandfather understands much about these things,' she adds.

Jake and I both wait for her to say more but she readjusts her files and turns to go.

'He's lucky to have you.' She looks from me to Jake and then she waddles off down the corridor.

If there's one thing Miss Tippet is right about, it's that he looks like he could do with a friend. And maybe he'll keep me company when Jake's off with Amy. I'm going to make sure I get to know Clay.

11

'Mum!'

I tumble through the door, dump my swim bag and my school bag in the hall and run into Mum's room.

'We have to hurry or we'll be late.' I flick my wet hair over my shoulders – the ends frozen into icicles.

I squeezed in a swim practice after school and Steph said my technique hadn't been this good in months and that if I kept it up I'd be in with a real chance of making it through the local trials and then the regionals. But right now I'm focused on something else. Ever since Mitch came round I haven't been able to stop thinking about how once I get Mum to the Slim Skills group, everything will start to get better.

'Steph and Jake are outside with the people carrier. She's taken the seats out of the back so there's loads of room.'

'Steph's here?' Mum asks.

I didn't tell Mum until the last minute; I didn't want her to use it as an excuse to back out of coming. Plus, by forcing them together I'm hoping they'll talk and make up.

'I'd rather your dad took us,' Mum says.

'Dad's out on a job.'

'Fine,' she mumbles, though her tone says the opposite. I wish she'd see how much Steph loves her and how much effort she's going to.

I run up to my bedroom and come back carrying a massive bin liner.

'I've got a surprise, Mum.'

'What on earth?'

I pull out the gigantic, blue coat I got from the Age UK shop in Newton. I shake it out and lay it on the floor in front of Mum.

'I thought you should have something smart to wear for your first trip out.' I hold it up to Mum. 'I measured it. And the colour will bring out your eyes.' I take a breath. 'Plus, it's to celebrate you losing all those pounds. Did Nurse Heidi come again today?'

Mum nods.

'And?'

'She said I'm doing well,' Mum says.

Mum told me she's lost another stone since she's been back from hospital. I can't see it yet, but I guess that's normal. It will take stones and stones before we notice a real difference.

'You'll see, Mum, as you lose weight and feel healthier, you'll start enjoying clothes again. We'll go shopping together—'

'Maybe,' Mum says.

All the bounce Mum had the other day when Mitch Banks came round has disappeared. I guess it's normal that she's nervous about the meeting.

'Here, try it on.' I guide Mum's arms through the sleeves. One of Mum's wrists gets stuck in the cuff.

She takes in a big breath.

'I don't think it'll fit—'

'Just push your arm through harder, Mum.'

Mum breathes out and the seam between her shoulder blade rips.

I take the coat away and stuff it back into the bin liner.

'It doesn't matter, Mum.' I give her a kiss. 'It's not that cold out.'

I measured Mum's sweatshirts really carefully to make sure the coat would fit. I don't understand.

Mum glances at the slit in the lounge curtains. In a few months it will be spring. And then summer. Mum doesn't talk much about the time before she stopped going out but once she mentioned that she liked summer: the picnics in Willingdon Park and everyone out on The Green. Mum hasn't felt the sun on her skin for over a decade.

Mum leans towards the window.

'Who's that?' she asks, pointing through the slit.

I open the curtains a little and look out. The vicarage is across The Green, bang opposite our cottage. I notice Clay standing by the front door in running gear. His legs look so thin poking out of his shorts that I get a stab of pain in my chest. I get how Mum put on weight but I can't get my head around how someone can get so thin. You have to eat to stay alive, don't you? Standing there in his running gear, Clay barely looks alive at all.

'That's Clay,' I say. 'He's American.'

Mum takes in a sharp breath.

'Mum?'

'How long's he been here?'

If Miss Tippet is right about Clay's mum still having contacts in Willingdon, maybe she knows Mum and Dad.

'I'm not sure… a few days? Do you know him?'

Mum shakes her head.

Maybe she's just worried about there being another person in Willingdon to gawp at her. I don't know what the word for people-phobic is but Mum's got that phobia along with her water phobia and her hospital phobia and her going-out phobia.

I want to tell her that I like him and that he's the first real-life (rather than TV) guy I've seen that have made my insides flip. Because I always tell Mum what I'm feeling. But she doesn't seem in the mood.

'I think he's nice...' I try out.

'He's too old for you.'

Which is a really weird comment for Mum to make. You know how I said that Mum was better than any of the other mums around because she takes time to listen and because she doesn't have all these unrealistic expectations of me and because she laughs at the same stuff I do and sees the world in the same way? Well, that means she doesn't shoot me down when I say I like something. Especially when that something is a guy.

'Too old for what? I just said he was nice.'

'You've got Jake,' Mum says, wiping the back of her hand across her brow. She's gone into convection heater mode.

I put the bin bag to one side and wheel over Mum's chair.

'Come on, Mum.' I slip my arm under hers. 'Let's get outside, the fresh air will make you feel better.'

I've got a technique for getting her from armchair to wheelchair. Only today, it doesn't seem to work. Mum's body feels like this big bag of bricks. It won't budge.

'I'll bring the chair closer,' I say. 'Or maybe we could try walking to the car. I can get Jake to help.'

'Maybe I can go next week,' Mum says.

'Come on, Mum.' I put pressure under her arm and heave her up. 'One, two, three…'

Mum makes it to standing and sways for a bit; her feet are really small, too small to hold her body in balance.

'It's all about first steps, Mum. You'll get used to it.' I guide Mum to the lounge door. 'You'll see, the people in the group are really nice. They'll support you, and you can support them.'

'Give the sales pitch a rest, Feather.'

'We're nearly there, Mum. Steph's parked right outside the front door.'

Mum takes a deep breath and we set off again.

The front door is open. Sharp January sunshine falls into the hallway.

'Is anyone looking?' Mum asks.

I lean out of the front door. Jake and Steph give me a thumbs up smile.

'It's fine, Mum.'

'You're telling me there's *no one* out on The Green?'

'Only Clay. And Mrs Zas.' She's standing on the doorstep looking out, a bright pink headscarf on. 'But you don't need to worry about them, Mum, they won't even notice. And if they do, it's not important, just ignore them.' I kiss Mum on her cheek. 'You're doing something amazing, Mum. You should be proud.'

Through the front door, I see Steph standing by her car, the back door of her people carrier open, her brown hair gold in the sun. Mum looks at her too and, even though she'd never admit it, I know what she's thinking: that she's missed her best friend.

Across The Green, I see Clay jogging down through the cemetery, past the children's graves and out onto the road.

Jake's staring at him too. And so's Mum. I bet they're thinking the same thing I am: that someone that thin shouldn't even be able to run.

'Come on, Mum, we're going to be late.'

She keeps staring at Clay.

'Jake – give us a hand,' I say.

Jake comes over and takes Mum's other arm. We help her over the doorframe. And then Mum freezes. She's staring at a flier wedged into the letterbox.

'Come on, Mum, or we'll be late.'

Mum reaches out for the flier but tilts off balance before she manages to grab it. Jake gets it for her.

'Cool!' he says.

He hands Mum the flier.

I lean in and read the headline:

Lido: Grand re-opening on Willingdon Day, 1st June.
And then the line underneath it: *New venue for this year's Junior UK Championships.*

'It's opening again?' My insides are doing somersaults. 'And they moved the competition from the Newton pool!'

I get goosebumps thinking about it opening again. It'll be the first time in the history of the competition that it's outside: swimming in the sunshine must be the best feeling in the world. It was exciting enough knowing that the national championships would be in Newton but now it's even better – it's going to be right here in the village. I'm going to train even harder to make sure I make it into the regional team. My whole body is buzzing: this is the most exciting thing that's happened to Willingdon ever.

Mum shuffles backwards and grabs hold of the side table by the front door. It makes a sharp cracking sound under her weight.

'Mum?' I put my hand on Mum's back. 'What's wrong?'

I look at the flier in her hand. There's a picture of the lido as I've never seen it before: bright sunlight, a thousand colours, the pool filled with water and children and families splashing around. And then it hits me. Mum hates water. And crowds. If what the flier says is true, there are going to be loads and loads of people coming down to Willingdon this summer.

'People are looking at me,' Mum says.

I look out onto The Green. 'There's no one there, Mum. Only Steph.'

Mum shakes her head. The flier is scrunched up in her hands. 'They're whispering. And they're staring.'

Mum sways beside me. Jake and I try to hold her but she's so big I don't have the strength.

'Steph—' I call out. 'It's Mum!'

Mum's legs buckle.

'Mum!' I grab her arm and Jake tries to hold her from behind, but she slips away from us.

Steph runs into the house.

Mum crumples to the floor and I fall with her. My hip bashes into the floorboards. And then a thud as Mum hits the floor, so loud, a tremor shakes the foundations of the cottage.

Jake scoots down beside me. 'Feather… are you okay?'

I bat him away. Ignoring the pain tearing through my hip, I sit up and take Mum's hand. 'Mum—'

Steph kneels beside us. She looks from Mum to me and then leans over, prises the flier out of Mum's hand and shoves it into the back pocket of her jeans.

'I'm sorry, Mum,' I say. 'I should have let you take the wheelchair.'

Mum doesn't answer.

'Do you think you can get up?' I ask. 'If we help you?' I look up to Steph and Jake.

All the strength has gone from Mum's body. I'm worried she'll never get up ever again.

I glance at my watch. If we don't go now we'll miss the meeting.

Mum closes her eyes and nods. 'I want to go back to my room.'

'But…' I start. 'The meeting…'

Mum shakes her head, her eyes still closed.

'Mum? You promised.'

Mum opens her eyes and looks at Steph. 'I'd like you to leave, now,' she says.

Blood whooshes in my ears.

'I told you this would happen, Jo,' Steph snaps back. 'I said you had to talk to Feather…'

'Talk to me about what?' I ask.

'Nothing!' Mum yells and then she fixes her eyes back on Steph. 'I said, I'd like you to leave.'

'But Steph and Jake came to help, Mum.'

'It's okay, Feather,' Steph says softly.

'No,' I say, 'it's not okay. Mitch is expecting us. And we don't have time to wait for another week to go by.' My voice trembles. I know Mum's had a shock and I know she's nervous about going out of the house and that she's upset that the village is going to get swamped by people and that she'll have to face them all. But that's ages away. She'll be better by then.

Steph rests her hand between my shoulder blades. 'We just need to give your mum a bit of time.' She turns to Jake. 'Come on, let's go home.'

I stand up, my fists tight knots at my side.

'But we don't have time, do we?' My hip throbs. 'We have to do something now, or—' I break off and hang my head.

'We'll get your chair, Jo,' Steph says. 'And then we'll go.'

As I watch Steph and Jake disappear into the lounge and as I watch Mum rocking back and forth as she sits in the middle of the hall, I suddenly feel really tired. Every time I get Mum to take one step forward, it's like something out there yanks her right back to square one. Worse than square one. Maybe all this is pointless. At least before New Year's we were happy.

12

I slam the front door behind me.

Mum promised she'd come, I mutter through gritted teeth. *She said she was going to make an effort to get better.*

I hate myself for thinking it but a little part of me wonders whether Mum collapsed on purpose, whether maybe she had no intention of going to the Slim Skills meeting.

I take Mitch's card out of my pocket and dial his number.

'It's Feather.'

'Feather? Everything okay?'

'Not really.'

'I thought you were bringing your mum?'

'So did I.'

I kick at a clod of earth on the drive.

'What happened?'

My eyes sting.

'She chickened out.'

'Oh, I'm sorry.' There's a crackly pause down the line, then he says, 'It's daunting to join a new group, especially for someone like your mum.'

'But we planned everything – Steph was here with her people carrier.' I sniff. 'I even bought Mum a coat.'

'She can come next week, Feather. Try not to worry.'

Try not to worry – after what those nurses said? After what Jake and I found out about Mum's BMI? It's like no one gets it: that we don't have a choice, that if we don't do something, Mum's just going to get worse and worse. And then one day, it'll be too late to do anything about it.

'Hope it's a good meeting,' I say and hang up.

Jake comes up behind me.

'You okay?' he asks me.

'Not really.' I look down the road. 'You think he saw Mum collapsing?'

'Who?'

'Clay.'

Jake shrugs. 'I don't think he'd care.'

Jake doesn't get that it's not about Clay caring – it's about me caring. It's about me wishing that for once in my life I didn't have to deal with Mum, that she'd be the grown-up and take care of herself.

Steph comes out of the house.

'Your mum's resting,' Steph says.

'She's always resting.'

'You can't expect changes overnight.'

'I don't. I just expect her to try.'

'She is, Feather. More than you know.'

I look at Steph and wonder why she's taking Mum's side when Mum's been blanking her since Christmas.

'Did she talk to you? I mean, properly?'

'A little.'

Which means no. Whatever it is Mum's holding against

Steph, I wish she'd get over it. Steph's the nicest person in the world, and she's always been there for us.

I notice a bit of white paper poking out of the back pocket of Steph's jeans.

'Is that the flier?'

Steph nods. 'Thought it was best to take it.' She sighs. 'Though I don't think Jo's going to let it go.'

'Let what go?'

'Oh, nothing, just that she's pretty wound up.'

Steph's car is still open, ready to whisk Mum through the streets of Willingdon. Steph even put blankets across the back bench so that Mum would be comfortable.

I look back at Steph's car.

'I've got an idea.'

Steph smiles. 'Oh dear.'

'How many people does the carrier fit?'

Jake scans the seats. 'Two and the driver on the front bench, and then another three in the middle... and two in the boot...'

'That's eight – including the driver. That should be enough.' I smile. 'Let's go.'

Half an hour later, we're back at the house.

I step out of Steph's car with Mr Ding and Allen, the reporter from the *Newton News*, and the others from the Slim Skills meeting. They're standing in a huddle around Houdini; he's bleating and head-butting their hands and nodding his head to make his bell clang against his chest. Jake went home to catch up on some homework and Steph's inside getting things ready.

I look at Mum's window. The curtains are drawn. Once she sees the trouble we've gone to so that we can have the Slim Skills meeting at our house, she's bound to come round, isn't she?

I head into the kitchen. Dad extended it with a conservatory to give Mum a bit more room. It's the only space in the house that will hold everyone. Mum isn't in there yet.

Steph fills up the kettle.

Mitch puts the scales down on the kitchen floor. 'You thought I'd forgotten these, didn't you?' he says, smiling.

'I've made some healthy treats.' I pull out a tray of granola bars from the fridge. I was going to give them to Mum later tonight as a thank you for having gone to the meeting. 'They're made with bananas rather than sugar.'

I look down at the grey slab of oats.

When Mr Ding and Allen and the two people from Newton called Mark and Sally are sitting down with their cups of tea and bits of grey granola, I go and get Mum.

As I skip to her room, I think about how she'll be so proud of me for organising all this.

I knock lightly on the door.

No answer.

'Mum?'

Still no answer. Maybe she's fallen asleep.

I walk in.

Mum's in her purple love seat, her feet up on the stool. On her knees, she's got the spiral pad I gave her to write down things she wants us to get her from the supermarket.

She's just sitting there, chewing on the end of her pencil, staring at the wall where the TV used to be.

'Mum?'

She closes the notebook and puts the pen down on the side table.

'I've got a surprise,' I say.

I thought she'd ask about all the noise and footsteps and about where Steph and I have been for the past half-hour, but she just sits there, zoned out.

'They're all here, the people from Slim Skills. And Mitch too. They're in the kitchen. We're going to have the session here.' I gulp. 'Just for you.'

She shifts her head and looks at me.

'I'm tired, Feather.'

'But Mitch is going to give a talk about why he started the group; he says that testimonials are really important. All you have to do is to walk across the hall – I can help you. It's not far. Not nearly as far as going all the way to Newton Primary.' I look at the chair. 'I can wheel you in if you like.'

'I'm not up to visitors.'

'But Mum, they're *here*—'

'We don't need other people, Feather. We're fine, just the two of us.'

'They're not other people. They're our guests and they've gone to all the trouble of coming here. And they're waiting for you.' I've got a burning feeling in my chest.

Mum goes back to the staring at the wall.

'Mum? Are you coming?'

'Not today.'

Blood rushes to my ears.

'Fine,' I say and go to the open door.

Then I spin round.

'You know what, Mum? We're not fine. *You're* not fine. Not if you don't let me help you get better.'

A burning feeling rushes up my throat and pushes up behind my eyes.

The nurse's words come back to me.

Six months – if she's lucky.

Except luck has nothing to do with it. It has to do with us all pulling together to make sure Mum gets better.

I did some more research on Jake's phone while we were driving back from the pool and came across the statistic that one in every eleven deaths in the UK is now linked to obesity. None of the people sitting in our kitchen are anywhere close to obese. They just need to lose a few pounds to feel healthier. And they're making an effort and listening to Mitch. Mum's the one who's really sick and she's not even making an effort.

I rush to the front door.

'Feather?' Steph comes after me into the hall, but I ignore her.

It's dark but I grab my bike anyway and pedal down the drive and along the street. I need to get away from it all. I need to get away from *her*.

I pedal harder and harder. The wind pushes against my face. It feels good to be out in the cold night air.

A shadow jumps out in front of me.

I slam on the brakes.

My wheels skid. The bike slips from under me and I put my hands out to break my fall. For a second, I feel numb and then my hands burn.

There's a figure a little further on from me, lying in the middle of the road. God – I knocked someone over.

I push my bike away from me and stand up. My whole body's shaking.

Straight away, I notice it's him: his light blond hair glows under the street lamp. His face that makes me feel like I've known him his whole life. And then it hits me: he's been running this whole time. He must have run for miles.

I kneel down. 'I'm sorry—'

Clay stands up, drops his headphones from his ears and brushes himself down. From the light of the street lamp, I notice blood on his knee.

'I'm sorry,' I say again, my voice shaking. 'I'm so, so sorry.'

He's wearing bright blue Nike trainers and music leaks through the big black headphones he's got clamped around his neck, the beat sounding like one of Jake's Macklemore albums.

I pick up my bike.

'Sorry,' I say again, because it's all I can think of. And then I burst into tears. Big, embarrassing, blubbery tears.

Clay looks up and down the street – no doubt to check that no one's seen him with the sobbing daughter of the obese woman.

Thinking that makes me blubber even more.

He touches my shoulder. 'Let's get out of the road.'

The warmth of his hand presses through my T-shirt. He's really hot from running and there's sweat glistening on his brow, but it doesn't gross me out like sweat usually does. It makes my stomach go warm and kind of melt into itself. I don't ever want him to take his hand away.

Clay goes over to pick up my bike. As he pushes it over to me, the wheel clicks and I notice a spoke sticking out.

'Here.' He hands me the water bottle he's been clutching.

'Really?' I can't believe he's going to let me drink from the same bottle as him.

He nods. 'It'll help.'

I take the bottle and tip the water into my mouth so that I don't touch the rim – I reckon he wouldn't want my snotty slobber all over his bottle. 'Thanks,' I say and hand it back to him.

He leans forward, takes my hands and pours water on my palms. Then he brushes the grit off.

'I used to skateboard,' he says. 'I grazed my hands and knees all the time.'

My palms sting so much I want to yank them away but I don't want to take them out of Clay's hands.

'Looks like you were in a hurry to get somewhere,' Clay says.

I shake my head. 'I've had a tough day.'

He pauses, like he's hesitating, and then he says, 'Want to talk about it?'

'Not really.' The words just come out. I don't mean them: even before I knew who he was, when I saw the suitcase with the I LOVE NYC sticker outside Rev Cootes's front door, I've been dying to talk to Clay. But I'm worried that if I talk to him I'll make even more of an idiot of myself. And anyway, he hesitated, didn't he? I bet he just offered to be polite.

'Okay.' He pulls his headphones up over his ears again and flicks through his iPhone.

If I don't say anything now, he'll go and he'll think I was rude and he won't want to speak to me ever again.

'You live with Rev Cootes?' I blurt out.

'Grandpa?'

Grandpa? Wow, not in a million years did I think I'd hear anyone call Rev Cootes that.

I nod. 'Yeah, your grandpa. You staying with him long?'

He shrugs.

Any minute now, he's going to take off.

I touch his arm. 'Maybe…'

He looks up and frowns.

'Maybe we could talk… just a bit.'

He takes his headphones off again.

'But not here,' I add quickly.

I need to get away from the house and The Green and everything that reminds me of Mum.

'Sure.'

And then my chest goes tight because I think of Jake and how he's the one I tell about Mum and how we don't ever take anyone to our special place. It feels like I'm betraying him twice over. Three times over, seeing as he wants to get to know Clay too.

'So, where are we going?' Clay smiles.

I lock my bike to the lamppost by the park gate, put the bike light in my pocket, and take Clay through a gap in the fence.

As we walk across the empty park, the wet grass seeps through our trainers. He follows me, without asking questions, as if breaking into a park is the most normal thing in the world.

When we get to the Lido, I take my bike light out of my pocket, switch it on and sweep it across the pool.

Clay hangs back.

'What is it?' I ask.

For a few seconds, he doesn't answer.

'Clay?'

I hear him swallow. And then he says. 'Nothing, it's just bigger than—'

'Than what?'

He doesn't answer.

'You've seen the Lido before, haven't you?'

He looks back at me and blinks and there's a long pause.

'Yeah. But it was a long time ago. I was so young I don't really remember anything.'

But do you remember me? I want to blurt out, only Jake's right, it'll just come out sounding desperate.

He clears his throat. 'What I actually meant is that it's bigger than the public pools we have back home.'

'I thought everything was bigger in America.'

'We don't really have pools like this.'

'Come on,' I say and usher him to the edge of the pool.

He peers over. 'Isn't it dangerous?'

One thing I hadn't expected from Clay was that he'd be scared of stuff, especially of a plain old empty Lido. He seems like the kind of guy who'd dive into things headfirst and think about whether it was dangerous later.

'Not if we don't throw ourselves off the deep end,' I say, laughing. 'Come on.'

He joins me and we walk to the far end of the pool.

'It's been shut for years.' I shine my bike light down into the big, empty shell, littered with leaves and twigs and piles of Willingdon dirt, and gathered in heaps in the corners. Weeds grow through the cracks in the tiles. 'They used to fill it on the first of May every year and it would stay open until mid-September, but that was when I was too little to remember. They closed it when I was one'

'It must have been amazing,' he says.

I often think about what the Lido must have been like when it was still in use – a happy, blue, sparkly place filled with children swimming and laughing in the sunshine. People came from all over the county.

And then I remember the flier from earlier today.

'They're opening it again,' I say. 'They're holding the Junior UK Swimming Championships here this summer.'

Just saying that makes me feel a glow of pride for the village.

Clay nods. 'Grandpa showed me the flier.'

I clear my throat. 'I'm going to compete… Well, if I get through to the regionals… I mean, it's going to be tough…'

I wish I hadn't said it. If I don't make it through I'm going to look like an idiot.

'You swim?' He sounds surprised.

'Fly – butterfly stroke.'

'That's hard, isn't it?'

I feel a swell of pride again but this time for me.

'Yeah, it is. I love it though.'

'Cool.'

'Will you still be here?' I ask. I think about how, if I do make it through, I'd like for him to see me swim. That maybe if he was there I'd swim even faster to impress him. That maybe I'd win.

He pauses. 'Maybe.' He looks out across the dark Lido. 'I'm not really into swimming.'

'You're not?'

I know it's ridiculous but the first thought I have when Clay says he's not into swimming: *Can you love someone who doesn't love what you love?* Swimming means everything to me. But then Mum won't go near water and I love her.

I shift my bike light to show him the ladder that goes half way down the tiled inside of the pool.

'Want to go in?' I ask, looking down the ladder. 'We'll have to jump down for the last bit, and scramble a bit on the way up.'

He hesitates for a moment and then steps onto the first

rung of the ladder. I light his way and wait for him to get far enough down to start following.

I hear his feet land on the tiles and jump down beside him. Then I take his hand.

He looks at me and then stares down at our hands.

I'm glad it's dark and that he can't see me blush.

'Sorry,' I say. 'It's a habit I have with Jake... my friend. We hold hands when we come here.'

Clay smiles and squeezes my fingers. 'It's okay, I like it.'

This time, all the organs in my body flip inside out. No boy (except Jake) has ever:

a) held my hand; or

b) said he *likes* holding my hand.

'You okay?' he asks.

'Fine,' I say, but my voice sounds wobbly, which makes my cheeks burn up even more.

Clay lets go of my hand but I can still feel the warmth of his palm pressed against mine.

'I'll show you the best bit,' I say and walk ahead of him across the tiles. Dry leaves crunch under our feet and, when we reach one of the side walls, I pull Clay down beside me and we sit with our backs against the tiles. I switch off the bike light and, for a moment, we sit in the dark. Everything is still except for the sound of our breath and the skittering of leaves on the tiles of the Lido.

'Look up,' I whisper, pointing at the sky.

Framed by the trees of the park, there's a big clearing of sky. And a thousand stars.

'Wow!'

'You'll see stars from most parts of the village,' I say. 'But here it's like the sky's putting on a show just for us.'

We stare at the night sky and I feel him smile.

'Cool that you found this spot.'

'Yeah.'

Jake and I first started coming here five years ago. Houdini had gone missing – again. After spending hours scouring Willingdon without any luck, we spotted the gap in the park fence and had the impulse to go in and look for him there. We found him bleating his head off, looking down into the big empty Lido. It's a miracle he didn't go over the edge and break his neck. Anyway, since then, whenever we're sad or need to talk or want to get away from things, Jake and me come here to talk.

'Were you having a party?' Clay asks. 'At your house?'

I laugh. 'Not exactly. It was something I organised for Mum.' I crush a dry leaf between my fingers. 'I guess you've heard about her.'

'Heard what?'

Rev Cootes must have told him about Mum.

'She's obese.' I think of those NHS articles I read with Jake. '*Morbidly* obese.'

'She didn't look that bad.'

'She got sick a few weeks back and had to go into hospital. They used a crane to lever her out of the window.'

He pauses. Then he asks, 'How much does she weigh?'

'Think of a brown bear.'

He laughs. 'A bear?'

'I looked it up. I wanted to know what else weighed thirty-seven stone – besides Mum, that is.'

'I hope you haven't told her.'

I like how easy it feels, talking to him about Mum. As easy as talking to Jake. Easier maybe even than that.

'It's one of the better comparisons,' I say.

And brown bears are disappearing from the earth, I read

that too. They're an endangered species, which is what Mum's heading for if she doesn't start looking after her health.

'I'm trying to get her to lose weight. The people you saw going into the cottage, they're from this group called Slim Skills.'

His eyes go wide. 'Seriously?'

'What?'

His eyes pop out of his bony face. 'You invited a weight-loss group over to your house?'

'Mum won't leave the house. It was the only way.'

Clay brushes his pale blond hair out of his eyes. His wrists make me think of the tiny bones of a bird skeleton. I want to ask him about why he's so thin, whether it's because he's ill, but I'm scared it will make him clam up just when we've got talking.

'Has she always been... the way she is now?' Clay asks.

'No. I mean, I don't think she was ever skinny, but she's definitely been getting bigger over the years.'

It strikes me that I've never seen a photograph of Mum young.

'There must have been a trigger then,' Clay says.

'A trigger?'

'When it started. Something that happened to make her start eating.'

Maybe if Clay has to see a counsellor to talk about whatever it is that's making him sick, it means he understands about people going crazy; about people eating too much and being scared of everything and locking themselves indoors.

Maybe Clay can help me get my head around Mum.

'If there was a trigger, I'd remember – or Mum would have told me,' I say.

'Everyone has their secrets.'

I straighten my spine. 'We don't. We tell each other everything.'

He smiles, which annoys me.

'I get it,' he says, 'you're close. But still, in my experience, when something goes wrong in someone's life, really wrong, there's always a trigger. And finding it will help more than forcing your mum to go to weight-loss sessions.'

'Is that what your therapist in New York said?'

'My what?'

Our eyes lock.

'I'm not forcing her—' I start.

'No?' He gives me a crooked smile, which makes me relax.

'I'm just trying to help her.' My voice wobbles. 'Someone has to.'

My phone buzzes. It's Jake.

I consider leaving it because I don't want to spoil the moment with Clay – but I always pick up when it's Jake.

'Hey, Jake.'

I mouth *Sorry* to Clay.

'How was the Slim Skills meeting?' Jake asks.

'A disaster.'

'I'm sorry,' he says.

I hear bleating in the background.

'Where are you?' I ask.

'I went to your house. You weren't there and your bike was missing – and Houdini was straining at his lead. So we thought we'd take a walk and look for you.'

I look at Clay, sitting in the spot where Jake should be and feel guiltier than ever.

'So are you going to tell me where you are?' Jake asks.

Clay gets up and walks around the bottom of the Lido. He keeps looking back up at the sky, his mouth open.

'I'm okay,' I say. 'I'll come by later.'

I can't explain why, but I want Clay to myself for a bit longer. And anyway, I can't tell Jake that I've brought a stranger to our special place without asking him. Especially a stranger he's desperate to get to know.

'You sound weird,' Jake says.

'I'm just a bit upset – you know, about Mum ruining everything. I'll get over it.'

'You're not giving up, are you?' Jake asks.

'Never.'

I look over to Clay, who's staring at the far end of the pool, the shallow bit where Steph says Jake and me splashed around when we were babies.

'I'd better go, Jake.'

'Sure.'

'See you later.'

And then we hang up. And I feel like I've betrayed Jake again. For not telling him where I am and who I'm with. For not asking him to join us.

I get up and walk over to Clay.

'Was that Jake?' Clay asks.

'You remember his name?' They only met once, outside Miss Tippet's office at school.

He nods.

'Yeah, it was Jake,' I say. 'He's a friend.'

A friend? What's wrong with me? My *best* friend. Besides Mum, Jake's the single most important person in my life.

'He helps me with my swimming. And his mum's my swim coach.'

They're my family, that's what I meant to say. I'm not doing so well at talking about me so I decide to change tack and focus on asking Clay questions.

'So what made you leave the most exciting city in the world for the nothing-ever-happens village of Willingdon?'

He looks up at the stars again but doesn't answer.

'I told you about Mum,' I say. 'It's your turn to share.'

He looks back at me and laughs. 'To share?'

'Isn't that what they say in America?'

He does his crooked smile thing again. 'Only in bad teen movies.'

'You're avoiding the question.'

'Mum thought it would be good for me to get away,' he says.

'From her?'

He nods. 'She's kind of intense. Lives for her job.'

'What's her job?'

'She's the principal of a private school in New York. It's famous.'

I think of Newton Academy and how pathetic it must seem next to Clay's mum's school.

'What's it famous for?'

'Rich people's kids go there. And it's religious.'

'Religious like your grandpa?'

'Mum must have got it from him, yeah. But her kind of religion is a hundred times worse.'

'Worse, how?'

'She thinks that there's only one way to believe in God and that everyone else is wrong.'

'I thought New York was meant to be really liberal and progressive.'

At Newton Academy, the Head is always saying that every faith has its place and that, in the end, we all believe in the same God, which she basically has to say because there are loads of Muslims who live in Newton because of the mosque there.

Clay flicks his hair out of his eyes.

'After 9/11, things changed. Mum decided that the school needed to have a clearer direction.'

Even though I was really small, I remember sitting on Mum's lap, watching TV, staring at those towers burning down. I thought we were watching a film.

'So, you were a pupil there?' I ask.

'I was Mum's shiny advert: the son of the principal, a straight-A student, ice-hockey captain, in the chapel choir… I even believed the religious stuff for a while. And then I realised it was all crap.'

I think me getting straight As is about as likely as Mum being a size zero. I might scrape a B in History, but that's only because I like thinking about the past. Mum says it's okay to have a different kind of intelligence, to be practical, like Dad. That's why I want to take over his business one day.

'She must be proud of you,' I say.

'I said I *was* Mum's shiny advert.'

'What happened?'

'Things changed. I changed. And she found it embarrassing.'

'She found *you* embarrassing?'

'It's complicated.'

I'm about to ask him what's so complicated and why

he ended up living in New York with his mum when his grandpa lives in England, but I get distracted by footsteps on the tarmac path leading to the Lido.

At the exact same moment, we look up.

Jake and I have been best friends for so long that I could spot him a mile off. The way he holds his head and his shoulders and how his arms dangle awkwardly at his side. I can tell he's looking down at us both, wondering who the hell I've brought to our place.

13

Jake ties Houdini's lead around the bench by the Lido and then climbs down the ladder and runs over to me and Clay.

Clay smiles at Jake. 'Thanks for the album.' He holds up his iPhone.

'You liked it?' Jake asks.

Clay nods.

I stop breathing for a second. The music coming out of Clay's headphones wasn't *like* Jake's Macklemore album; it *was* Jake's Macklemore album. Which means that they've met more than once. Wow, I'm naïve.

'You lent him one of your albums?' My voice comes out wobbly. Jake never lends his music out, not even to Amy.

They both turn round and look at me as though they'd forgotten I was there.

'Yeah,' Jake says, as though it's the most normal thing in the world that he's met up with Clay without telling me.

'When?'

Clay looks at me and frowns, probably because I'm sounding really lame, checking up on Jake like this.

'We met when I was doing the paper round.'

Jake does the round to help his mum out with the bills.

He looks at me and I can tell he feels guilty, just like I feel guilty for bringing Clay here. I guess we're even.

'I saw your bike outside the park.' He keeps looking right at me. 'What are you doing out here?'

Clay breaks the silence. 'Feather basically ran me over with her bike.'

'I had to get out of the house,' I add. 'And, yeah, I might have crashed into Clay...'

'She does that,' Jake says, smiling at Clay.

'Anyway,' I interrupt, 'I thought Clay might like it down here.'

It's like there's more air and space between the three of us all of a sudden. We go back over to the wall of the Lido and sit down. Clay sits between Jake and me.

'Cool sweater.' Clay touches the outline of a black cat on the front of Jake's jumper.

'Thanks. Mum made it.'

'Seriously?' Clay asks. 'That's awesome.'

'I'll tell her.'

Steph knits – I mean, really knits. She started knitting – like she started going to church – when Jake's dad left. She does these amazing jumpers with animal silhouettes on the front. We all say she should start a business, that everyone's into retro knitted stuff at the moment.

'Are black cats bad luck or good luck in the UK?' Clay asks.

'Bad luck—' I start.

'Neither!' Jake butts in.

Clay smiles. 'You guys should start a double act.'

'Feather's superstitious,' Jake says. 'She flips out about umbrellas inside, walking under ladders, Friday the thirteenth – black cats. I don't believe in that stuff.'

Flips out? Jake knows that I like Clay, why's he making me sound so lame?

'Do you think your mum would knit me one?' Clay asks, still staring at Jake's jumper.

Jake shrugs. 'Sure.'

Sure? He's known Clay what, like ten seconds? It takes Steph ages to make those jumpers. I got one for my birthday last year and that was the most special present I've ever had. It's red and has a picture of Houdini on the front.

'What's your favourite animal?' Jake asks.

'Hummingbirds,' Clay says.

'I'll let Mum know,' Jake says.

Jake and Clay are so locked into their conversation, I might as well not be here. I take back feeling guilty about not telling Jake I was at the Lido with Clay.

'I'd better get home,' I say, standing up. 'I have to clear up after the meeting. And make sure Mum isn't eating rubbish.'

I wait for Jake to say he'll come with me but he just sits there.

'Jake? I'm going now—'

'Okay,' Jake says.

Okay?

'Want me to show you around Willingdon?' Jake asks Clay.

I don't know if this is payback for me not telling him where I was when he phoned, and for taking Clay to our special place, or whether he's just being an idiot and doesn't realise that I need him right now and that this isn't the time to play tour guide – especially as a tour of Willingdon would take, like, five minutes.

'A tour would be cool,' Clay says.

'You coming?' Jake asks me.

Which makes me feel guilty for thinking he was trying to leave me out.

'I'd better get back to Mum,' I say as casually as I can, though what I really want is for Jake to come home with me. I don't think I can face Mum on my own.

'Okay, later then,' Jake says.

Clay raises his hand to wave.

I turn my back on them, run over to the end of the Lido and scramble up the ladder, still hoping that Jake will come after me.

Only he doesn't.

When I look back, I see him shuffle up closer to Clay. He points up at the stars and they start talking. They were meant to be going on a tour of Willingdon but it looks like they're not going anywhere.

As I walk away from the Lido, I hear them laughing like they've known each other for years and part of me wishes I could go back and join them, but I know that Mum needs me. And what I said to Jake was true: I'm not giving up on her. Not even close.

14

For the next week, I go to train at the Newton pool every day, sometimes twice a day, and when Steph and Jake can't come with me I take the bus and go on my own. I train so hard that my shoulders burn and my legs ache, but it feels good to be getting back to my training schedule and to feel my body getting stronger. And sometimes, when I'm worming through the water, my mind goes still for a bit and I forget about Mum and my chest opens and I breathe again.

On Saturday afternoon, when Steph and Jake drop me back home after an extra-long training session at the pool, I find Houdini straining so hard at his lead I worry he's going to choke. So far, Houdini has broken two out of his four legs, had a shard of glass from a Heineken beer bottle stuck in his hoof, got his head stuck in the Willingdon Park gates and been electrocuted by the fence Mr Warner, the farmer, put up to keep his cows from running across the motorway. So we don't have any choice but to tie him up. Though Houdini's so cross about being pinned to one place, one of these days, I reckon he's going to find a way to escape again.

'Come on then, just a few minutes of freedom,' I say, unclipping the lead. 'Just don't tell Dad.'

Houdini head-butts my hand and then scampers around the driveway like a mad thing, leaping and bleating and pirouetting. I reckon Mum should sign him up for the next round of *Strictly*.

For a while, I sit on the wall, keeping an eye on him. I'm grateful to have an excuse not to go into the house yet. Things have been awkward between Mum and me since I stormed out the other night. She's been expecting me to say sorry – but I'm *not* sorry. And how am I meant to bring her tea and wash her and help her get into her PJs and settle her into bed, all when we're still mad at each other?

Houdini munches the grass and goes round and round in circles like he's chasing his tail, his bell tinkling. Sometimes, I think he must have been a dog in his past life.

For a second, I close my eyes and let the afternoon sun warm my face and pretend that I've got a normal life with normal parents and a best friend who's not more interested in hanging out with a guy he's only just met than he is in me. Jake's been just as weird with me as Mum has. The two people I love most in the world feel like strangers right now.

When I open my eyes, Houdini is lying in a warm patch of grass, his eyes closed too.

I pull out my 'Mum Action Plan' list and scan the items.

Joining a support group. Well, look how that worked out. I'll have to go and see Mitch and apologise for all the trouble he went to and how Mum let everyone down.

I look down at the item I added last night: *Staging an intervention.* I saw them doing that in a film once. I know it would have to be a last resort, I mean, picture Mum having to sit in the middle of all her friends and family as they tell her how much she's hurting them by not even trying to get healthy. If it didn't work, she wouldn't talk to me ever again. But with what happened today and with Dad not helping, it's looking like one of the only options I have left. And maybe Mum not talking to me ever again might be an okay price for her staying alive.

Just as I'm relaxing a bit at the thought of having a new strategy to work on, I hear a burst of music from Mum's room. Jive music. I spin round and look up at the window of the lounge.

It's the theme tune from *Strictly*.

She's got the TV back.

I dig my nails into my palms.

Mum doesn't leave the house. And even if she did, she couldn't have wheeled herself out of the house and down the ramp and all the way to the garage by herself. And she wouldn't have been able to open the garage door. And she definitely couldn't have hauled the fifty-inch TV back to her room.

So it had to be Dad.

I jump off the wall, run to the side of the house and yank open the rusty garage door.

When Mum was still working for Dad, she converted the garage into an office. She organised his tools onto special hooks and bought a filing cabinet for his paperwork and put a desk and chair in the corner. Now the tools hang at weird angles because they're on the wrong hooks. One of the filing cabinet drawers is stuck open, yellowy bits of paper spill out of its metal mouth; mouldy mugs of coffee stand on Dad's desk – there's mould on everything, the walls and the cardboard boxes and the seat pad of Dad's office chair. Cobwebs hang from the ceiling and the air smells damp. Dad's put a bucket in the corner of the garage to catch the leak in the ceiling. Even though it hasn't rained in days, the ceiling's still drip, drip, dripping this reddy brown liquid onto the garage floor. Dad's so busy doing jobs for people he never has time to fix things at home.

At the far end of the garage, there's a pile of boxes stacked from floor to ceiling. They're supplies. Enough food to feed every resident of Willingdon and Newton combined for at least six months. Tinned fruit and tinned potatoes and tinned condensed milk and tinned hot pot and tinned spaghetti hoops and packets of rice and packets of pasta and cartons of long-life milk and a whole load of other stuff that won't go off for another zillion years. Mum says it makes her feel safe, to know that we'll never run out of things to eat.

Steph and I had propped the TV against those boxes. Of course, it's gone.

Just as I'm getting myself ready to go into the house and explode at Dad, I notice that the lid's come off one of the boxes next to his desk. The bare light bulb hanging from the ceiling reflects the glossy paper inside.

I go over and read the label on the side, which is in Mum's handwriting:

Insurance Papers

But they're not insurance papers. They're photographs. Piles and piles of photographs.

I feel so dizzy, I have to close my eyes. Red dots swim around in a sea of black.

Then I take a breath, open my eyes and look back down at the photos.

Shuffling through a few of the pictures from the top of the pile, I notice that they're from when I was really little.

So Mum and Dad *did* have a camera. And there was a time when Mum did like pictures. I look at myself in a pink tutu at a ballet showcase, another one from when I was a baby, lying in a pram, my fists held up beside my head in a pea-on-fork sleep. Then I see one photograph that gives me the same feeling I had when I found Mum lying on the floor on New Year's Eve: like the bottom's just fallen out of my life.

Mum's sitting on the edge of the Lido, her legs dangling into the water.

'Feather?'

I look up. Dad stands at the door that leads from the kitchen into the back of the garage.

'What are you doing?' he asks, walking over.

I stuff the photograph into the back pocket of my jeans.

'Nothing.'

He puts the lid back on the box and carries it over to a filing cabinet.

'Please don't play around with my work papers,' he says. 'I'm finding it hard enough to keep everything in order.'

I want to blurt out that I know he's lying, that they're not work papers, that they're a bunch of photos from when I was little – from *before* I was little – hundreds of them, and that if the one I found is anything to go by, he and Mum have some serious questions to answer.

I look back over to the box where Steph and I had put the TV.

'Why did you bring the TV back in, Dad?'

He shoves the box under a dustsheet with a pile of other boxes.

'Your mum asked for it,' he says.

'Of course she asked for it, Dad. What did you expect?'

'She's allowed to have some entertainment, Feather.'

'But it's not helping, Dad, is it?' I hear my voice thicken. 'Like you cooking her fatty, sugary things isn't helping. Like nothing you've been doing for Mum for the last five years has been helping.'

Dad stares at me for a moment, as though he doesn't recognise me. And maybe he's right. I feel like something's changed in me too; I feel like, no matter how much I want to, I can't go back to the person I was before New Year's Eve.

Dad takes some tools off the hooks and puts them in his box.

'I've got a late call-out,' he says. 'Mum's been waiting for you.'

'Dad – you can't keep ignoring this.'

He looks at me for a second and then blinks and says, 'This isn't something you can fix, Feather.'

Why does everyone keep saying that?

'Yes, it is. If you help me, we get Mum better.'

He checks his phone. 'I'll be back late,' he mumbles and walks back through the kitchen door.

I grab a box of nails from his desk and hurl it at the wall. The plastic container splits open and a shower of metal falls to the floor.

Why doesn't anyone understand how important this is?

Mum needs you. Dad's always saying that.

'Don't you get it, Dad?' I shout at the door he's just walked through. 'If we don't help Mum get better, she won't need us ever again!'

I go back out through the garage door to the front garden.

Houdini's bell lies in the patch of grass where he was sunning himself just a few minutes ago, next to his snapped collar.

Please, no.

I scan The Green but can't see him anywhere.

Dad's van is still on the drive, so he must be in the house. He won't have noticed that Houdini is missing. Not yet.

I run up the ramp, open the front door and yell, 'I'm taking Houdini for a walk! I'll be back in half an hour!'

And then I slam the front door and run down to the road. Crap. Crap. Crap.

15

'Houdini!' I yell as I run across The Green.

Why the hell didn't I keep him tied up?

'Houdini!'

Every time Houdini escapes, he gets more adventurous. Last time, Dad found him by the bus stop, like he was waiting to hop onto the 474 to Newton. A little further from there, the motorway starts. And I'm not talking about a small village motorway a couple of lanes wide with cowpats and tractors and a takeaway van in the lay-by. I'm talking a proper, full sized, lorries rattling past in the slow lane and idiots speeding in the fast lane, get yourself killed if you step out into it, motorway.

Anyway, my gut's saying that Houdini is heading straight to that motorway.

I run past Rev Cootes, who's collecting empty Coke cans and crisp packets and other rubbish from the front bit of St Mary's, and I run past the bus stop and then past Mr Warden's field (checking to see whether Houdini is there because he likes cows) and then out to the roundabout that leads to the M77.

The air from the whooshing cars nearly knocks me over,

as does the smell of petrol wafting off the tarmac. Part of me doesn't want to look, in case I see a Houdini-shaped splat in the middle of the road, but I force myself to scan up and down the motorway anyway; Houdini's had so many narrow escapes, it wouldn't surprise me if he'd magically got through to the other side of the road.

'Strange place to take a walk.'

I spin round to see Jake standing there.

'You're here,' I say, smiling.

'Clay said he saw you running like a maniac from the house.'

'Clay said…?'

'Amy wanted to meet him, so I took her over.'

My chest goes tight. Jake never brings Amy to Willingdon. Although we've never spoken about it, it's like a deal we have – that, in Willingdon, I get to have Jake to myself. He knows that it's my way of coping with him having a girlfriend I can't stand.

'You actually left Amy with him?' I ask. If Jake's at all interested in impressing Clay, he's just gone and blown it.

'Amy thinks that just because he's from New York, he must know loads of A-list celebrities. She begged me to let her come over.'

I've heard Amy and her friends talking about Clay. Jake's right: everyone's totally psyched about him being American. For those of us who live in Newton or Willingdon, coming from New York is as exotic as coming from the moon.

'Houdini's escaped,' I say.

He smiles. 'Right, let's get looking then.'

And right there, I love him again. In the end, he always shows up when I need him.

'And I can't stop worrying about Mum,' I say.

Jake was there when the nurses spoke about Mum not having long left to live. He must get how serious it is.

'Your mum's going to be okay, Feather,' he says.

A Tesco lorry roars past. We both step back. And just like that, I realise Jake doesn't get it. He's dismissing how serious things are, just like Dad is.

'You been to the Lido?' Jake asks.

I shake my head. But he's right, that's where we should look next. Houdini likes it there. And there are loads of leaves and bushes and lots of grass in the park.

'Well, let's go then.' He takes my hand.

On the way to Willingdon Park, we scan people's front gardens. Houdini could munch his way through all the gardens in Willingdon and still have room for pudding.

'It'll be amazing to see it open again,' Jake says, looking across the empty Lido.

'Yep.'

Steph, who works as a cleaner for the Newton council, said they closed it because they couldn't afford to keep it open, but from what I can gather, the Lido's one of the only things that's ever made the village money.

'What's this?' I ask, walking up to a tree with a laminated sign.

We go up and read it:

NO! TO THE LIDO! There's a hand-drawn picture of a pool with a big red cross through it.

'Mum says there have been some letters of complaint at the council,' Jake says. 'It's really driving people crazy.'

'Why? It'll be amazing for the village.'

'I guess people don't like change. And they think it will cause noise and disruption to the village. There was a big piece about the dispute on the front page of the *Newton*

News. Apparently, a local resident wrote a really fiery letter to the editor.'

Jake gets to read the front page of the *Newton News* before anyone else when he collects the papers for his round from the corner shop.

'It doesn't make sense. Having the Lido again will make us special, it will bring people to the village. And having the swimming championships here this summer will be amazing.'

I stare out at the empty Lido.

'Do you think I'll be good enough to get through to the finals?' I ask.

I imagine the sun beating down on the water, the lanes divided up, me standing on a starting block, ready to dive in.

'Of course you are. You've been training like crazy and you're the most determined person I know, you're bound to make it.'

'Even against Amelia?'

Amelia's a girl who represents North London in my age category. We always come up against each other in the final.

'She won't even come close,' Jake says.

I slip my arm under his and lean my head on his shoulder.

'I wish Mum could have reacted better when she saw the flier. She knows how important the competition is to me.'

Jake doesn't answer. He and Steph are really close, so close that I sometimes wonder whether she tells him stuff I don't know about. Stuff about Mum. Like why they had that row at Christmas.

As I look out at the Lido, I think about the picture of Mum in the back pocket of my jeans. As soon as Dad's out on a job, I'll go and dig out that box in the garage. Who knows what else I'll find out about Mum and Dad and what life was like before she stopped leaving the house?

My eyes go hot and stingy and every cell in my body feels tired.

Tired of trying to help Mum and getting it thrown in my face.

Tired of trying to persuade Dad that he has to get on board.

Tired of fixing things between Mum and Steph.

Tired of hoping that maybe this century I'll find a guy who'll actually like me.

And tired of spending my life looking for a goat.

I sit down on the edge of the Lido.

'Hey, it's going to be okay,' Jake says, sitting down beside me and putting his arm around my shoulders.

I stare down at a couple of leaves chasing each other along the dirty tiles.

'Do you think that someone can go from loving something to hating it so much that they won't go near it?' I ask Jake.

'Like what?'

I take a breath and pull out the old photo of Mum and put it in Jake's hands.

He holds the photo up to his eyes.

'Wow, the whole village is in the pool!' He looks up at me. 'Who took this?'

My throat goes tight. 'I don't know. Dad, I suppose. I wasn't meant to find it.'

He waits for me to continue.

'You know Mum and Dad,' I say. 'How they've always said they don't have any photos from when I was little because they couldn't afford a camera and because they thought memories were better kept in our heads rather than on paper…'

'Yeah, I remember the speech…'

'But *everyone* takes photos of their kids, right? It's just what parents do. Even parents who aren't into taking photos. And it's not like they couldn't have found a cheap, second-hand camera.'

'Where did you find the photo?' Jake asks.

'In this old box in the garage.'

Jake traces his fingers over the bit of the photo where Mum's sitting on the edge of the Lido. It's hard to make her out because it's full of kids and mums and dads splashing around, and there are balloons and banners because it's Willingdon Day – but I'd know that long, shiny hair anywhere. And that smile.

'Dad once said that every man in Willingdon fancied Mum,' I say. 'I thought he was just trying to make Mum feel better about being overweight, but I guess he was telling the truth.' I take the photo and point at Mum's legs dangling into the water. 'And look, she's totally okay with the pool.'

Jake goes quiet again, so I go on:

'And Mum doesn't even let me talk about swimming, even though she knows it's one of the things I love most in the world and that every time I take part in a competition I swim harder because I want to make her proud, which is just stupid because she won't ever see me.' The words tumble out.

My vision goes wobbly. I sniff back the tears.

Jake draws me in tighter and maybe it's because I'm too tired to move or maybe it's because of the shock of finding out about Mum, but I drop onto his shoulder and start sobbing.

'I'm sure there's an explanation,' Jake says. 'Maybe you should talk to your mum. Ask her right out.'

'No. She'd just freak out.' I straighten my spine and sniff back the tears. 'Could you ask your mum?'

Steph would have known about Mum going to the Lido and being happy when she was younger – which means she's been lying to me too.

'It's complicated…' Jake says.

I stand up. Whenever I think that he's going to help, that he understands, he says something to undo it all.

'I'd better keep looking for Houdini.'

We walk back to The Green without saying a word. Then Jake gasps and points at Rev Cootes's front garden:

'Look! Over there!'

Houdini's right in front of Rev Cootes's house. His white fur is covered in soil, his jaw's grinding from side to side and his pink tongue's chewing the life out of what looks like a pot plant.

And behind Houdini, Rev Cootes stands on his front doorstep, staring right at me.

16

On Sunday morning, after an early morning training session with Steph and Jake at the pool, I stand on Rev Cootes's doorstep, holding a Fuzzy Deutzia.

When I dragged Houdini home from Rev Cootes's garden the other day, I yanked what was left of the plant out of his mouth and took it to The Willingdon Seed. One of the gardeners at the shop poked at it and then spent ages looking it up on the internet. It's got these delicate star-like flowers – it's not really the kind of plant you'd imagine Rev Cootes picking out. Anyway, the guy ordered me another one and I went to collect it yesterday, only he didn't warn me how expensive it was and by the time he'd wrapped it up and put it through the till, I didn't feel I could ask him to send it back. So I had to eat into my savings for Mum's gastric band – and all the other things that are going to help her get thinner. I'll definitely have to get a job now.

I knock on the door because Rev Cootes doesn't have a buzzer, and pray that Clay answers. He hasn't been at school for days, so I haven't been able to spend time getting to know him.

The other reason I hope Clay answers is because it would

mean I didn't have to talk to Rev Cootes. No one goes to see Rev Cootes out of choice. Besides the walk between the vicarage and St Mary's and the gardening he does in the cemetery, Rev Cootes doesn't go out. And he doesn't have Mum's excuse of not being able to walk on his own. I reckon he just doesn't like human beings very much. And, judging by how he yells at Houdini, he doesn't like animals either. He probably doesn't like anything alive. Poor Clay.

I clench my hands to stop them from shaking.

Squeaky footsteps walk towards the front door. Then it opens, just a crack; the security chain is still on.

'What do you want?'

It's definitely not Clay. Clay's got an American accent. And his voice doesn't sound like it would graze your skin if you got too close.

I thrust the Fuzzy Deutzia into the gap above the security chain so Rev Cootes can see it.

'It's a new plant. To say sorry.'

A pause.

'What am I meant to do with a plant?'

My heart hammers against my ribcage. I should just go. But then I think about what Mum's always saying about how being brave is one of my defining characteristics.

I take a breath.

'It's the same one. I checked. I thought you could put it back in the earth. And you don't need to worry about Houdini digging it up again: Dad's got him on a double padlock.'

'I don't need another plant.'

'Okay.' My mouth feels dry. 'I'll put it down here then, in case you change your mind.'

I place the Fuzzy Deutzia on his doormat and turn to go.

I'm halfway down Rev Cootes's driveway when I hear the click and drop of the door chain.

'Feather?'

I turn back round.

'Do you like tea?' he asks.

'Eh – yes.'

I'm more a hot-chocolate-with-squirty-cream-and-marsh-mallows kind of girl, but I don't want to say anything that might trigger Rev Cootes's temper.

He opens his door wider, picks up the Fuzzy Deutzia with one hand and does this weird over-the-shoulder gesture with the other, and starts walking down the hallway.

I don't move.

He stops and turns round again. I look at him under the dim light. I wish Clay would come out of his room.

Rev Cootes's black cassock fades into the dark of the hallway, which makes him look like his head's floating in the air without a body.

'Are you coming in, then?' he asks.

The other day, Miss Pierce told us how it's the people you least expect who end up doing all the crazy stuff in the world. That most of the time, crazy mean people are in disguise, like dictators who make people think they've come to save the world but end up blowing it to pieces instead; like your neighbour who wears a dog collar but spends his free time chopping children into little pieces and storing their pickled body parts in jam jars in the basement.

'Yes, I'm coming,' I say.

I take a breath, walk back up to Rev Cootes's front door and follow him down the hall.

However you imagined the inside of Rev Cootes's house

(shotguns, axes, stag heads dripping with blood), you'll have been wrong.

The house is dark, sure, but that's because Rev Cootes has angled the shutters to keep out the sun. Once your eyes adjust to the dark, you'll see the pink roses and white birds and a blue sky painted on the walls; you'll notice the blossom-pink walls and the pieces of furniture with spindly legs – and you'll lose count of all the china ornaments: fairies and dancers and squirrels and hedgehogs. And weirdest of all, you won't be able to stop staring at the easels scattered around the open rooms, holding half-painted canvases, splashed with pastel paint.

'I didn't know you were an artist,' I say as I follow Rev Cootes into the kitchen.

He shakes his head. 'Oh, those are Rosemary's.'

Rosemary?

'She likes to have several projects on the go,' he adds.

As far as I'm aware, Rev Cootes has always been single. But then I glance at his left hand and spot a thick, yellow band clamped onto his wrinkly finger. I guess I've never got close enough to see it before.

I strain my ears to see if I can pick up the sound of Clay moving around in one of the rooms, but the house is completely quiet.

When we get to the kitchen, Rev Cootes puts the Fuzzy Deutzia on the table and stares at it for a minute.

'They're Rosemary's favourites,' he says, brushing the white star-like flowers with the pads of his fingers.

Then he picks up a tray from the counter and carries it over. It's got a big teapot on it with pink roses growing up the side and china cups with the same roses growing up them too and a silver sugar bowl with silver tongs and silver milk jug and silver teaspoons and a silver tea strainer. The silver things are so shiny you can see your wonky face reflected in them like in those crazy fairground mirrors.

Rev Cootes points at a chair, 'Take a seat, Feather.'

I feel like I'm about to have tea with the Queen. Or an axe-murderer.

Behind Rev Cootes, on the kitchen wall, I spot a photograph. I can't be sure because the guy in the photo is really young and he's got a pencil moustache but it's definitely Rev Cootes. And poised in Rev Cootes's arms, in mid-waltz, stands the prettiest woman you've ever seen: black-and-white-movie-star pretty. *Beautiful* pretty. So she's real. And there was a time when Rev Cootes left his churchyard – with Rosemary, whoever she is.

There's a small brass plaque attached to the photo frame: FINALISTS: THE WILLINGHAM WALTZ, 2000.

'You dance?' I ask.

He looks round at the photo.

'Rosemary's the talented one. I do what I can to keep up.' He smiles. 'We dance for ourselves now, that's enough.'

I'm not very good at grammar and tenses and that kind of stuff, but whenever he talks about Rosemary, it sounds to me like she's still alive. And living here in the vicarage.

Rev Cootes goes quiet. And then he says, 'We were in the final against your parents once.' It's the first time I've seen him smile. 'Josephine and George were the most beautiful couple in Willingdon.'

I think I'd have been less surprised if Rev Cootes had admitted that he was in fact an axe-murderer and that he was going to kill me and then pickle me in jam jars along with those other children in his basement.

'Mum and Dad – *dancing*?'

Dad's so gangly he's bound to have two left feet and he and Mum just aren't the kind of couple who do stuff like that together. I mean, if Mum made a wrong step, she'd squash him. They love each other because they're married, but they're not into that romantic, slushy stuff.

'If there's someone to rival my Rosemary on the dance floor, it's Josephine Tucker,' he says.

And then it hits me. Rev Cootes would have known what Mum was like before she locked herself indoors, before she had me – when she wasn't scared of the water yet and sat by the Lido.

'Do you still dance?' I ask.

'Only at home. Rosemary is too tired for competitions. She taught ballroom dancing in Willingdon and Newton for forty years.'

And then it hits me that for all their differences, Rev Cootes and Mrs Zas both love ballroom dancing. Maybe when he knows that about her, he'll like her more. Plus, they're both the same age and they're both kind of lonely. It would make sense for them to spend some time together. Unless Rosemary really is around. Which looks unlikely.

'Did you know that Mrs Zas teaches ballroom dancing?' I ask.

He furrows his brow and his eyes go dark and he gives me the look he gave me when Houdini had shredded his Fuzzy Deutzia.

'It's not the same,' he says.

'Not the same as what?'

'Rosemary gave proper lessons. She was classically trained. She took dancing seriously.'

So that's why he doesn't like Mrs Zas: he knows she's been giving lessons. And it makes him sad because he feels like this mad woman who goes round in coloured headscarves and jangly jewellery and fancy-dress costumes has replaced his beautiful wife. Plus, Mrs Zas doesn't believe that the waltz should be a competition.

'Rosemary and I did a different kind of dancing,' he adds.

Isn't a waltz a waltz? I mean, I get that there are different techniques, like how I do butterfly stroke differently from other people, but basically the dance must be the same, whoever does it.

'I don't understand,' I say.

'I don't expect you to understand,' he snaps back, which gives me a jolt and reminds me that only a few minutes ago I thought he might be an axe-murderer.

'Sorry,' I say.

He doesn't answer so I lean over the china cups and notice they're filled with hot water. Rev Cootes picks them up, carries them to the sink, empties them and brings them back to the table. He places one of the steaming cups in front of me.

'You need to heat the teapot *and* the cups,' he says. 'A steaming teapot opens the leaves and a warmed cup keeps your tea hot. Serving tepid tea is criminal.' He makes a sucked-on-a-lemon face when he says the word *tepid*.

I've never been scared of having a cup of tea before.

He picks up the milk jug and fills the bottom of my china cup.

'There's some disagreement as to whether the milk should go in before or after but I'm with the Royal Society of Chemistry: when poured into hot tea, milk separates, which causes degradation. You'd need a microscope to see it but you can taste it. This does not happen if you add the milk first.'

Rev Cootes pours tea into my cup: it looks like liquid gold and sunshine and honey all at once.

'Wow,' I say.

'Not a word I would choose, but, yes, tea is a small miracle.' He picks up a white-crystal lump with the silver tongs. 'One or two?'

'One please,' I say, hoping it's the right answer.

He plops in the sugar, gives my cup a quick stir with a silver spoon, pushes the cup and saucer towards me and sits back in his chair.

Then he stares at me.

'So, are you going to try it, Feather?'

I'm not sure how. I mean, I've obviously drunk liquids out of cups ever since I was a toddler, but not like this, not proper tea from a teapot in a warmed china cup with milk poured in first. I'm worried about slurping and spilling and generally doing something to upset him.

And then I have a thought: maybe this is Rev Cootes's way of luring in his victims. Maybe he goes through this whole ceremony and really the tea's poisoned and the person he's about to murder is so hypnotised by his whole tea ceremony thing that they don't realise that they're about to die. The fact that he hasn't poured himself a tea and that he's just watching me confirms my theory. But would he kill me with Clay in the house? Maybe he's killed Clay too – maybe that's why Clay hasn't been at school. People kill their own family members all the time, more than strangers—

Rev Cootes's eyebrows scrunch together.

'The tea's getting cold, Feather.'

My hands shake, like they did when I stood on the doorstep.

He won't stop staring at me.

I blink, look down at my tea and lift the cup from the saucer. I make sure to keep my little finger down because I remember watching a film with Mum where posh people all had their little fingers in the air when they were drinking tea and she said that the director had got it all wrong, that *real* posh people think it's vulgar to do that and that it's only people who want to pretend to be posh who put their pinkies in the air and that it's a dead giveaway that they're really not posh at all.

I close my eyes and take a sip.

Please don't let me die, I say to myself.

I feel the liquid going down my throat and the corners of my mouth lift. If it is poison, well then, poison tastes totally yummy. Warm and fresh and light and rich all at once.

'So, your verdict?'

I put down the cup.

'It's perfect.'

And then, for maybe the first time ever, I see Rev Cootes smile – and I realise that, putting aside the fact that he's ancient and that he might be a serial killer, he's actually quite handsome. A Clay kind of handsome.

'Good.' He pours himself a cup. 'You've met our grandson?'

I nod. At last I'm going to find out what's up with Clay.

'We're worried about him. Rosemary, especially. I thought that perhaps, being of a similar age, you might be able to help.' Rev Cootes drops a second lump of sugar into his tea. 'He has a modern condition that I am finding a little difficult to understand.' He takes a sip of his tea.

I'm grateful to see that he doesn't lift his little finger; at least I got that right. I send Mum a silent thank you.

'A modern condition?'

He nods. 'Clay has decided to stop eating.'

'Oh.'

I don't know what to say. I've never considered that a boy might get an eating disorder. But it all starts to make sense. How painfully thin Clay is, how grey his skin looks, the bags under his eyes, how he goes running all the time and keeps himself to himself. Apart from the stuff they taught us in PHSE, and finding out that a girl called Daisy, who was in my class a few years back, had to go and stay in a special hospital in London because she had to learn to eat again, I don't know much about anorexia. And I don't get why someone as cool and interesting as Clay would want to damage himself like that.

'He's in need of a friend or two.' Rev Cootes looks out through a crack in the curtains. 'I saw you talking to him the other day.'

He really is like Mum, spying on the world from inside his house.

'Yes, we chatted.'

'He needs to spend time with people his own age.'

It's what Steph keeps saying about me. I mean, I spend time with Jake, obviously, but when I'm not with him I'm with Mum.

'Maybe he's happy the way he is,' I say. And anyway, he's got a new friend, I want to say – *my* best friend.

Rev Cootes shakes his head. 'Clay isn't happy.'

He puts down his cup, stares into it for a moment, and then stands up.

'So it's settled then,' he says.

'Erm—' I haven't got the foggiest what we're meant to have settled.

'You will be his friend,' he says. As though being someone's friend is as easy as picking up a pint of milk from the corner shop.

It hits me then that maybe Rev Cootes has never made a friend in his life.

'I have your word?'

My word? Who even speaks like that any more?

'Yes,' I say, mainly because I don't think I have a choice in the matter.

Rev Cootes walks into the hall and then stops and looks round. 'What are you waiting for, Feather?'

With a bit of regret, I leave my cup of tea and follow him.

Clay's room is so dark, I can't see where he is. Maybe he left when I was talking to his granddad.

I look over my shoulder and watch Rev Cootes disappear down the hall. Then I turn back to the room.

'Clay?' I whisper.

The air smells of sleep.

I feel around for the light-switch.

'Clay…'

I wonder whether Jake has been in here. I find the switch and flick it on.

'Don't.' A mumble from the corner of the room.

Clay sits curled up on his bed, his hands over his eyes. It makes me think of Mum on her bad days.

'Turn it off,' he says.

I switch the light off again but push the door open a little more so that at least there's enough light for me to see where I'm going.

'Are you okay?' I ask, walking over to the bed.

He sniffs. 'I've got flu.'

So that would explain why we haven't seen him around school for the last few days. Only he doesn't sound like he's got flu, his voice is way too clear.

I go over and pull back the curtains and open the window: I'm not going to stay in this room talking to him in the dark, breathing in old air.

When I turn to face him, it's like I'm seeing one of those famine victims from the news, all hollow cheeks and hollow eyes and jutting-out collarbones. I mean, he looked thin the first time I saw him, but now, I may as well be looking at a skeleton – a skeleton wearing PJs. Clay doesn't have flu: he's starving. Mum may be freakishly overweight, so overweight that she's made herself ill, but her extra pounds have never shocked me as much as seeing Clay in front of me looking like a ghost.

'You've been cooped up in here since Tuesday?' I ask.

He nods.

I'm waiting for him to ask me what I'm doing here – and to ask me to leave – so I leap in and explain before he gets the chance:

'Your grandfather asked me to come and say hello.' I clear my throat. 'Are you feeling better?'

He shrugs. And sniffs again.

'It's not just the flu, is it?' I burst out, and then I regret it because calling someone a liar isn't usually the best start to a relationship.

But he doesn't get angry. Instead, he juts his chin towards his bedside table – I go over and find a handwritten letter covered in really neat, tight writing. The envelope has a NYC stamp on it.

When he doesn't say anything else, I pick it up and start reading:

Dear Clay,
I hope that, with a bit of time and distance, you've had the chance to think about what you did and how your actions have consequences…

I suck in my breath. 'Wow.'
'Yeah.'
'Your mum?'
He nods.
He gets off the bed and grabs the letter with his skin-and-bone fingers and shoves it under his pillow.
'She likes to check in every now and then to make sure I remember how much I've disappointed her.'
Once again, like when we chatted by the Lido the other day, I want to ask him what he did that was so bad, only if he wanted me to know, he wouldn't have snatched the letter away, would he?
'I'm sure that's not true,' I say. Though I'm not so sure; I mean, she made her feelings pretty clear in that first line.
'Oh, it's true.'
I look around the room, at how dark and gloomy it is, at how Clay probably hasn't been out for days.
'You want to come round to mine?'
'I thought your mum hated visitors.'
'She does. But she'll like you.'
For the first time since I came into his room, he smiles, a smile that makes me think of Rev Cootes when I said I liked his tea.
'You sure?' he asks.

'As long as you promise not to take photos of her and sell them to the *Newton News*, or force her to eat salad, and as long as you don't look at her like she's an alien, just because she's overweight—'

'Damn, there go all my plans...'

I smile at him. 'So, you coming then?'

He looks out through the window, his eyes so blue they're transparent, and then he blinks. 'Sure. Would you mind stepping out while I get changed?'

I feel myself blushing. 'Of course.'

I go out into the hall. And as I wait I imagine him pulling off his T-shirt and his PJ bottoms. And then I picture his ribs sticking out and his stomach caving in rather than sticking out and his hipbones poking into the waistband of his boxers. And thinking of all those things gives me goosebumps, because when you're that thin, your body starts to close down, just like it did with Daisy, that girl in Year 7.

He steps out of his room, pulling a hoodie over his head. Then he pushes his fingers through his hair and smiles. I wish I could do something to help him get better but I feel as clueless about how I'm meant to do that as I feel about how I'm meant to get Mum to a healthy weight.

'Ready?' I ask.

He nods.

As we walk into the hall, I hear old-fashioned waltz-music, like one of the CDs Mum puts on. It's crackly, like a vinyl. The door to the lounge is open just a crack and through it I see Rev Cootes sitting on his sofa, staring into space. He doesn't look scary at all – he looks small and frail and alone.

'Is he okay?' I ask.

'He misses Grandma.'

'She died?'

'No.' He pauses. 'It's worse than that.'

I can't think of anything worse than the person you love dying.

'She's in a nursing home. She's got Alzheimer's. When she stopped recognising who he was, he gave up visiting.'

'He doesn't visit her?'

'It broke his heart, seeing how much she'd changed.' His eyes go sad. 'And she doesn't recognise him any more.'

'But he talks about her like—'

'She's still here?'

I nod.

'It's his way of coping. If he focuses on what she used to be, how she danced and painted, and how happy they were together, he doesn't have to think about what she's like now.'

'He really doesn't go to visit her?'

I can't imagine loving someone that much and then cutting them out of my life completely.

'I've been working on him. But you can't force people to do things.'

It reminds me of what Clay said about Mum the other day and about what Mitch said too. But sometimes you have to force people to do the right thing, the thing that's going to make them happy – that's going to save them – don't you?

17

Clay looks over his shoulder at the lounge door.

'Your mum really spends all her time in there?'

Seeing it through Clay's eyes, the room looks even smaller than usual.

'Mum doesn't like to move.' I lower my voice: 'Though it's on my list of things to change. When Mum gets fitter, we'll eat in the kitchen again.'

He raises his eyebrows. 'Your list?'

'Yes, my list.'

I know he's thinking what he was thinking the other day at the Lido: that I'm forcing things. That I should just let her be. But he doesn't get that that's not an option for me.

As we stand at Mum's door, Clay turns and looks at me.

'Are you sure it's okay for me to be here?'

'Definitely.' I push open the door. 'Mum…' I walk in. 'Mum – I want you to meet someone.'

Mum sits in her love seat, her eyes clamped shut. Snoring. *Don't be embarrassed*, I tell myself. If Clay and I are going to be friends, he has to see Mum for who she is.

'Mum,' I say, louder this time. 'It's lunchtime.'

Mum jolts her head and snores louder. My cheeks are burning up so much, I must look like I've got sunburn.

'She'll wake up in a minute.' I say to Clay. 'She has lots of naps. It's her medication, it makes her tired.'

I go and kneel beside her and stroke Mum's arm.

'It's Clay – from next door.'

Mum's eyes fly open. She stares right past me at Clay. The sunlight presses in behind him through the open door.

Mum blinks.

'Is that you?' she asks.

'Mum?'

She sometimes gets a bit disoriented when she wakes up after a nap.

'It's me and Clay – Clay Cootes.'

Mum doesn't take her eyes off him.

Clay smiles at Mum, steps forward to shake her hand. For a moment she just stares at him and doesn't respond and I'm worried she's going to be rude and not take his hand and blank him and that I'll have to tell him to leave.

'Mum...'

She blinks and finally holds out her hand. His fingers get lost in her big, fleshy palm.

'Turns out Rev Cootes has a long-lost grandson he didn't tell any of us about,' I say.

'You're visiting your grandfather?' Mum asks.

Clay smiles. 'I'll probably stay for a bit.'

I get that warm feeling at the pit of my stomach again. I'd like that, to have Clay around for good.

'You don't have a family to go back to?' Mum asks.

I worry he's going to be put out by her being so direct but he leaps right back in.

'Mum's basically disowned me.' He clears his throat. 'And I never met Dad.'

Hearing Clay say that makes me think of Jake and how he doesn't have a dad around either. Maybe that's why they get on so well.

'I'm sure your mother loves you,' Mum says.

'Maybe.'

I hear the front door open. Dad comes into the lounge and looks from me to Clay to Mum, back to Clay. I don't know whether it's because it's the first time I've brought a boy round who isn't Jake, but Mum and Dad are being properly weird.

'This is Clay from next door, Dad.'

Dad clicks back into the present.

'Good to meet you, Clay,' he says. 'You staying for lunch?'

I freeze. We haven't had a proper Sunday lunch together since New Year's.

'I've made a healthy roast chicken,' he says. 'I took inspiration from your cook book, Feather.' He turns to Clay. 'Want to help me set up?'

I shoot Dad a look. Asking Clay to prepare food? Can't Dad see that that would be a crazy idea? But then I remember that it's only an hour or so ago that I found out why Clay was so thin. Dad wouldn't have the first clue about eating disorders.

'You don't have to…' I whisper.

'I'd love to,' says Clay.

I stare at him and blink.

'Let's get to work then,' Dad says. As he slaps him on the back, I can hear the dull thud echoing through Clay's body.

Mum and I watch them go out into the hall.

I go over and open the curtains fully and then come back and sit on the armrest of Mum's chair

'I think he did something to upset his mum,' I whisper. 'Back in New York – that's why she sent him away.'

I gather up Mum's hair, slip it over her shoulders and tie it in a knot so it's not in her way when she's eating.

'Be careful,' Mum says.

'Careful of what?'

'He's not right for you.'

I feel like I've just been punched in the stomach.

'What do you mean?'

'What I said: he's not right.'

And that makes me really mad. It's not like I'm bringing boys round every two seconds – it's not like I've ever even *talked* about liking boys. And all she has to say is *Be careful*? She doesn't even know him.

In a moment, Dad and Clay are back with the fold-up table. They lift it into the room and press it up against Mum's armchair. Without being asked, Clay goes to grab a chair from the kitchen. I carry in the food with Dad. Only one chicken. And no roast potatoes. Just piles of broccoli and carrots and peas. If I weren't so worried about Clay, I'd be hugging Dad for finally making an effort to make Mum proper food.

Dad and I lever Mum up in her armchair so she's sitting upright and then we sit down at the table with Clay.

Houdini pokes his head through the window and Dad reaches over and feeds him a bit of broccoli.

'Houdini likes to join in our Sunday lunch,' I explain to Clay.

I place a piece of white breast-meat on Mum's plate.

'You see, Mum, you can still eat chicken.'

Mum nods and smiles but I can tell she's not impressed. The fatty, golden skin is the bit she likes best.

'Help yourself, Clay,' Dad says.

Clay empties a small spoonful of peas onto his plate.

Mum leans forward and pushes the roast chicken towards him. 'George's roast chickens are famous. Dig in.'

Clay's cheeks flush pink.

I grab the serving dish and help myself to a leg. 'Clay ate with Rev Cootes before he came out,' I say quickly. 'He's just joining us for the company, aren't you, Clay?'

Clay nods, but goes even pinker.

From the way Dad looks at Clay, I know he's thinking the same thing I thought when I first saw him: he looks like a ghost, a flesh-and-bone ghost.

'You found the wishbone, Dad?'

Dad pulls the chicken meat from the bone.

'It's there,' Mum says, spotting it under the brown skin.

Dad hands me the wishbone. I wipe it with a piece of kitchen roll and hold it out to Clay.

'We take one side each and snap it and make a wish.' I hold out the bone to Clay. 'On the count of three.'

We lock eyes. He smiles. I screw my eyes shut, count to three, then we pull.

The bone snaps.

For a second, the room holds its breath.

There were so many wishes I wanted to make. The biggest, being that Clay will like me back. But I know that I can't waste wishes on stuff like that right now, so I wished what I've wished every day since Mum went into hospital: *I want Mum to live.*

When I open my eyes, Clay's still looking at me. I wonder

what wish he made and I can't help hoping it might be about me.

'Keep it,' I say, nodding to the half-wishbone in his hands. 'As a souvenir.'

Clay puts the piece of bone into his pocket. He looks past me and his eyes go massive.

'Wow!' He points at the bookshelf. 'Those yours, Feather?'

I look over at the books.

'No, they're Mum's.' I roll my eyes. 'Boys' adventure stories aren't really my thing.'

Clay stands up and walks over to the books.

'Why don't you sit down, Clay,' Mum calls over to him.

Dad puts his hand on Mum's shoulder and I hear him whisper: 'It's okay, Josie.'

'I have the whole collection of these back home.' Clay reaches up for one of the books. 'Mum used to read them to me every night – I never got sick of them. I didn't know they existed over here.' Clay pulls a book down.

'*Max's Marvellous Adventures…*' He flicks through the pages and shakes his head. 'Wow, this takes me back.'

I don't know how she does it but somehow Mum gathers up enough strength to swing her body up out of her armchair. The table skids away from her. Clay's plate falls to the floor and smashes. His peas roll over the floorboards.

'Mum?' I hiss. 'What are you doing?' I stand up and hold my hand out to her. 'Sit down, Mum.'

Mum ignores me and pushes herself up to standing.

'These look like the real deal,' Clay says. Dust flies up as he pulls another one off the shelf. 'First editions, I reckon. They're collector's items.' He looks up at Mum. 'Did you know that, Mrs Tucker?'

When Mum doesn't answer, Clay keeps flipping through the pages.

Mum pushes over the table. The rest of the crockery and glasses smash and roll around the floor.

'Mum!' What the hell is she doing?

'Leave the books alone,' Mum says, her voice tight. 'Please.'

Her legs are shaking. She breathes hard and starts walking.

'Josie!' Dad says.

Mum doesn't hear Dad either. She keeps tearing forward. I don't remember the last time I saw Mum move this fast.

'What are you doing, Mum?'

My hand grabs the hem of Mum's sweatshirt. She yanks it away.

'Leave it, Feather,' Mum says.

Her face has gone bright red and her brow has beads of sweat all over it and her eyes are bulging like she's about to turn into the Incredible Hulk.

Clay drops one of the books.

The spine cracks as it hits the floor.

As Mum grabs Clay's wrist, she nearly falls on top of him.

'Leave my books alone.' She pushes Clay away and pulls the second book out of his hand.

I run over and take Clay's hand out of Mum's grip. 'Why are you doing this, Mum?' My eyes well up.

No, I don't know Mum any more.

Clay's gone even paler than usual. And he gives Mum the same look he must have given his mum back in New York: a look that says, *Why the hell's everything always my fault?*

He makes for the door.

Dad comes over, picks the book up off the floor, eases

the other one from out of Mum's hands and puts them back on the shelf.

Mum's whole body is shaking now, which looks scary on someone as big as her.

'They're my things.' Her voice is quiet and steady.

'I'm sorry,' Clay mumbles.

'You have nothing to be sorry about,' I blurt out. 'You didn't do anything wrong. They're just a bunch of dusty old books.'

I've never taken sides with anyone against Mum before. But right now, I don't want to have anything to do with her, let alone fight her corner over those stupid books.

'Come on.' I join Clay at the door. 'Let's go.'

The way Mum looks at me, not angry any more but sad and scared, tells me everything I need to know: she wants me to stay. But I've had enough of this.

I walk to the door.

For a moment, Clay doesn't move. He looks at the shelf of books and then at Mum and then, as if becoming aware of them for the first time, at the mess of broken plates and glasses and food all over the floor.

'Sorry that I spoilt your meal,' he says and then turns and walks out into the hall.

I spin round and look at Mum. 'How could you?' I throw at her and then follow Clay out to the front door.

18

Clay and I walk silently back to Rev Cootes's house.

'I'm sorry,' I say.

Clay pushes open the front door.

'I don't know what came over her…' I add.

Clay looks back at me and shrugs. 'It doesn't matter.' He pauses. 'See you around.' And then he disappears inside.

I know what *See you around* means: it means, *I hope I don't see you ever again.*

I run back to the cottage and then, as I stand outside the front door, I realise that going back in and seeing Mum is the last thing I want to do right now.

'Come on, buddy,' I say to Houdini, 'let's go for walk.'

I untie him and yank him out across The Green, his bell ringing ahead of us like a warning.

As I walk, I think about how Mum's been acting lately: the fact that she isn't even trying to make an effort to lose weight; that weird photo of her at the Lido, which means she's been lying all this time about being scared of the water – and just now, how rude she was to Clay. It's like a whole different Mum woke up from that diabetic coma.

I want to talk to Jake, but things have been a bit weird

between us lately. I'm beginning to wonder whether I can rely on anyone to stay the same.

'Feather?'

I look up. Mrs Zas is sitting on the doorstep of her shop. She's wearing a three-piece suit and a bowler hat over her purple headscarf and, like always, between the puffs of her electric cigarette, she's humming that tune that does circles on itself: *To everything there is a season... turn... turn... turn...*

'I'm trying to quit,' she says, holding the e-cigarette. Her nails are purple too.

'At least you're making an effort.'

She switches it off, and then she stands up.

'I think I might have a job for you, Feather.'

I want to tell her that I don't need a job any more. Mum won't even come for a walk with me, so persuading her to have personal training or a massive operation to have a gastric band fitted isn't exactly likely, is it? But then I think that maybe the job will give me an excuse for getting out of the house and at least I won't have to keep scrounging off Jake for money all the time.

'Would you like to come in?' Mrs Zas asks.

I nod then tie Houdini's lead to a lamppost.

'Don't go anywhere.' I pat his head.

He tilts his head and gives me one of his cheeky goat-grins. I don't trust him to stay in one place any more than I trust Mum to stay away from prawn cocktail crisps.

Mrs Zas disappears into the shop and comes back holding a purple cabbage.

'There you go, Houdini, that should keep you busy.' She places the cabbage in front of him and then turns to me. 'I used to have goats, back home in Ukraine.'

'I thought you were Russian.'

She takes the electric cigarette out of her mouth, glares at me and says, 'What did you say?'

I've never seen anyone snap so quickly from friendly and relaxed to scary – scarier than Rev Cootes.

'It's what most people say… that you're Russian.'

'Russia and Ukraine are as different from each other as the sun and an electric light bulb.'

From her tone, I take it that the Ukraine is the sun.

'Sorry,' I say.

'It's all right. It is what you English people call, a *sore point* for us Ukrainians. The Russians and the Ukrainians do not get on very well.'

I think of a way to make Mrs Zas flip back to happy mode. 'So you had goats, in the Ukraine?' I ask.

Her shoulders relax. 'Yes, for milk. And cheese. We loved them too.'

I wonder who she means by *we*, but I'm scared to ask another question in case I upset her.

Houdini starts munching through the cabbage and making all these happy grunting sounds.

As I follow Mrs Zas into the shop, I'm reminded of how amazing this place is – the smells, the colours, the clashing fabrics, it's like the costume cupboard at school: millions of characters just waiting to be brought to life.

'Are you any good at sewing?' Mrs Zas asks, leading me to the storeroom at the back of the shop.

I look around at the heaps of costumes and the two old sewing machines set up on a rickety trestle table. No, I'm not good at sewing.

'I'm a fast learner,' I say.

'I cannot be in two places at once, especially on a Saturday afternoon when I have the greatest number of customers. I cannot be here, mending things, and out there, welcoming customers. Perhaps we can take it in turns to sew and to welcome?'

'I'm good at being welcoming,' I say.

'That was my feeling when I met you,' she says. 'And I imagine you will know most of the clients, though we do get visitors from further afield. Or people who used to live in the village who come back to visit and stop in the shop because it's new.'

Meeting people from outside the village would be like a breath of fresh air. And maybe I can ask some of the old villagers questions about Mum and what she used to be like. Just as I'm thinking of new people, I glance through one of the storeroom windows and spot Clay jogging across The Green.

Mrs Zas follows my gaze. 'You like him, don't you?'

I shrug. 'Not really.'

I've decided to put a stop to my feelings for Clay. Fancying him is pointless. He's never going to be interested in someone like me and even if there was the tiniest chance he might like me in the asking me out kind of way, Mum's scared him off. Maybe I'm just not made for having a boyfriend.

'Would you like some of my special warm cinnamon milk?'

After the morning I've just had, warm milk sounds like heaven, especially as my lunch ended up on the lounge floor.

'I'd love to.'

I follow her to the flat above the store. Mrs Zas leads the way, humming.

'What's the song?' I ask.

'The Byrds and the Bible, I think.' She clears her throat. 'To everything, turn, turn, turn... There is a season, turn, turn, turn...' Her voice is rich and deep and gravelly.

'What does it mean?'

'It means that things come and go, that there's a time for everything – that we can't always fight it.'

That's the sort of thing that Miss Pierce would say.

'Come on, let's get you some milk.'

The flat upstairs has two bedrooms and a bathroom and a tiny kitchen with two spirally rings for a hob. She takes a bottle of full fat milk out of the fridge, adds a splash of cream, tips it into a dented saucepan and heats it up. I think about how different this is from Rev Cootes's tea ceremony.

'How do you make it?' I ask

She snaps a cinnamon stick into the saucepan and, when the milk is nearly boiling, she pours it into two mugs. Then she dollops a spoonful of honey into the milk along with a few scrapes from a vanilla pod and gives the mugs a stir.

The room fills with the smell of cinnamon and vanilla and everything bad from the day floats away.

I take a sip and close my eyes. It's delicious. Delicious in a completely different way from Rev Cootes's sunshine tea. It's thick and sweet and tastes like Christmas.

I notice a photo frame on the kitchen wall. It's of a woman with the same red lips as Mrs Zas and eyes as brown and silky looking as Mum's Galaxy bars. Which makes me think of Mum again and how she flipped out at Clay. Maybe the diabetes or the meds are upsetting her hormones or getting to her brain or something. I wish I could get Mum out of my head, even for a few minutes.

The woman has a headscarf too, a strawberry-red. Maybe headscarves are a Ukrainian thing.

'She's very pretty,' I say.

Mr Zas nods. 'She was my little sister, Irinka. We lived together before I came here.'

My throat goes tight. 'She's not your sister any more?'

Mrs Zas takes off her bowler hat and puts it on the table and then she stares down at the picture.

'She will always be my sister.'

I wait for her to go on.

'She was very ill.'

My stomach churns even more as I think of how, if Mum doesn't lose weight, she won't be around for much longer and it'll be me looking at a picture of her with tears in my eyes. I can't stop worrying, even when I'm meant to be angry with her.

'I'm sorry,' I say. 'About your sister. Her being ill must have made you very sad.'

'Yes. For a long time, I was very depressed. My heart could not understand that such a young, beautiful girl should be allowed to get so ill.' She sniffs. 'I kept thinking – it should have been me.'

'Was your sister a dancer, like you?'

'She was a much better dancer than me. At the age of twenty, she was the ballroom dancing champion of Ukraine.' She takes a sip of her cinnamon milk. 'I coached her.'

'Wow – you coached the Ukrainian champion?'

That's another thing Rev Cootes should know about Mrs Zas. He'd be really impressed if he found out how good she was at teaching.

'It must be strange,' I say. 'Going from preparing people

for national competitions to running a waltz competition in the smallest village in England.'

She shakes her head. 'People are people. Dancers are dancers. It doesn't matter where you are.' She glances out of the small kitchen window, which overlooks The Green. 'And I like it here.'

'You can teach *anyone* to dance?'

I think about how clumsy I am and how I couldn't do ballroom dancing in a million years. If it's true about Mum and Dad doing competitions with Rev Cootes and his wife, their dancing gene must have run a mile when I was conceived.

'Yes, I believe I can.' Mrs Zas looks around the shop. 'My gift – if I have one – is that I make people believe they can dance. And once they believe they can dance, they begin to dance well.' She smiles. 'Look at children, at how they move their bodies when they hear music – dancing is a natural part of who we are.'

'Why did you come to England?'

'It was my sister's idea – she dreamt of us opening a costume shop in a beautiful small village.' Her eyes are bloodshot and I'm worried she's going to cry.

'She loved dressing-up even more than I do,' Mrs Zas goes on. She takes out a blue handkerchief and blows her nose really loudly.

'She'd be happy that the shop is doing so well then,' I say.

Mrs Zas sniffs and then she gives me one of her massive, red-lipped smiles. Then she steps forward and hugs me. I can smell the menthol from her electric cigarette and mothballs from her three-piece suit and perfume and nail polish. She holds onto me so hard that I think I'm going to suffocate, but it feels good too, especially as I haven't been getting any hugs from Mum lately.

When she lets go, she looks at me and says:

'You are a very special young lady, you know that, don't you?'

I shrug. I don't feel very special. Not in a good way, anyway. But maybe, if I help Mrs Zas and if I find a way to get Mum healthy, at least I'll have done something good. Plus, I reckon that if I spend time talking to lots of people in the village, I could ask them questions about what life was like when I was born – before I was born. Maybe I could find out about Mum and why so many things I thought I knew about her don't add up any more.

We both stare out of the window. Clay's come back from his jog, he's doing stretches in front of the rectory.

'So, are you going to explain to me why you don't like that boy?' she asks.

Which is a weird way to put it.

'There's no point to liking him. He'll never notice me.'

'Why on earth not?'

'I'm not pretty…' I look down at my baggy jumper and jeans. 'I don't wear the right clothes. And I don't have the right hair. And I don't even know how to put on make-up.'

Every single girl at Newton Academy seems to have had a masterclass in hitching up their skirts and putting on eye-liner and sparkly lip-gloss and shiny nail polish. Whenever I see Amy, she looks like she's done a detour via the John Lewis make-up counter. Mum says I don't need make-up, and I don't even like make-up, or I don't think I do, but boys notice those girls and they don't notice me so there must be something in it.

I look at Mrs Zas's red lips and her long, black eyelashes and her shimmery eye shadow.

'Could you show me?' I blurt out. 'I mean, how to put it on?' My face burns up and I realise how pathetic I must sound and wish I could take back the words.

There's bleating and clanging outside. I'd forgotten about Houdini. I stand up and push in my chair.

'Don't worry. I'd better get him home, Houdini's getting impatient… And Mum will be waiting.'

Mrs Zas catches my hand.

'Wait here, Miss Feather.'

She dashes out of the kitchen and comes back a minute later with a small wash bag.

'Sit down for a moment.' She kneels in front of me and unscrews her mascara wand. 'The secret is to enhance your beauty, not to distort it. And to be true to your character.' She leans in. 'Open your eyes wide.' I stretch my eyeballs and eyelids and then feel a tickling sensation as Mrs Zas brushes the mascara up through my top lashes and then dabs at my bottom lashes. She hums a few lines from her *turn, turn, turn* song and then says, 'You see, some of us are like the bold, bright flowers of the world.' She leans back, closes the mascara and smiles. 'Red roses and yellow tulips and pink carnations. Like me.' She takes a small pot of pearly eye shadow, dabs her little finger in it. 'Close your eyes.' I feel her fingertips brushing my eyelids. 'And there are others, like you, dear Feather, who are like delicate flowers.' She takes a small mirror out of her wash bag and holds it up. 'Like bluebells and snowdrops.' I stare at my reflection. My eyes sparkle. Half of me doesn't recognise the person or the eyes in the mirror and part of me feels like the girl looking back at me is a brighter, clearer, truer version of me than I've ever seen before.

'A light touch, Miss Feather, that's all it will take to turn his head.'

I gulp and nod. 'Thank you.'

She presses the mascara and the pot of eye shadow into my hand. 'Take these. You can practise.'

At that moment, I wish Mrs Zas were my mum. A mum who actually goes out of the house and shows me stuff. Who understands what it's like to be a teenager. And then I feel guilty – Mum's been my best friend ever since I can remember.

'I'd better get back home,' I say.

As we step out of her shop, Jake comes running across The Green.

'Hey – Feather...' he says out of breath.

I wonder whether he went to see Clay before he came to look for me. And then I brush away the thought and feel grateful that he's here. I give him a big hug and close my eyes. I need him right now.

When we stop hugging, Jake steps back, frowns and says: 'You look different.'

I look down at my feet, wishing I could wipe off all that stupid make-up.

'Good different,' Jake says.

I look up and Mrs Zas gives me one of her winks.

'Thanks...' I say.

I untie Houdini.

'I'll see you next Saturday then?' Mrs Zas calls after me.

I nod. 'I'll be here.'

Mrs Zas goes back inside. Jake looks over at Rev Cootes's house.

'Why don't we go and see Clay?' he says.

'No.'

'I thought you liked him?' He pokes me in the ribs. 'You could dazzle him with your new look.'

'Mum was horrible to him.'

A beat of silence.

'He met your mum?'

Jake knows that Mum doesn't like visitors.

'Yeah. I asked him over. It was a disaster.'

'Want to talk about it?'

I nod and tuck my arm under Jake's and lean my head on his shoulder.

Next to the Lido, the chestnut tree in the middle of The Green is one of the places we go to talk. We started climbing it when we were seven and since then we've spent hours sitting in its branches, spying on the village. Jake gives me a leg-up and follows.

We sit on one of the top branches for a good hour. I tell Jake about everything that happened with Clay and Mum and he listens, like he used to listen, like he understands and cares.

'You're doing an amazing job with your mum,' Jake says.

'I'm not doing an amazing job with anything right now,' I say. 'I wanted to help Clay and he ended up getting shouted at by Mum.'

Jake laces his fingers into mine.

'He'll understand.'

'I don't think he will.'

'He's got his own demons to fight, Feather. Your mum's the least of his worries.'

I take my fingers out of Jake's. He's doing it again, talking about Clay like they've been friends their whole life. Like they're us.

'And it must be weird, him coming back to the village after all this time.'

'He spoke to you about that?'

Jake nods.

'He doesn't really remember it, of course. He was only three at the time. But I suppose there's a kind of subconscious remembering.'

I wonder what else they've been talking about without me and then I tell myself to stop being so pathetic. Jake's allowed to have other friends and I'd rather he'd hang around with someone like Clay than with Amy.

'I'd better get home,' I say. 'I need to do Mum's hair.'

Sundays and Wednesdays are Mum's hair-washing days. And even though I'm angry with her, it still needs to be done.

'Sure,' he says and we jump down into the grass.

I tie Houdini back up in his kennel and as I look up, the garage door catches my eye.

'Can I show you something?' I ask Jake.

'Sure.'

If I'm going to piece together what happened between the time when Mum was happy and smiley and liked swimming and being with people to how she is now, I'm going to have to see more of those photos.

I guide Jake into the garage and walk over to the dust-sheet, which covers Dad's old boxes, and lift it into the air. The boxes I saw the other day are still piled high. There must be loads of evidence in those.

'What are you doing?'

'You know the photo I showed you?'

'Of your mum at the Lido?'

I nod. 'This is where I found it.'

I pick up the top box, the one that was full of photos, and realise, straight away, that it's way lighter than it should be. I put it down, open the flaps and look in. It's empty.

'There were millions of them.' I stare into the empty box.

And then I notice a photo, face down, under one of Dad's filing cabinets. I kneel down, pick it up and turn it round. Jake looks over my shoulder.

'It's you at the Lido!' He says. 'As a baby.' He makes a cooing noise. 'What a cutie.'

And he's right, it is me, it has to be, only I'm not the only one in the photo. Sitting beside me is a little boy with blond hair and transparent skin and blue eyes and I understand then why Clay feels so familiar: it's three-year-old him, sitting there right beside me, smiling, the Lido sparkling behind us.

February

19

After everything went wrong with Clay and Mum and not getting any further with my investigations about Mum's past, I decide to take a different tack. I'm giving No. 3 on my list another go: *Get Mum and Dad to be happy with each other again*. Everyone says you lose weight when you're in love and Mum and Dad haven't been in love for years. People think they're really close because Dad's so nice to Mum and they *are* close and he *is* nice (Dad would do anything to make Mum happy), but that's not the same as loving each other romantically, and that's how you're meant to love each other when you're married, otherwise you might as well just be friends, like me and Jake.

When they danced and won competitions – when, like Rev Cootes said, they were the most beautiful couple in Willingdon – they must have been in love with each other. Properly in love. And that doesn't just disappear.

I'm going to do everything I can to make it come back to life. And maybe when they're in a better place, they'll tell me more about what life was like when I was little and how Mum got to be sick.

One of the ways I've planned to bring Mum and Dad

together is a romantic Valentine's supper. Yesterday, after swim training and a Slim Skills meeting, I went to M&S in Newton and bought lots of posh ingredients. I've spent most of my savings but I'll make it up with the money I earn working for Mrs Zas and, anyway, if it works, if it makes Mum and Dad notice each other again, it'll be worth it.

Amazingly, Rev Cootes has allowed me to use his kitchen to do the cooking. With his whole tea-ritual thing and liking things just so, I thought he'd freak at us making a mess, but it was his idea: he said that we'd have more room to cook here than at Steph's.

'When you get home, you'll need to store these in the fridge.' Clay puts the tray of strawberry tarts on the table.

It's like he's completely forgotten the disastrous Sunday lunch with Mum. I guess I was wrong about him never wanting to see me again.

He's wearing Rev Cootes's navy pinstriped apron, his hair and eyebrows are dusted with flour and his cheeks are flushed pink. It was Clay's idea to make a fancy meal. Turns out he's this gourmet chef, which you'd think was weird considering he doesn't eat anything, but Mum and I watched this programme on anorexia and how one of the symptoms is being obsessed with food and cooking. Apparently, some people with eating disorders like to go shopping and to cook and to breathe in food smells but then won't even take a bite when the dish is made. It made me think of Mum, but sort of in reverse, how she likes watching other people cook these amazing meals on TV but doesn't make anything herself and eats crisps and chocolate instead of proper food. I wonder how we all got so screwed up about food.

I'm glad that Jake's not here yet; it's nice to have Clay to myself for a bit. I keep blinking at him, hoping he might notice my eyes: I've been practising with the mascara and eye shadow Mrs Zas lent me.

I grab an onion for the risotto, peel off the skin and balance it on the chopping board.

'So you've been to Willingdon before?' I try to sound casual. 'When you were little?'

Clay stops arranging the strawberries.

'Yes.'

I press the knife down into the moon-glow flesh of the onion.

'You were visiting your grandpa?'

'I was born here.'

He slices up another strawberry.

'You were born here?'

I want to show him the photo of the two of us that I've been keeping in the back pocket of my jeans, to show him how we've known each other for years and years, how we've got a special connection. But I'm scared about how he'll react.

My eyes have started to run from the onion fumes so I rub them with the back of my hand.

Clay runs tap water into a glass and hands it to me.

'Here, drink this, it'll ease the stinging.'

Clay's fingers brush mine as I take the glass.

'Thanks,' I say.

I'm not doing very well at the putting a stop to my feelings thing. Which is why I feel totally embarrassed that my nose and my eyes are streaming. I picture my face as this gross, blotchy mess. And then I see the back of my hand, smudged black. I try to get a look at myself in the kitchen window but there are too many reflections. I bet I have these ridiculous splotchy panda eyes. I was stupid to think

I could pull off wearing make-up, or that it would make Clay like me more.

'You okay?' He asks.

I nod and sniff. Clay's got panda eyes too, except his are from the big shadows he has. Maybe he finds it hard to sleep, like Mum. His cheekbones jut out even more than they did when I first met him. And his skin's kind of yellow. I wonder what happens to your body if you stop eating altogether. I want to touch his cheek and to tell him that I can help him.

He steps away.

'You can add a few more strawberries to the plate when you serve up,' he says. 'And dust them with icing sugar.'

He's as much of a perfectionist about his baking as Rev Cootes is about his tea. Clay made the pastry for the strawberry tarts from scratch. We tried to find healthy versions of everything so that I didn't feel guilty about feeding Mum food that would make her worse, but we still made sure it would taste nice so that Mum and Dad felt it was a treat. I questioned Dad until he told me that they'd had risotto and strawberry tarts at the restaurant when he proposed.

I go back to chopping my onion. 'Your dad wasn't around, even back then?' I ask Clay.

'No. It was a one-night stand. Mum never told him.'

'That doesn't sound like your mum – I mean, like the mum you've described.'

He laughs in a kind of cold way that I don't like. 'What? Not telling my dad that he had a kid? That sounds *exactly* like Mum. She wanted to be in control of my life from the word go.'

Whenever he talks about his mum, his words get all these sharp edges.

'That must be hard for you. Not knowing your dad, I mean.'

Clay goes over to the sink to wash the strawberry stains off his hands.

'You know, Feather, there's loads of crap we don't know about our parents.'

A few weeks ago, I would have leapt right in and disagreed with Clay. I thought I knew everything about Mum and Dad. But things are different now.

'Do you love her?' I ask. 'Your mum?'

Clay comes over to the table. He brushes his hair out of his eyes and looks right at me. 'It wouldn't make a difference.'

'What do you mean?'

'She'd still hate me, even if I did love her.'

'What did you do that was so bad?'

He pauses and looks at the door to the kitchen. Rev Cootes is in the lounge practising his sermon for Sunday.

'I wrote an article for the school newspaper. For *her* school newspaper. She didn't like it.'

'What didn't she like?'

'I wrote about how screwed up I am.'

I take a breath. 'You mean because of you being ill?'

'Yeah, I wrote about being anorexic.'

I suck in my breath. It's the first time he's used the word.

'She didn't like it,' he adds. 'And she didn't like the language I used either.'

I think about what Miss Pierce said about how some situations require strong language. I bet Clay used just the right words.

Still, writing an article isn't enough of a reason for a mum to disown her kid and send him a whole ocean away.

'Was that all you wrote about?'

He stares down at his hands and rubs at the strawberry stains on his fingertips.

'I said that it was her fault. That schools like hers were making kids sick.'

'Wow, you wrote that?'

He nods. 'Mum doesn't get it. She thinks she's this amazing Head, who gets her pupils to achieve these incredible results, that it's down to her that so many of them get into Ivy Leagues and become lawyers and bankers and senators. She even thinks it's because of God, because her school's religious and it has this special blessing from heaven. She doesn't get that you can't force everyone to be the same, that if you stop them from being who they really are, you're doing more damage than good.'

I wait a beat and then I ask, 'Who are you then... really?'

Clay looks up at me for a second and I know that he's weighing up whether he can trust me.

And then the doorbell goes.

Jake. Damn it. Just when I was getting somewhere with Clay.

A moment later, Jake comes in, dragging Amy behind him.

She jumps onto one of Rev Cootes's counters and crosses her long legs. Even though it's below zero outside and the pavements are frozen over, Amy's legs are bare – and tanned. She's wearing a short skirt and knee-high boots. I wonder whether her legs are longer than my entire body.

'Smells *delish*, Clay,' Amy says, passing her tongue over her lips.

I wish Jake would wake up and dump her.

'My mum says it's the wine that makes the risotto.' She jumps down off the counter, grabs the bottle of white I bought for Mum and Dad to have with the meal, unscrews the cap and splashes it into the pan that Clay's stirring.

Clay laughs. Which makes me feel sick. Surely he can see through Amy?

Amy takes a swig of wine and wipes her mouth.

'It's so much fun hanging around with you guys.' Her eyes swim, which makes me wonder whether she started drinking before she came here.

Jake grabs the bottle from out of her hands and for a second I hope that he's going to tell Amy to stop being such an idiot, but before he has the chance to say anything at all, she leans forward and kisses him right on the mouth.

Jake pulls back.

He's never said it out loud but I know he doesn't like to do things like kissing when other people are watching.

A moment later, Amy, Jake and Clay are standing over the pan, laughing and pouring in more wine, the wine that I paid a fortune for. And I feel invisible. It's like Jake's replaced me twice over: first, with his girlfriend and, second, with Clay, his new best friend. And you know what I feel like, watching them together? Like maybe Jake just put up with me as a friend until he found someone better, that he was only friends with me because our mums were close and because he didn't have any other options. I feel like I've been a stopgap.

'You'll need to heat up the risotto before you serve it,' Clay says. 'If it looks dry, you can use a bit more wine – like Amy said.'

Like Amy said? So he's sucked in by her too?

Jake leans over Clay's shoulder and stares at the strawberry tarts. 'You could totally win *The Great British Bake Off.*'

'The what?' Clay asks.

'It's a cooking competition on TV,' I explain. 'Mum's obsessed with it.'

'So, what can we do to help?' Jake asks, looking around the kitchen.

I look at my watch.

'Dad will be back from work soon and we have to set up the conservatory.'

I've planned it all. Candles. Rose petals. Soft music.

'Okay – so, why don't Amy and I stay here and help Clay clear up,' Jake says. 'And you go and set up?'

I look from Clay to Jake to Amy and try to think of a way to counter this suggestion without sounding pathetic.

'Can you manage on your own?' Clay asks me.

I nod but don't look at him. 'Sure.'

I place the pan with the risotto at the bottom of a jute bag and balance the tarts on top of it and walk out of the kitchen.

I wish I could have stayed with them but at least now I'll be able to leave the card for Clay without him seeing that it was me. I mean, he'll obviously know it was me because he'll find it in his bedroom, but we don't have to talk about it, not unless he wants to.

It's the first Valentine's card I've ever written. And I know that it could spoil everything, that he could freak out and never want to speak to me again, but it's the only thing I could think to do to let him know how I feel.

There's a saying Dad's used whenever I've been scared of doing something important: *If you don't let go of the edge, you'll never learn to swim.* I remember it more than any of the other things Dad has said because it's about swimming and because it's true: when you're a kid and you're still a bit scared of going into the water on your own, you have to just jump right into the deep end and trust that your body will know what to do: that you'll be able to keep your head out of the water and that your legs will start kicking and that you'll be able to swim.

I put down the bag, grab my duffle coat from Clay's bed and pull my Valentine's card out of the pocket. My heart's banging away like the crazy beat in one of Jake's Macklemore albums.

It feels kind of exciting to be in here without Clay and a bit wrong too.

I look around for the best place to put the card. And that's when I spot it. The wishbone I gave him when he came round to the house for lunch. He's tied a piece of red string around it and used it to bind up a small notepad that looks like it might be his diary. So he kept it. And it means something to him. Blood rushes to the surface of my skin and I'm glad he's not here to see me standing in the middle of his room, pink as a lobster.

And then I notice something else.

An envelope on his bedside table. The first thought I have is that it must be from Clay's mum. Only, when I get closer, I see there's a heart on it, and bright pink writing: *My Secret Valentine.*

I swallow, hard. I look to see if there's a postmark, thinking that maybe it's some girl from New York, but it's been hand-delivered. Why am I so surprised? Even though Clay's had loads of days off school, he's already caught the attention of the girls at Newton Academy. I bet the card's from one of Amy's friends. I bet Amy brought it over herself and slipped it into his room before coming to the kitchen.

As I stuff my card back into my coat pocket, I get a

glimpse of myself in the long mirror behind Clay's door, and I'm hit by how gross I look: my hair's frizzy and my skin's flushed and my eyes are still bloodshot from chopping the onions. And my cheeks are smeared with mascara.

Why did I ever think he might fancy me?

I'm about to go when I notice something on Clay's desk. My heart thumps even more than when I saw the Valentine's card.

I walk over and pick up the first book in the series of *Max's Marvellous Adventures*.

My hands are shaking as I flip open the cover and read the inscription:

For my little adventurer. Mum x.

It's Mum's handwriting.

And she must have written the inscription for me. It's what she calls me sometimes, her *brave little adventurer*.

I flip through the pages of the book. It's all about Max's adventures at sea.

I don't believe in stupid books about boys going out and saving the world while girls stay home plaiting their hair and playing with dolls. That's what I'd told her when, a couple of years ago, she asked me whether I'd like to read them with her.

I'd rejected them. And she'd never told me that they were meant for me.

'Feather?'

I spin round. Rev Cootes stands in the doorway.

I put the book back down on Clay's desk and grab my duffle coat from his bed.

'I was just getting this,' I say.

He looks over at the book for a second and blinks and looks back to me.

'It was nice of your mother to call.'

She *called*? Mum's got the same crap phone as I do and only has two numbers stored in her contacts: mine and Dad's.

'When did she call?'

'Yesterday.' He looks across the road at Mum's window. 'It was nice of her to think of Clay.'

I used to know everything about Mum's day: when she got up and when she sat in her chair and what programmes she watched and what she ate and when she went to bed. And now she's doing all this stuff without telling me.

'He loved those books when he was small.' He looks at the cover. A little boy with curly blond hair, sitting in a sailing boat on an open sea with big waves crashing all around him. 'His mother read them to him every night.'

His eyes go sad. Then he picks up the jute bag and gives me a smile, which makes his face go all soft and kind.

'Why did Clay's mum go to New York?' I ask.

I think back to what Clay said back at the Lido the night when it was just the two of us. That there has to be a trigger. That people don't just flip their whole lives upside down for no reason.

Rev Cootes looks out of Clay's window and I know he's staring at Mum's window.

'Willingdon was too small for her.'

'I know how she feels,' I say.

I'd always thought Willingdon would be enough. That once I'd taken over Dad's business, I'd meet someone and that we'd have a family and live close enough for me to see Mum every day. I thought that would be enough. But I'm not so sure any more.

'It must have been hard for her to move country when Clay was so small. To do it on her own.'

'Rosemary has family in New York. She's American. So Eleanor had some help finding her feet.'

'How did you meet Rosemary?' I ask.

'At vicar college. She was one of those Americans who fell in love with England. She dreamt of having a small parish like Willingdon.'

'So you were *both* vicars?'

With parents like that, no wonder Clay's mum went so religious.

'Rosemary never finished her training. Dancing turned out to be her true calling.' He gives me a crooked smile just the same as Jake's. 'She always had a bigger following than I did.'

It's at times like this that I wonder how I could ever have thought that Rev Cootes was a child murderer. He's just about the sweetest old man in the world.

Rev Cootes picks up the jute bag and looks inside.

'You're a kind girl, Feather Tucker,' he says.

And then it hits me that it's not just Rosemary: he's lost his daughter too. At least he's got Clay.

'Your parents are lucky to have you,' he goes on. 'I'll carry this to the gate for you. Rosemary likes me to be helpful.'

I've got so used to Rev Cootes talking about Rosemary that it's like I know her. It makes me feel sad that he doesn't go to see her.

I follow Rev Cootes out of the house. As I look at the back of him, I realise how old he is, old and stooped and frail. As frail as one of those birds he's forever feeding.

When we get to the gate, I take the bag off him.

'Thank you for the help,' I say.

He nods and I can feel his eyes watching me as I walk across The Green. A hollow feeling settles in my chest. It's not right that Rev Cootes shouldn't see his wife any more, or his daughter. And it's not right that the first guy I've ever fancied should have got a Valentine's card from someone other than me. And that he should be with my best friend and some random girl I don't even like, having fun without me. And it's not fair that he should have talked to Mum behind my back.

As I stand at the bottom of the ramp that leads to our front door, I think about doing what Clay's mum did – escaping my crappy old world and going far, far away, somewhere no one knows me, somewhere I can be a whole new person.

Houdini's bleats break up my thoughts.

He walks over to me and nudges me with his horns. I squat down and give him a cuddle.

I know, I know, I whisper into his ears. *I've got a job to do.*

20

After I've set everything up in the kitchen, I tie a red bow to Houdini's bell and scatter silky red rose petals on the gravel (Mrs Zas let me have some from her Valentine's window display). And then I sit on the ramp, waiting for Dad to come home. It's freezing out here but there's a bit of sun left and I need some air after all that cooking and rushing around decorating the kitchen.

'Smells good in there,' Nurse Heidi says as she comes out through the front door.

She came by to check on Mum before heading home. I'm sure she comes round more often than she's paid to.

'Dad proposed on Valentine's,' I say.

Nurse Heidi smiles. 'What a romantic.'

'He was. I'm trying to get it back – the romance.'

'That's wonderful, Feather.'

'Mum's doing okay, isn't she?'

Nurse Heidi shifts her nurse's bag on her shoulder.

'She told me that she's lost weight.'

Nurse Heidi smiles at me and says, 'It's getting late, I'd better get home.'

'Aren't you happy with her progress?' I ask.

'She still has a way to go, Feather. I'm sure she'll be fine.'

Which isn't an answer.

I notice that Mum's notes are tucked under her arm.

'She hasn't lost weight, has she?'

Nurse Heidi gets her car keys out of her bag to avoid looking at me.

'Has she?' I say again.

'It's a long process… And it's not all about losing weight.'

Which basically means no.

'I'd better go.' She walks down the ramp. 'I hope it all goes really well tonight,' she says. And then she gets into her car and drives away.

I go inside and put on Dad's Lionel Richie CD. Mum and Dad had 'Endless Love' as the first dance song at their wedding. I haven't heard Dad play it in years. I thought it would be nice for them to have it tonight. That it might remind them of how much they love each other and how life used to be.

Then I go and untie Houdini from his post and walk him over to the ramp. I sit down and he flops down across my lap.

'Mum and Dad are going to like it, aren't they, Houdini?'

He nudges his head against my leg and I lean over to kiss the top of his head.

Houdini's been around longer than I have; I wish he could tell me more about what Mum was like back then. And what happened when Clay came over to talk to her yesterday.

Then I look over to Rev Cootes's house and think of Jake and Amy and Clay having fun in there without me.

By 10pm, my lips are blue, it's gone dark and Dad still hasn't shown up. And I still haven't seen Jake and Amy come out of Clay's house.

I wait for Houdini to nestle into his kennel for the night and then I go back inside.

After switching off the CD player that's been playing 'Endless Love' on a loop, I scrape the risotto into the bin – it's got this gunky crust over it, and it's gone cold. I throw the strawberry tarts into the bin too, squishing them down with a wad of kitchen roll until they're a gloopy, sticky mess. I tip the wine down the sink and gather up the cutlery and the crockery and the glasses and stuff them back into the cupboard any old how.

And for a second, it feels good. But only for a second. After that, I just feel empty.

As I close the cupboard door, I glance at the calendar, where I'd scrawled *28 days to break a habit!* under the February heading. Right now it feels like nothing's changed at all. In fact, everything's worse.

I haven't eaten anything since lunchtime but I don't feel hungry so I climb straight up the stairs to my bedroom.

When I'm halfway up, I worry that I haven't tied Houdini up again. The last thing I need is for him to go missing.

I was right, I had forgotten to tie him up. Except he hasn't made a run for it, he's just standing at the bottom of the drive, looking up the road, and I can tell that, like me, he's waiting for Dad.

'Come on, Houdini, time for bed.'

He won't budge.

I yank at his lead. 'I'm tired, come on.'

As I grip his collar and pull him back towards the house, he pulls in the opposite direction and he's so strong that I end up stumbling behind him until we're both standing in the middle of the road.

I shake out my hand, which is aching from where his collar dug into my palm.

Houdini head-butts my shin.

'Houdini, what is it?'

He looks at me for a second and then runs across The Green.

'Dad will come home!' I yell out. 'He's just on a late call-out.'

If it's my job to look out for Mum, I reckon Houdini sees it as his job to make sure Dad's okay.

As I run past the Lucky Lantern van, Mr Ding pokes his head out.

'Everything okay, Feather?'

'It's fine!' I yell over my shoulder and keep running.

But it's not even a bit fine.

For a moment, I consider letting Houdini go. It's only a matter of time before he runs away and breaks his neck by tumbling into the Lido or gets squashed on the M77, and there's nothing any of us will have been able to do about it.

But then I think about Dad and how much he loves Houdini and about how I love Houdini, too.

So I keep running.

Past St Mary's with Jake's bike still tied up against the cemetery railing.

Past Mrs Zas's fancy-dress shop with its inflatable hearts glowing in the window.

Past the mobile library.

Down Twirl Street and past Jake's house, where there's only one light left on, shining out from Steph's bedroom.

And bang into Allen, the reporter from the *Newton*

News. He's standing outside one of the houses on Twirl Street, writing something in his notebook. I try to walk past him without him seeing, just like I try to avoid him when I go to Slim Skills meetings – I don't trust him since the photo he printed of Mum at New Year's.

But he looks up at just the wrong time.

'Feather – just the person I wanted to see.'

'I'm in a hurry.' Houdini's just turned the corner at the end of the street.

'I've been canvassing local opinion about the opening of the Lido – finding you is just perfect,' says Allen. 'You'll have an insight from the eye of the storm.'

I haven't got a clue what he's talking about. I know that people in the village are getting really het up about the Lido debate but it doesn't have anything to do with me. And if I don't move now I'm going to lose Houdini.

'I really have to go,' I say and run off down the road before he has the chance to say anything.

I run all the way to the motorway, barely keeping up with Houdini. And then he stops dead.

I nearly crash into him… and then I see it, parked in the lay-by: GEORGE AND JO'S EMERGENCY PLUMBING VAN.

'Dad?' I knock on the window. 'Dad?'

Houdini lifts his body up and places his hooves on the door handle.

I knock again. 'Dad, it's me!'

Cupping my hands, I press my face to the window and look in.

Dad's sitting there with a blanket pulled up to his chin, his head bowed, and his eyes shut. He's sleeping.

'Get down,' I say to Houdini and push his hooves off

the door. Then I try the handle. It's creaky and rusty and I need to give it a good yank but it's unlocked.

Dad's eyes fly open.

'Feather?'

He sits up. The blanket drops down. Houdini jumps in ahead of me and sits on the passenger seat.

Under the orange light that shines in from the street lamp, Dad looks as grey as a ghost.

'Hey, little guy,' Dad says, then gives Houdini a stroke under his chin. It's not the first time I feel like Dad's happier to see Houdini than he is to see me. 'Gone for a wander again, mischief?'

Houdini bleats.

I push him into the back of the van and sit down next to Dad.

'What are you doing here, Dad?'

Dad rubs his eyes. 'Just having a rest.'

I take a breath to keep my voice steady.

'Why don't you have a rest at home?'

'Oh, just waiting to be called out for another job. I didn't want to disturb your mum.'

I clench my jaw. 'You didn't want to *disturb* her?'

'You know Mum doesn't sleep well.'

A lorry drives towards us, a soft toy in the shape of a red heart pinned to its fender. Dad's van shakes as it whooshes past.

'You know what day it is, Dad?'

In the grainy darkness of the van, I see his shoulders drop.

'Dad?'

He looks at his watch. 'I guess I'll risk going home,' he says. 'If someone calls, I'll head out again.' He turns the key in the ignition.

I pull his fingers away from the key.

'I asked you a question, Dad.'

He sighs. 'What's wrong, love?'

'It's Valentine's Day, Dad. That's what's wrong. The day you and Mum got engaged. The story you told me over and over when I was growing up – how you loved Mum so much that you wanted Valentine's Day to be more your day than anyone else's – remember?' I gulp. 'And now you're sleeping in your van…?'

'We can talk about this later, Feather.'

'How about a bunch of flowers? Or a box of chocolates? That would be in line with the crap you feed her. Or maybe you could have just stayed in and given her a hug. Done just one thing to show her you love her.'

Dad stares out at the motorway.

'Mum doesn't like a fuss, you know that, Feather.'

'Well maybe if you tried a bit harder – if you made it special, if you showed her how much you cared about her.' Words are flying out of my mouth so fast, I hardly know where they're coming from.

Houdini bleats and shifts on the seat. I look back and notice what a mess everything's in. Tools jumbled in a heap on the floor. Ripped cardboard. Sawn-off bits of tubing. Screwdrivers. Scrunched-up kitchen towel. When Mum helped Dad with the business, she would never have let it get into such a state. He doesn't deserve to have her name on the front.

'Just forget it,' I say.

And that's when I notice the jobs book poking out of the glove compartment. I yank it out and flip through the pages, scanning Mum's neat handwriting, columns and columns of clients and dates and job details and payment references.

The last entry was made almost six months ago, in Dad's scrawly writing.

'You haven't been making a note of jobs.'

He rips the book out of my hands and dumps it on the floor beside him.

'Leave it, Feather.'

Dad's been tearing around on so many call-outs that maybe he hasn't had time. And paperwork hasn't ever been his strong point, that's why Mum did it all for him.

'I could help you,' I say. 'I could do what Mum did.'

Dad turns away and stares out of his side window.

We sit in silence, listening to the night traffic rushing past.

'Dad?'

He sniffs and turns round to face me, his eyes shining. Then he rubs the sleeve of his overalls over his eyes and nose.

I've never seen Dad cry before.

I put my hand on his arm.

'I'm sorry, Dad,' I say. 'I shouldn't have said those things.'

He starts properly crying now, big heaves and gulps.

And then it falls into place. The fact that no one in Willingdon has been mentioning Dad doing jobs for them. The fact that we don't have money to fix anything in the house. The 'Private & Confidential' letters from the bank. Dad not letting me come to help him like he used to.

Dad hasn't been forgetting to make a note of the call-outs. And he hasn't been rushed off his feet working day and night. He hasn't had a job since September.

I lean forward and put my arms around him and hold him tight.

'It's okay, Dad. It's all going to be okay.'

March

21

'Will you walk in a straight line?' Jake nudges me to the side of the pavement.

'Hey, I'm practising!'

Mrs Zas has been teaching me basic waltz steps when the shop's quiet. It turns out that being clumsy doesn't affect dancing that much. I can't stop practising. Even at night, when I'm in bed, I feel like my feet are twitching to the beat. One two three... one two three... Plus, practising steps is taking my mind off the regional heats this afternoon.

It feels special to be doing something that made Mum and Dad so happy when they were young.

'Your dad okay?' Jake asks.

He's the only one I told about Dad and the business.

'Sort of. I've been helping him sort out the van and his books, and I've been calling his old customers to let them know he's still in business.'

After our heart to heart in the van, Dad promised he'd make more of a go of the business and that he'd stop feeding Mum rubbish. And he's been insisting that she come to the kitchen for meals. Proper meals. And I've made sure I'm there whenever Nurse Heidi weighs Mum so that I can keep track of her progress.

'You're amazing,' Jake says, tucking his arm into mine.

Jake's been spending a bit more time with me lately, though he never comes to The Green without stopping by to see Clay.

I lift Jake's arm up and twirl under it until I'm dizzy.

I wobble off the side of the pavement and Jake holds out his hand and spins me round and round until we're dizzy and laughing and stumbling around all over The Green.

I haven't felt this good in ages.

Jake collapses on the ground.

'You know you're going to be amazing this afternoon, right?'

He's talking about the regional swim heats.

I'm still spinning so hard I can't answer.

'I know you're scared,' he adds. 'You always act bonkers when you're scared. But you're going to be awesome.'

I shake my head. 'I haven't been practising enough.'

After that burst of training a few weeks back, I've let it slip again.

'You'll step up a gear once you're competing, and we can do loads of practice for the national swim competition this summer.'

Steph and me have been going to the pool alone lately, Jake keeps saying he has to work or to see Amy. I guess that's another reason I haven't been practising so hard; it's not the same without Jake standing by the side of the pool yelling my name.

'I'd like that,' I say. 'I thought Mum might come this time, but she said she wasn't feeling well.'

'Maybe she isn't.'

'She never feels well when I want her to support my swimming.'

I haven't had the courage to ask Mum about the photo of her in the Lido yet.

Jake steadies me and we walk the rest of the way to Bewitched.

I dance up and down the steps of Mrs Zas's shop.

Jake laughs and pokes me in the ribs. 'Let's go inside, people are staring.'

He's only pretending to be embarrassed. I know Jake's happy that things are going better with Mum and Dad – they're his hope that there are some parents who don't fall out of love and break up.

'Morning, Rev Cootes!' Jake calls over to the church-yard.

Rev Cootes looks up from watering his plants. Mrs Zas says he fusses over his plants too much, watering them and giving them special fertiliser and poking and prodding at them. *If you want something to grow, you've got to leave it alone long enough to do some living*, she says. Poor Rev Cootes.

'Hi, Rev Cootes!' I call out.

I'm working on him too. If I can get him to see how amazing Mrs Zas is, they could dance together. And maybe we can get Rosemary to come and watch. It doesn't matter if she doesn't understand what's going on, she'll still like it, watching the dancing. Mrs Zas says that your body remem-bers things as much as your mind does; all those years and years of dancing, it's bound to trigger something.

Rev Cootes gives us a nod.

I unlock the shop. Mrs Zas had a key cut for me for the

days she does her dance classes. Today, Jake's going to do some sewing in the back while I staff the shop.

Rev Cootes is still staring at us like he wants to say something but then, when he notices us staring back at him, he bows his head and goes back to his flowers.

'Apparently, Rev Cootes was really sociable when he was young – the life and soul of the party,' Jake says.

'Really?'

Jake smiles. 'Yeah, Clay told me.'

I feel a thud in my chest. If I could get a pound every time he says, *Clay told me this* and *Clay told me that*, I'd be able to get Dad's bank balance out of the red.

When we reach the storeroom Jake goes over to the rack of ballroom dancing costumes. 'These are awesome.'

'Mrs Zas has made loads of them herself. I've asked her to make one for Mum.'

'You think your mum will agree to wear a dress?'

'I've got to try, right?' I touch one of the purple velvet dresses with a full skirt. 'You should take lessons, Jake. Women love a man who can dance – Amy would swoon...' I hold my hand to my forehead and pretend that I'm falling backwards.

Jake blushes.

I stand up straight. 'Seriously, you'd be good.'

He tugs at his earlobe. And then he looks at his feet.

'What?' I ask.

'Nothing.'

'You're not acting like it's nothing.'

'Things aren't great between me and Amy.'

I'm hoping that Jake isn't picking up on the voices in my head saying, *At last!* And *Thank God!*

'What happened?'

'She keeps complaining about us not spending more time together.'

Only, I reckon they've been spending more time together than ever recently.

'Hasn't she always complained about that?' I ask.

'Yeah. But it's got worse. It's like she keeps checking up on me. Calling Mum to ask where I am. Turning up at my house.'

'Well, she obviously cares about you,' I say. And I actually feel a bit sorry for Amy because she's probably feeling the same thing as me: that now that Jake's found a new best friend, he's slipping through our fingers.

'Clay says Amy's not right for me.'

I've said that Amy's not right for him like a thousand times. Maybe Jake needed to hear it from a guy. At least it's reassuring to know that Clay can see through her.

'Yeah,' Jake says. 'He thinks I'm going out with the wrong type.'

'So what type should you be going out with?'

He shrugs. 'He didn't say.'

I get this crazy thought that maybe Clay meant me. I mean, you can't get more different a type of girl to Amy than me.

'I'm sure it will work out,' I say, kind of feeling bad as I do because really I hope it won't.

'We'll see,' Jake says.

I point at the storeroom. 'Mrs Zas asked if we could fix the astronaut costume.' I laugh. 'Its arms have fallen off.'

Jake takes off his coat, grabs the astronaut costume and settles down behind Mrs Zas's workbench and I go back into the shop.

'Jake?'

He looks up and smiles. He's wearing his favourite knitted sweater, the one with the black cat on the front. As I look at him I realise that he's giving up his time to help me in the shop and I remember how I love him more than just about anyone in the world.

'Thanks,' I say.

'What for?'

'For being awesome.'

I go up and hug him and hold him so hard I can feel his heart beating against my chest.

'I can't breathe!' he says, doing a mock gasp.

I step away. 'Better get sewing,' I tease. 'When Mrs Zas isn't here, I'm the boss, remember?'

Just as I go back to the counter to look for any notes Mrs Zas might have left in the diary, the bell above the door rings and Rev Cootes comes in. I don't think Rev Cootes has ever been in Mrs Zas's shop and I wish I could freeze time and go and get her and drag her back just so that she can see it. Maybe he waited for Mrs Zas to be out to come in.

'Hi, Rev Cootes,' I say.

Behind me, I can hear Jake rustling the astronaut costume.

Rev Cootes looks around the shop. 'I was hoping to borrow a costume…'

I gulp down my amazement and say, 'Of course!'

Rev Cootes walks over to the superhero section of the shop.

'It's for my sermon. I thought my words could do with being brightened up by a prop or two.' He touches the Superman cape. 'I'll be talking about heroes on Sunday.'

'That sounds interesting.'

'Maybe you'd like to come along – with Josephine?'

Mum would kill me. She hates religion.

'I've got swim training on Sunday,' I say. And then vow to actually go to the pool to train.

'Oh… of course.' He goes over and picks up a Spider-Man mask. 'Clay said I should try to be a bit more relevant…' He takes a Superman cloak off the rail. 'Isn't it interesting how human beings have always believed in heroes?'

'I suppose it is,' I say.

'It's the ordinary heroes that impress me,' says Rev Cootes. 'The everyday people who do remarkable things.'

'Shame there aren't many heroes in Willingdon,' I say.

'Oh, there are heroes everywhere,' Rev Cootes says. 'You know that, when she was a little younger, your mother was regarded as a hero in the village.'

'Really?'

He nods.

'She's the reason Willingdon doesn't have a motorway running through the middle of it.'

'I think you must have got Mum mixed up with someone else.'

The sewing machine Jake's using in the storeroom stops whirring.

Rev Cootes shakes his head. 'No, it was Josephine Tucker. I didn't always agree with her activist methods but I admired her courage.'

'Her *activist* methods?' I ask.

'She hasn't told you the story?'

Jake comes into the shop and stands beside me. 'What kind of costume were you looking for, Rev Cootes?'

I squeeze Jake's arm to get him to shut up. This is the most interesting thing I've learnt about Mum since that photo I found in the garage.

'You were saying, about Mum and the motorway…' I say.

Rev Cootes nods.

'They were going to build the M77 through the middle of the village. Your mother was the one who got everyone to protest and write letters to Downing Street. She even slept out in the middle of The Green for a week. Refused to move when the diggers came in. There were articles in the national news.' He smiles. 'With the fire Josephine Tucker had in her belly, we all thought she'd be running the country within a few years.'

Except she's not running the country. She's hiding inside a tiny cottage.

I know that Mum did first aid and that she swept to people's rescue when they were choking and having heart attacks and everything but I've never heard of her sitting in the middle of The Green leading a protest. I can't imagine her doing stuff like that. It makes me feel proud. And then it makes me feel sad and angry and confused. Why hasn't anyone told me any of this stuff before?

Jake smiles. 'How about a piece of kryptonite?' He picks up a green glass stone from the shelf above the Superman costume. 'That would be a good prop.'

Rev Cootes nods. 'That sounds nice and simple.' He blushes. 'I'm not really one for dressing-up.'

Which is funny, considering he spends his life wearing a dog collar.

Jake hands him the green stone. 'We'll let Mrs Zas know you borrowed it.'

Rev Cootes blushes even more.

I don't understand why Jake's focusing on a stupid prop for a stupid sermon when we could be quizzing Rev Cootes more about Mum.

'Thanks for this,' Rev Cootes says, holding up the green

stone. 'I'll be sure to return it.' He walks back out through the door and over to St Mary's.

I'll have to find an excuse to go over and talk to him.

And then Mrs Zas's computer catches my eye and I have an idea.

'That astronaut costume fixed yet?' I ask Jake.

He smiles. 'Nearly.'

He hesitates for a second and then shuffles back into the storeroom.

An astronaut, that's what I'd like to be right now: locked in a bubble of air, floating in space, far away from everyone and everything I know.

When Jake's out of sight, I switch on the computer Mrs Zas has on her counter. She does lots of mail-orders, which is part of what she asks me to help her with. Except I don't go into her orders file to check whether anything needs to be bagged up and taken to the Post Office. Instead, I click on Google and type:

Josephine Tucker M77 Motorway Willingdon.

Mrs Zas's computer is so ancient that the page takes ages to load. The coloured beach ball spins and spins and spins. *Come on...*

The screen blinks to life.

My breath catches in my throat and it's like I've forgotten how to take the next one. I press my hand to my neck.

There are *loads* of articles about Mum. Why did I never think to do a search on her?

I click onto the *Newton News* website and then click on the archive button and Google *Josephine Tucker.*

There's a picture of Mum sitting cross-legged in the middle of The Green, her hair hanging long down her back. She's holding a placard: SAVE THE GREEN.

I open another article:

Local swim teacher completes a twelve-hour swimathon to raise money for the new Lido...

Local *swim* teacher?

There's a picture of Mum in the Newton pool, wearing goggles and a swim hat, her arms propped up on the edge, grinning.

She raised money for the new Lido to be built? None of this makes any sense.

I click on a third article:

Josephine Tucker, an advocate of Baby Dippers, has taught just about every child in Willingdon to swim...

I Google *Baby Dippers* and open the *Wikipedia* page:

Babies have a natural instinct for the water. Dipping them under the water when they are a few weeks old will give them a natural confidence in water...

'You okay, Feather?'

Jake's standing behind me; I can feel him looking over my shoulder. I shut down the screen.

I'm light-headed and dizzy. 'Fine.'

Jake looks at the blank screen for a moment and then smiles and holds up the astronaut costume. 'It's done.'

I take a breath to calm down, lean in and kiss his cheek. 'You're a genius.'

As we both get back to sorting out the return costumes and packaging up the mail-order items, I think about everything that's happened in the last few minutes: Rev Cootes telling me about Mum being a local hero and then me finding those articles about her being a swim teacher, articles which told me that my water-phobic mum not only hung around the Lido getting a suntan (like the photo I found in the garage suggests), but that she taught half of Willingdon to swim, that she *loved* the water. And I've made a decision. I'm not going to go tearing in this time. I'm not going to ruin the good stuff Dad and me have got going right now, or how Mum's making loads of progress with getting her health back on track. I'm going to keep going as normal, or make it look like that at least. And when no one's looking or asking questions, I'm going to make sure I find out why everyone's been lying to me this whole time.

22

Steph drives us to the Newton pool and I can't help looking at her face in the rear-view mirror. She would have been around when Mum protested against the motorway and when she taught all those kids to swim. I think of all the times I moaned to Steph about how much I'd love Mum to come and watch me compete; every time she'd give me a hug and say we had to respect Mum's decision, that water made her nervous, that there was nothing we could do about it.

Steph's face doesn't give away a thing. I bet she's got so used to making stuff up about Mum, she's lost track of what's true and what's not.

And that's the thing. I'm not angry at Mum. There's obviously a reason why she's scared of everything from water to hospitals to stepping out of the house – it's normal she wouldn't want to talk about it. But there's no excuse for everyone else lying to me. Like Steph and Dad. They could have helped me to understand. I wouldn't have brought it up with Mum, not if they thought it would upset her. I have a right not to be lied to by the people I love, don't I?

I bite my tongue and remind myself I have to keep quiet until I've done some investigating of my own. Then I'll ask everyone in my life why they've been lying to me.

For the second time today, I look over at Jake and feel grateful to have him as my best friend. He's just about the only person I can trust right now.

I take his hand and lean my head against his shoulder.

'Thanks,' I say.

He turns to face me. 'What for?'

'Just for being you.'

I sit in the whipping area, Steph and Jake beside me, waiting for the race to start. As I breathe in and out, I force my mind to go blank: if I'm going to qualify for the regionals, I have to let all my thoughts about Mum float away.

Only, the thoughts won't stop shooting in.

I scan the crowd that's come out to support the Willingdon team. I know lots of them are here for me, which should make me feel happy. But the only thing I can think is that, like Dad and Steph, they've been lying to me. The whole Slim Skills bunch is here; I wonder whether they know too. And there's Allen of course, sitting there with his camera because he's covering the competition. Our parents had to sign forms to say it was okay to have photos taken in our swimming costumes. I should probably quiz Allen about Mum: with all his snooping around, he probably knows everything that's going on.

I bet even Mitch knows stuff about Mum that I don't. Maybe they have meetings when people first arrive in the village to warn them: *Whatever you do, don't tell Feather Tucker anything.*

I look over at Mrs Zas. She keeps coming back from her

dance classes really drained. But she never stops smiling. She catches my eye, holds up her hand and waves.

I wave back and force a smile but I can't breathe. Not with all those people looking at me. Not when I haven't got a clue whether I can trust any of them any more.

I scan the benches to see whether Clay showed up.

I understand that if Clay has body issues, he won't want to get into swim trunks, but he could at least have come to support me. One moment he acts like we're friends and like he cares about me, and the next he acts like I don't even exist. I wanted him to see me swimming; I thought that maybe if he watched me win a race, he'd be impressed and that it would make him like me. Which I realise now is totally lame. First, because guys don't suddenly fancy girls because of their swimming skills. And, second, because no guy in the world would fancy me in my high-necked navy swimsuit and orange swim hat.

'Did Clay say he was coming?' I ask Jake.

'He's not well today, he needs to rest.'

Those are the other words Jake uses about Clay all the time: *He's not well.*

'I'm sure he'll come another time,' Steph says.

I wonder whether she's worked out that I like him. She's good at stuff like that.

One of the officials moves forward with the starting gun.

I'm so angry at thinking about all those lies I've been fed that my body feels on fire.

'I'm going to get some air.'

'The race is about to start, Feather,' Steph says.

'I'll only be a second.'

Before she has the chance to answer or Jake has the chance to stop me, I grab my towel and dash out to the changing room and through the fire-escape door that leads to the back of the pool.

I take in big gulps of air.

I close my eyes and listen to my heart beating.

'Feather?'

I open my eyes. It's Mrs Zas, standing in the fire-escape doorway. The sun reflects off her glasses.

'Is there something wrong? You looked upset out there.'

Everything's wrong, I think.

'I'm fine.'

'Are you nervous about the competition?'

I shrug. 'It's just a stupid race.'

She shakes her head. 'I don't think you believe that, Feather.'

'I've got other stuff to worry about right now.'

Goosebumps rise on my arms and my teeth chatter.

Mrs Zas unwinds the purple shawl from around her shoulders and puts it around me. It feels soft and warm and, for a second, I close my eyes and imagine it's one of the superhero costumes in her shop, one that's actually got magical powers in it, and that, maybe, if I wrap it around myself tightly enough, it'll make me disappear.

'Thanks,' I say.

Mrs Zas nods. 'I understand that this is a hard time for you, Feather. With your mother.'

And at that moment, I want to tell her everything. About Mum and how I'm tired of worrying about her and looking after her and persuading her every day that she needs to get better. How, for some reason I don't understand, everyone's been lying to me about the past. And how I've never felt this alone in my whole life.

But something makes me keep my mouth shut.

'I'd better get back to the race,' I say.

She steps away from the fire-escape door. 'Of course.' Then she kisses my cheek lightly. 'Break a leg – isn't that what the English say?'

I nod. 'Thanks.'

I can hear the official's voice booming through his megaphone.

'Feather?' She calls after me.

I turn round.

'You can come and talk to me any time you want to, you know that?'

'Thanks, I'll be fine.' I walk back through the changing rooms to the pool.

'Thank God you're here!' Jake's eyes are wild.

As I step onto the block, the official looks at me and shakes his head.

'I told him you needed the loo. Girls' issues,' Jake whispers.

'You did *what*?'

'It's the only thing I could think of to make them wait for you.'

I want to hit him and hug him at the same time.

'Thanks for covering my back.'

He kisses the top of my swim hat. 'You'll be brilliant,' he says and walks over to sit with the other spectators.

The official whistles and then hands over to the starter.

'Ready…'

I kneel down, curling my right foot over the edge of the block and look ahead at the empty lane. Mrs Zas was right. This isn't a stupid race: it matters to me. It's what I've been training for.

A loud beep.

I dive in.

As my body slices in and out of the water, shouts rise and fall from the crowd.

I've never been this in tune with my body: my arms and legs feel like they're part of the water – and I know that I'm going faster than usual.

I want to make Mum proud. I can't stop thinking that if she used to love swimming, maybe as much as I do, then me winning matters more than ever.

Feather! Feather! Feather!

I hear a chant, led by Jake.

I swim harder.

I'm going to win this race: it's the one thing no one is going to take away from me.

Go Feather! Go Feather! GO!

I push against the side and swim to the end of the pool.

Our Beautiful Butterfly, Dad called me at breakfast this morning. He's been trying to be really encouraging about my swimming. Mum didn't say a word.

Is it all my fault? Am I the reason Mum didn't want to come to the pool again? Why she went off swimming? Because I was a disappointment?

I push my arms harder over my head. I snake my legs through the water, dolphin-kicking as hard as I can.

Feather! Feather! Feather!

I push harder and harder. Blood roars in my ears. The taste of metal pushes up the back of my throat. My heart pounds.

And then I slam into the end.

I gasp for breath. I can't see anyone on either side of me. And I realise I made it. I came first.

Only, I don't feel a thing.

23

Dad drops me off at the house before heading out on a plumbing job, his first proper job in ages: one of Mr Ding's pipes are blocked in the takeaway van.

I'm worried that if I see Mum, I'll blurt out what I found out about this morning, so I plan to go straight up to my bedroom. Only, when I get into the hall, I hear voices coming through the kitchen door.

I ease shut the front door, take off my shoes and pad over to the kitchen.

Through a crack in the door, I see Clay sitting by the window, the afternoon sun so bright behind him that he glows: he looks like he belongs to a world made of air and light and shadows. And he looks thinner than the last time I saw him. Much, much thinner.

Mum's sitting in the special wooden chair Dad got from The Willingdon Seed garden centre – it's big enough for her to be able to sit at the kitchen table with us for meals. He got her a walking stick, too, to wean her off the wheelchair, and that's propped up against the table.

'Thank you for bringing it back,' Mum says.

She nods at the first in the series of *Max's Marvellous Adventures* lying on the table.

So that's why Clay didn't come to the pool: he wanted to talk to Mum without me here.

'Reading it brought everything back,' Clay says. 'Or most of it.' He pauses. 'I called Mum last night.'

Clay called his mum? Clay *hates* his mum.

Mum must have had the exact same thought because her head snaps up she and looks right at Clay.

'You called Eleanor?'

He nods. 'She explained everything. Or the bits I didn't know, anyway.'

The light from the conservatory shines right into his eyes, a washed-out blue.

'And then she hung up,' Clay says.

'Eleanor will come round,' Mum says.

They're talking like they're old friends.

Mum picks up the book, opens the front cover and strokes the first page.

Clay plays with the rim of a glass but he doesn't drink from it. His lips look dry.

'I don't think she will.'

My chest goes tight. My wet hair drips down my back.

'It was my fault that it happened,' Clay says.

Maybe Clay's told her about the article he wrote and how he embarrassed his mum.

'Eleanor said that?' Mum asks.

Clay pushes his glass away.

'She didn't need to say it, I knew that was what she was thinking.'

Mum leans over and takes his hands. 'It wasn't your fault.' She grips his fingers hard. 'Look at me,' she says.

Clay lifts his eyes to her.

'It was *my* fault. It was all my fault,' she says.

Mum's fault? How could it have been Mum's fault?

I get that same feeling that I did this morning, when I found stuff out about Mum that my friends and family, the people who are meant to love me, should have told me.

'I think you should speak to Feather,' Clay says.

My heart hammers so hard I'm sure Mum and Clay must be able to hear it. I take a step back.

'Not yet,' Mum says. 'She's not ready.'

Not ready for what?

Clay stands up. 'Well, you'd better tell her something – and soon – or she'll hear it from someone else.' He pushes his chair back under the table. 'Either that or she'll work it out. She's pretty smart.'

I'm angry that, this whole time, Clay's known stuff about Mum – which means *he* has been lying to me too. But at least he's trying to get her to talk; it's more than anyone else in my life has been doing. And he thinks I'm smart? Is that an equivalent to thinking I'm pretty or fanciable? I shake off the thought. There are more important things to worry about right now.

And then it hits me. Maybe Clay's been talking to Jake about this too – whatever *this* is. Maybe Jake knows a whole load of stuff about Mum that he hasn't told me either.

'I'd better go,' Clay says.

I move quickly back to the front door, open it quietly, make stamping sounds at the top of the ramp, jam the key in, push it open and run down the hall to, hopefully, give the impression I've just arrived.

I nearly crash into Clay.

'Clay – what are you doing here?' There's a tremor in my voice.

I wait for him to feed me a lie.

'I was just saying hello to your mum.'

'Feather?' Mum calls out.

I don't answer.

'I'll catch you later,' Clay says.

I stand there, watching him walk down the hall until he closes the front door behind him. He didn't even ask about the race.

I walk into the kitchen.

'I'm glad you're home,' Mum says. 'Dad called – he said you're through to the regionals.' She stretches out her arms but I don't move. 'He said he's never seen you swim so fast.'

Mum smiles but I can tell she's pretending. If it were down to her, I'd never swim again.

'I'm tired, Mum,' I say. 'I'm going to have a rest.'

And then I go over to her, kiss her forehead, turn back round, go up the stairs to my bedroom and close the door behind me.

April

24

Jake walks over to the research wall in my bedroom.

'Wow – this looks like something out of *CSI*.' He brushes his fingers across the photographs and Post-its and bits of string.

My stomach does a flip. Before this moment, I haven't shown anyone the wall. I'm hoping that, if Jake does know more about Mum than he's been letting on, seeing all my research will make him say something.

Every time I get a new bit of information about Mum, I add it to my board. I've got bits of string connecting pictures and Post-its with questions on them. Like the photograph of Mum at the Lido, which is connected to a Post-it with the things Rev Cootes told me and the stuff I found on the Internet: *Mum + swimming teacher? Raised money for Lido?* And then another Post-it with: *Motorway protest?*

When I asked Dad about Mum sitting in the middle of The Green for a week, he shrugged and said that was a long time ago.

Only it doesn't matter if it was yesterday or a hundred years ago. The point is that Mum used to be this amazing, brave person who loved to do things in public – and no one told me. It turns out I know next to nothing about Mum's past. That's why I'm doing all this research.

'You sure you want to be digging up all this stuff?' Jake asks.

'Wouldn't you want to know about your mum – I mean, if she had all these secrets in her past?'

He looks at me and frowns.

'I'm sure Mum was really different before she had me too, when she was still with Dad. People change, Feather, it's just what happens over time. Take me, for example.' He grins and looks down at his trainers. 'Who'd have thought that I'd have taken up jogging?'

Jake's been going out running with Clay. They set off really early because Clay doesn't like bumping into people. I haven't told Jake but I don't think them jogging together is doing Clay any good. I mean, he isn't going to get well if, on top of starving himself, he burns calories he doesn't have running around Willingdon all hours of the day and night. If Jake really wants to be Clay's friend, he should be looking after him.

'Yeah, but not this different. Mum's like a completely different person from who she used to be. And if we do change, there's always a reason. We don't just flip from loving something to hating it without something having happened.'

Jake rubs his forehead. 'I guess so.'

'If you ask enough questions and if you look hard enough, you'll find reasons.'

The floorboards creak downstairs. Mum's doing her afternoon laps of the lounge. When she moves, the whole cottage shifts with her. It's part of the exercise routine I've devised for her. She's been trying harder lately, which I guess is something.

Jake turns to face me. 'Feather, are you sure about all this?' He sits down on my bed. 'Sometimes, it's best to leave the past alone.'

Miss Pierce wouldn't agree. The past is what makes us understand now, that's what she says. Jake should know that: he's sat in her lessons, just like I have.

'I thought you understood how important this was to me,' I say.

'I just want to make sure you've thought it through.'

'I have.'

'Don't you think you should just talk to your mum – or your dad? Ask them straight out rather than doing all this digging around?'

'They won't tell me anything. Neither will your mum. Or anyone else who remembers far enough back. It's like the whole of Willingdon is conspiring to keep me in the dark about stuff.'

Right, now it's Jake's chance to say something.

'Everyone in the village loves you, Feather.' He blinks. 'Including me.'

Which doesn't tell me anything I need to know.

'People who love you are meant to tell you the truth,' I say.

Jake shakes his head. 'Not always. Sometimes it's because people love you that they keep quiet. Maybe, if they are keeping secrets, there's a good reason.' He sighs. 'Or maybe there's no reason at all. Maybe…'

'It's all in my head?'

'I didn't say that.'

'But you think that, right? You think I'm making all this stuff up? That I've gone mad or something.'

'Would I be here if I thought that?'

I hear Mum's door open downstairs.

Jake gets up off the bed and goes to the wall above my desk where I've printed off articles about people who've died from obesity.

'God...' he says. 'Are these stories really true?'

'Yeah, they're true.'

There's one about a woman in Austria who had so much body fat when she was cremated that it set the crematorium on fire: fire fighters got covered in sooty, burnt grease. Now they've capped how big someone can be to be cremated so I guess, if Mum does die, she'll have to be buried.

There's another one of a thirty-five-stone woman who died attached to the couch she was stuck to, she couldn't even go to the bathroom any more.

And then another woman who got to fifty stone and then had a gastric bypass, but refused to move afterwards even if it meant she'd die from a blood clot. She had a son called Dillon, who cared for her full time. I've been meaning to search for him on Facebook, it would be good to talk to someone who understands.

There's one story that makes me sadder than all the others. It's about a twenty-five-stone woman who fell off the couch and couldn't be lifted off the floor by her son and her husband. She died of the infected sores she got from sitting on the floor for so long.

The last article is the one of Mum from the *Newton News*. It's got a zoomed-up picture of Mum dangling in that net the firemen used to get her out through the lounge window. It's to remind me why I'm doing all this and why I shouldn't give up.

Jake looks pale. 'This stuff is horrible.'

'Yeah, it is horrible.'

I feel myself well up. Whenever I look at those articles I think about how, if she died, another picture of Mum would be splashed on the front page of the *Newton News*, a really unflattering one that she'd hate. And then there'd be a lame headline like THE WHALE OF WILLINGDON SNUFFS IT. And there'd be crap about me and Dad too, how it was our fault for not helping her enough.

'I need to be upset,' I say. 'I have to remember how important it is to get Mum better.' I stare at the picture of a woman lying in a hospital bed with her son handing her a brown paper bag with the McDonald's logo on the front. 'You know what two things all these stories have in common?'

Jake shakes his head.

'First, the overweight people didn't want to lose weight.'

'And second?'

'The people who loved the overweight people let them die.'

'That's a bit harsh.'

'Yeah, well, it's true. And I'm not going to let that happen to Mum.'

I look at the picture of the woman lying in an operating theatre with plastic all over her like a building covered in scaffolding.

I come and sit next to Jake on the bed.

There's a creak at the bottom of the stairs. Doing a few stairs every day is on the exercise plan I've devised for Mum.

I take a breath. 'You don't know stuff, do you? I mean, stuff that you aren't telling me?'

Jake looks at the door. He gulps and his eyes go watery.

'Why don't you have a talk with your mum?' he says. 'A proper talk. Ask her straight out about the things you've found out.'

Which, once again, isn't an answer to my question.

'She won't open up,' I say. 'I know Mum.'

I glance back at all the obesity stories and push the pads of my thumbs into the corners of my eyes to press the tears back in. Then I blink and look right at Jake:

'The nurse at the hospital said that if Mum didn't get healthy, she'd die within six months. That was in January.'

Jake takes my hand. His palm feels warm. 'I think it's amazing, what you're doing for your mum,' he says. 'How much you want her to get better.'

'She doesn't think it's amazing.'

'She does, I'm sure she does. You just have to give it time.'

'*She* doesn't have time, Jake, that's the point.'

'Just keep doing what you're doing, Feather.' He holds my hand to his heart and smiles. 'You're a real hero, you know that?' He uses one of those booming voice-overs from his zombie movies.

I think about the superhero costumes in Mrs Zas's shop and how all the characters who wear them have these special powers: they can climb up buildings or fly or have steel running through their veins. Even some of Jake's zombies have super powers. And me? Puny little Feather to the rescue. What a joke.

And then I spot something over Jake's shoulder. A bit of peeling wallpaper. I go over and scratch at it.

'What are you doing?' Jake asks.

'Have a look.'

He comes and kneels beside me on the bed. 'What is it?'

'It looks like someone painted on the wall.' I scratch a

bit more at the wallpaper. 'And then pasted over it.' I keep scratching. 'Probably the owners before Mum and Dad.'

I'd never thought of anyone living in our cottage before us.

I lean forward and look at the wall. There's a patch of bright blue paint. I pull at the bit of wallpaper that's coming loose.

'Maybe you shouldn't do any more,' Jake says.

I ignore him and keep scraping at the wallpaper until I've uncovered a patch as big as my palm.

'A fish…' I look at the red fins of a cartoon goldfish with bubbles coming out of its mouth. 'Maybe the previous owners liked the sea.'

I keep scratching and pulling. Next to the fish, there's an octopus and next to that a seahorse.

'Looks nicer than the stuff I have on my wall. I should take all the wallpaper down,' I say.

'Maybe ask your dad first.'

I shrug. 'He won't care.'

'Feather!' Mum's voice echoes up the stairs. 'Feather! I need you to come down.'

'Coming!' I yell back.

As I'm climbing off the bed, Jake catches my hand.

'You won't do anything stupid, will you Feather?'

'What do you mean?'

'It's just, you seem a bit wired, doing all this research about your mum. You should be focusing on your swimming, and on school…'

'I'll be fine,' I say.

But I'm not going to stop. Not until I know everything about what Mum was like before I was born. Jake hasn't seen anything yet.

25

I'm sitting at the computer in the mobile library. Penny, the librarian, asked me to keep an eye on things while she went to use the public loo across The Green.

I can't stop reading those articles about Mum and her life before me.

The door to the van squeaks open.

'No one's been in,' I say, clicking onto another article from the *Newton News*. It's about Mum cutting the ribbon at the opening of the Lido.

Penny doesn't answer so I look up.

It's Rev Cootes. He's standing in the doorway, his cheeks pink. And he's shifting from foot to foot like he wants to make a run for it.

'Hi Rev Cootes,' I say. 'Penny's popped out for a moment. Can I help you find something?'

Rev Cootes looks out onto The Green through the open door like he's worried he's been followed.

I stand up and go over to him. 'Rev Cootes?'

I'm kind of glad he's come in. Maybe here, in the library, without anyone else about, I can ask him stuff about Mum.

'Perhaps I should come back later…' Rev Cootes says.

'It's fine, Penny leaves me in charge all the time. Were you coming in for a book?'

He nods but doesn't say anything.

'What kind of book?'

He scratches his head. 'Erm...'

I've sat in the mobile library a few times when customers have come in to ask Penny for dodgy books, but I don't imagine that Rev Cootes would be into that stuff.

I go over to Penny's computer. 'Do you know who the author is?'

'No...'

'The title?'

He shakes his head.

Rev Cootes's house is filled with books. He's a booky kind of person. So it's weird that he doesn't know what he's looking for.

'What's it about?' I ask.

Though it's not like I'm going to know it. I can count on one hand the books I've read.

His cheeks go a brighter shade of pink.

'Clay...' he says really softly.

'A book about *clay*?' I ask. And then I get it and feel my cheeks blush too. 'Oh... you mean *Clay*, your grandson?'

He nods.

I really don't know what he's getting at. There's hardly going to be a book *about* Clay – is there?'

'About his eating...' Rev Cootes says really fast. He clears his throat. 'About his not eating.'

'Oh.'

'I thought there might be a book... to help me understand.'

I get that guilty feeling when you've been focusing so

hard on your own problems that you've totally missed the fact that someone else is struggling with things too. Possibly even worse things.

'Let me do a search,' I say.

I type *anorexia* into the search bar of Penny's online book catalogue.

A whole lot of books flash up onto the screen. The dust jackets are covered with pictures of girls.

Then I have an idea.

I type in: *male anorexia.*

'If it's too much trouble…' Rev Cootes says.

'No, not at all.'

One book comes up.

'I've found something that might help,' I say.

I swivel the screen round so he can see and watch as he reads the title:

Boys Get Anorexia Too by Jenny Langley.

He scratches his head again and his eyebrows go droopy.

I do a quick search on the computer to see if Penny's got it in stock but it doesn't come up. Which isn't exactly surprising: I'd be surprised if many people knew there was a book about boys and eating disorders. And the fact that there are millions of books on anorexia about girls and only one on boys kind of suggests that there isn't much of a market for the subject either.

'It's not in, but I'll leave a note for Penny to order it for you,' I say.

'Oh, no, no… that all sounds like a great deal of trouble.' He pulls at his dog collar. 'Let's leave it.'

'It's no trouble. Penny likes to order new books.' I've already started scribbling a note for her. 'There, it's done. She'll let you know when it's here.'

'Thank you...' Rev Cootes says in a small voice.

I lean forward and try to catch his eye. 'I think it's great. That you're trying to understand Clay. He needs that.'

'A mother's what he needs,' Rev Cootes blurts out. And then he puts his wrinkly fingers over his mouth. 'I'm sorry,' he mumbles.

'It's okay. You're worried.'

'Yes.' He clears his throat again. 'Well, thank you, Feather. You and your friend Jake have been a great help.'

I feel a stab in my chest. 'Jake?'

'I don't know what Clay would do without him. He's a wonderful boy.'

'Yes... yes, he is.'

I should feel happy for Clay that he's got someone to turn to. That he's got Jake. But I can't help wishing that he'd just said that about me instead.

He turns to go and I remember what I wanted to ask him when he first came in.

'Rev Cootes?' I call after him.

He turns back round.

'Could I ask you a question?'

'Of course.'

'What made Mum change?'

His bushy eyebrows shoot up. 'Change?'

'I've found out about what she was like before... before she got so big... before she locked herself in the house. And that she wasn't at all like she is now. Like the things you said the other day at Bewitched.'

He nods slowly.

'You must have known her really well – back then.'

He nods again.

'So, what happened?'

'Sometimes, the thing we love most in the world betrays us.' He pauses. 'And that changes us forever.'

'What do you mean?' I ask but he's turned round again and is heading out of the library door and down the steps. 'Rev Cootes – what do you mean?' I shout after him.

But he's gone.

26

I empty a jug of water over Mum's hair.

'Is the temperature okay, Mum?'

Mum's sitting in front of the kitchen sink, her head tilted back. Tuesday's come round again and I'm washing Mum's hair for the Slim Skills meeting. For the last month, they've been coming to the house. Mum's giving her testimony today.

'It's fine,' Mum says. 'Thank you, my love.'

I rinse out the last of the conditioner.

'You're going to look amazing, Mum.'

I wrap a towel around Mum's head and help her sit up.

'You've got your speech prepared?'

Mum nods, though I can tell she's nervous.

'Your mother is a brilliant public speaker,' Dad says.

He's wearing his apron and is busy arranging bits of smoked salmon and cucumber on a serving dish. He's been learning to cook healthy stuff for Mum. And the other day he spent hours clearing out his van.

'Mum's a good public speaker?' I ask.

I'm hoping she might say something about the demonstration or the other stuff she did when she was younger.

'That was a long time ago,' Mum says.

'You're always saying that, Mum.'

Mum doesn't answer.

I rub Mum's head with a towel, plug in the hairdryer and blast hot air at her head.

'Everyone's going to be so proud, Mum. Three stone in just over a month, that's amazing. Wait till Mitch hears!'

'Is Jake coming over later?' Dad asks.

'He's gone to Newton with Clay and Amy,' I say, hoping that my words get lost over the blast of the hairdryer. Because Dad's right. A few months ago, on a day like today, a special day for me, Jake would have been here in a heartbeat. These days, it feels like I have to compete for every minute of his time.

I bat away the thought. I have to focus on today and on Mum's testimony.

'Well, he's missing out – from what Mitch tells me, we're in for a feast,' Dad says.

Mitch asked everyone to bring a healthy dish – it was his *Challenge of the Week*.

Mum's hair has got thin lately from all the meds, so it doesn't take as long to dry as usual. I pick up her old make-up bag from the kitchen counter and rifle through it.

I pull out the mascaras and eye shadows and lipsticks.

'You really used to wear all this stuff, Mum?'

'I don't remember. Maybe,' Mum says.

I screw open one of the lipsticks and apply it to Mum's mouth. It's gone dry so I have to press really hard.

Mum's warm breath brushes against my skin.

'Not too much, Feather,' Mum says.

'You've got to look the part, Mum.'

Dad is staring at Mum, smiling. 'I remember that colour, Josie.'

'You do, Dad?'

Outside, Houdini bleats. A moment later, the doorbell rings.

I look at my watch.

'We're not expecting anyone until four.'

I put the make-up bag on Mum's lap and run out of the kitchen.

Houdini still hasn't stopped bleating.

Allen stands at the top of the ramp with his big Canon camera dangling round his neck.

'You're early,' I say.

'Didn't Mitch say?'

'Say what?'

'I'm doing a piece for the health and fitness section of the *Newton News* – about Slim Skills and how it's helping the community to get healthy.' He pats his stomach. 'Even my beer belly's gone down.'

'Mum won't like it,' I say. 'Especially not that.' I nod at the camera.

'I promise I'll do her justice,' Allen says. 'I'm out to write a feel-good story about how this amazing group of people has been coming together to support each other in leading a healthier life.' He smiles, revealing a row of small, coffee-stained teeth. 'It will help people who are struggling with their weight and their health. It will bring more people to the group.'

I suppose that would be a good thing.

'That's *all* you're going to write about?' I ask Allen.

'Yep. I'll pass the article past Mitch before it gets published.'

Houdini is straining so hard at his lead that I'm worried the bolts on his kennel are going to come loose. I go over and give him a stroke but he won't calm down. He head-butts my shins.

Allen walks over and strokes his horns. 'These are meant to bring luck, right?'

I nod.

Houdini yanks his head away from Allen.

'He's quite the character, isn't he?' Allen holds his camera to his face and clicks a photo of me and Houdini.

Houdini kicks his back hooves in the air. I yank on his lead. 'Calm down, Houdini,' I say.

He bleats and then lies down and puts his head on his hooves and stares up at Allen.

'So, are you going to let me in?'

'Can you ditch the camera?' I ask.

'Sorry?'

'Mum doesn't like cameras. And I think it's best if you don't tell her you're doing a piece.'

I don't lie to Mum. But then she's been lying to me about all kinds of stuff. And this isn't a bad lie, it's just to make sure Mum goes through with her testimony.

'I see.'

Allen goes and puts his camera in the boot of his car and then comes back up the ramp.

I guide him to the kitchen.

'Hi, Mum, Allen's come early to help set up.' I swallow hard.

Mum and Dad nod and smile and shake hands with him.

'I hear you're giving a testimony today,' Allen says. 'You're a real inspiration.'

'I've got a long way to go,' Mum says.

Allen looks around the kitchen, like he's taking a photo with his eyes instead of his camera. Then he says, 'May I use your loo – before everyone gets here?'

'Sure,' Dad says. 'To the right of the lounge.'

We watch Allen disappear through the door. I listen to his shoes squeaking down the hall.

I take a mascara wand out of Mum's wash bag.

'Here, Mum, let me do your eyes.'

She closes her eyes and I look at her face: her eyelashes are really long and thick and her skin is smooth and her lips are this perfect shape. She really is beautiful.

Houdini bleats – his face appears at the kitchen window. He must have yanked his lead loose from the kennel.

I put down the mascara. 'I'll go.'

I dash outside and tie Houdini back up.

'Please don't play up today.' I give him a kiss on the soft bit between his horns.

Houdini sits down by his kennel but I can tell he's going to start yanking again the minute I'm back inside.

'Today's an important day.'

When I come in I walk past the lounge and then I hear a squeaking. I push open the door.

Allen's standing bang in the middle of the lounge, scanning the room.

'What are you doing in here?' I hiss.

Allen spins round. 'Sorry, got lost.'

Getting lost in our cottage is basically impossible. Besides the kitchen and the lounge there's only one room on the ground floor and that's the loo.

'Well, the loo's this way.'

I wait for him to come out through the door and point at the loo door.

'Sorry, no sense of direction,' Allen says and closes the loo door behind him.

'Feather?' Mum calls out from the kitchen. 'Everything okay?'

'Fine!' I call back. 'Everything's fine.'

'So, this week, we're celebrating a very special milestone.' Mitch stands at the far end of the conservatory, his arms stretched out, staring at Mum. 'Jo – you ready?'

Dad and I are sitting on either side of Mum. Dad squeezes her hand and I lean over and give her a kiss on the cheek.

'You're going to be amazing, Mum,' I whisper.

It's a pretty big step, going from not leaving the house in thirteen years to speaking in front of a room full of people. The Slim Skills group has grown bigger recently and Nurse Heidi's come for moral support and so has Steph, even though Mum didn't say a proper hello to her. Steph's the most loyal person I know, I just wish Mum would get over whatever it is she's holding against her and realise that best friends like Steph don't come along every day.

Mum unfolds the piece of paper in her lap and looks down at her notes. She hasn't let me read her speech, she said she wanted me to hear it fresh, with the rest of the Slim Skills group.

I take her elbow, help her up and guide her to where Mitch is standing. Mitch shakes her hand and then sits down and I go back and sit next to Dad.

For a moment, Mum stands there in silence, staring out at the room, and I'm worried she's frozen up.

I look around at all the people waiting for Mum to say something.

Mr Ding smiles at me. He's lost a few pounds these last

weeks and he looks healthier for it: his skin is clearer and whenever I see him walk across The Green, he looks lighter on his feet.

Mitch beams at us with his big smile.

Allen's sitting on the back row. He gets out his notepad.

Mum clears her throat.

'My name is Josephine Tucker… and I'm overweight.' She clears her throat again. 'I'm more than overweight: I'm obese.' She pauses. 'Morbidly obese.'

I can't believe she's actually used those words. Apart from with Jake, I haven't said the term out loud. Maybe it was Nurse Heidi. Anyway, I'm so proud of Mum for being honest and facing up to being ill that I want to leap out of my chair and hug her. Instead, I lean my chin on my palms and focus every bit of my attention on Mum: I want to hear every word she has to say.

Mitch claps and the others join in.

I squeeze Dad's hand.

Mum goes on: 'I've been overweight for over ten years now. I suppose I kept kidding myself that I'd go on a diet some time, that it was just a phase. Only, every year, I got bigger.' She takes a sip of water from the glass on the table next to her. 'At about the same time as I started eating, I decided I didn't want to leave the house any more.'

All the members of the group are nodding and hmmming.

'It was easier, I suppose,' Mum says. 'Not to have to face people. The way they looked at me. I knew what they were thinking.'

Heads nod around me.

'I asked George to take the mirrors out of the house.' Mum pauses and smiles. 'I think it's called denial.'

'That's right, Jo,' Mitch says.

Laughter spreads across the room.

What Dad said about Mum was true: she's an awesome public speaker. She's funny and warm and real and has the kind of voice that makes you want to listen for hours.

'I guess that it's Feather here who made me wake up to myself.'

I feel myself blush but I love that she sees it at last, that all my nagging about healthy eating and exercise was because I love her and want her to get better.

'And George, too, of course.'

'What happened to change things?' Mitch asks, his voice gentle. 'What was the turning point?'

Mitch gave Mum tips for the testimony, key words and phrases to help Mum structure her speech, words like 'denial' and 'realisation' and 'trigger' and 'turning point'. I didn't think she'd taken any notice of them.

'I got very sick.' Mum takes a breath. 'I *am* sick.'

Be honest about where you are – Mitch had said that too.

'I have diabetes. And if I don't lose weight…'

My eyes well up.

'If you don't lose weight, Jo?' Mitch asks.

Tell the truth. That's what really matters. That's what I told Mum when she said she didn't know what to say.

Dad gets up and goes to fuss over the kettle at the back of the room.

'I want to be here for my family. For my Feather. For George,' Mum says. 'That's the point.'

'I love you, Mum,' I call over.

'I love you, too, my darling.'

'And are you going to tell us the good news?' Mitch asks.

I can't help it, I jump out of my seat and blurt out, 'Mum lost seven stone!'

Everyone starts clapping.

Mitch stands up, walks over to Mum and hands her a laminated certificate.

More clapping.

'So, before we tuck into your delicious creations, there's time for us to ask Jo some questions.'

'May I sit down?' Mum asks.

Dad and I grab Mum's chair and carry it over to Mum. She lowers herself into it. I notice that her hands are shaking. It must have taken a lot out of her, to stand up there and talk about herself like that.

Dad sits next to me and takes my hand again.

'She's doing well, isn't she, Dad?' I whisper.

He nods. I know he's as proud of Mum as I am.

'So, questions?' Mitch asks.

Allen's hand shoots up. I feel my jaw clench up.

'Yes, Allen?' Mitch says.

He's frowning. I can tell he's thinking what I am. That Allen's job is to sit in a corner and keep it zipped.

'How did you do it?' Allen asks.

'Excuse me?' Mum asks.

'Lose the weight. What helps you to stop eating – I mean, when you get tempted?'

Mum and Allen's eyes lock.

'I realised it wasn't fair on the people I love,' Mum says.

Allen nods. 'Good answer.'

'Any others?' Mitch asks.

'What's next month's goal?' Mr Ding asks.

'Nurse Heidi says we should aim for another three stone!' I pipe up.

'I'll try,' Mum says, giving me a smile.

This is turning out to be one of the best days ever. I even

stop caring about finding out about all the stuff in the past that I've been kept in the dark about. If Mum's committed to getting healthy again, none of that matters any more.

'By Willingdon Day, Mum's going to be healthy again,' I announce to the group, 'properly healthy.'

Mum shifts in her chair. 'Like I said, I'll try.'

'It's good to have a goal,' says Mitch. 'But remember, we need to take a step at a time.'

Mum nods.

Allen's hand goes up again.

I'm beginning to wish I never let him into the house.

'Allen?' Mitch asks. 'Another question?'

'How did it start?'

The room goes silent.

Dad's gone really red.

'What made you *start* eating?' Allen clarifies. 'What was the trigger?'

Mum folds up her notes and places them on her lap. Then she looks out at the room.

'I ate because I was sad.'

'You don't need to go into that, love,' Dad says, his voice wobbly. 'Does she, Mitch?'

'It's okay, George.' Mum smiles out at her audience. 'I don't mind.' She takes a sip of water and then wipes her mouth, and says, 'I suffered from post-natal depression.'

I watch her lips and I hear her words but they don't sink in. I don't understand.

Dad's hand goes limp.

'Dad?' I whisper. 'What does Mum mean?'

Dad shakes his head and looks into his lap.

'After I had Feather, I struggled to adjust.'

'You were sad because of *me*?' My voice comes out small and croaky.

Mum shakes her head. 'No, I was sad because of me. Because I wasn't very good at being a mum.' Mum lifts her chin and stares out at the room. 'Being a mum is the hardest job in the world. And I wasn't ready for it.'

You know what I said about Mum's voice being warm and funny and real? In a few seconds, all of that has seeped away. In fact, the words don't sound like they're coming from Mum at all.

I look over to Dad. He's closed his eyes.

'So you ate to make yourself feel better about yourself – and your situation?' Allen's voice rings across the room.

'I ate to survive. I ate to numb the sadness.' Mum swallows hard. 'I ate to give me the strength to face each new day.'

Mr Ding lifts his head. For a second, I forget about Mum and what she just said and how it changes everything I've ever felt about her and about us, and wonder what *his* sadness is and whether someone he loves made him sick like I made Mum sick.

Mitch comes to stand at the front.

He runs his fingers through his hair. His eyes dart around the room.

'Thank you for your honesty, Jo. It takes guts to share like that.'

Mum nods and looks at me like she wants me to say something, but what am I meant to say when I've just found out that Mum being ill is basically my fault?

27

I pull my body through the pool. I might as well be filled with lead weights: I can barely get my arms above the water. I imagine the official at the regionals, shouting, *Feather Tucker – disqualified!*

I try harder, pushing my arms up and over. My shoulders burn.

I haven't been able to stop thinking about Mum's testimony all day. School was a blur. I got told off three times for daydreaming. I came straight to the pool without telling Steph and Jake: I needed to train on my own today.

I breathe hard as I come out of the water and kick, kick, kick my legs.

Come on, make an effort, I say to myself.

When Mitch hung back after the meeting last night, he said, *You should feel positive, Feather. Your mum showed real courage, facing the past like that.*

But how can I be happy when she's just told the world that it was me who made her sad?

Which basically means it's because of me that she's obese.

And that she's got diabetes.

And that she might die.

In other words, if I'd never been born, Mum would be just fine.

But the thing is, it doesn't make any sense. Isn't having a baby meant to be the happiest time in your life? I must have been a really screwed-up baby to make Mum get depressed.

I get to the far end of the pool and climb out. There's no point practising today, my head's all over the place.

I get the bus back home, grab Houdini and head straight across The Green and down Twirl Street to Jake's house.

He's the only one I want to speak to right now.

I ring on the doorbell.

Steph opens the door. 'Feather...'

'Hi, Steph,' I say and look over her shoulder. 'Is Jake in?'

She looks past me up the street.

'I thought he was with you. He headed to The Green a while ago.'

'How long's a while?'

'An hour.'

My heart sinks into my stomach. If he went to The Green, and he didn't come to see me, it's obvious who he's with: Amy and Clay. The Three Musketeers.

'Was he with Amy?' I ask.

'You haven't heard?' Steph asks.

'Heard what?'

'They split up.'

I feel that same burn that tore through my shoulders at the pool, except this time it's in my chest and in my throat. I should be really happy: I've been waiting for Amy and Jake to split for close to a year now. But all I can think is that he didn't even discuss it with me. Worse: that he's probably talked to Clay about it instead of me. And what's more, Jake's never split up with a girl in his life. He doesn't want the hassle of breaking someone's heart; he always waits for them to finish it.

'I think he's better off without her,' Steph says.

'Yeah,' I say, 'I guess so.'

'You okay, Feather?'

'I'm fine.'

I wind Houdini's lead around my hand.

Steph catches my arm. 'You know I'm here to talk… any time…'

'You knew about Mum,' I say, 'and you didn't tell me.'

Steph's face drops.

'And please don't say it's complicated,' I add, 'because I'm tired of that excuse.'

'Your mum and I are best friends, like you and Jake are best friends. There are things that it's hard to talk about. I've told your mum that she should be more open with you—'

'I'd better get back home,' I interrupt. I'm not going to get any further talking to Steph now. Yanking Houdini behind me, I head back down Twirl Street to The Green.

'Mrs Zas!' I knock on the front door of Bewitched.

Friday is Mrs Zas's busiest day, it's when she sets everything up for the weekend. But the shop's dark and the door's locked.

I step back and look up to the windows of her flat. 'Mrs Zas!'

I see a light on in the kitchen, but no one answers.

Across The Green, Rev Cootes looks up from under his hat. He's watering the Fuzzy Deutzia I gave him. He holds up his hand and gives me a crooked smile and it makes sense now, what he said about the thing you love betraying you. Mum loved me – or she thought she'd love me because everyone thinks they'll love their baby. And then she had me and I did what Rev Cootes said – I betrayed her.

I get out my keys and unlock the door to the shop. I need to talk to Mrs Zas. I should have come to her to start with. Jake wouldn't get what's happening with Mum. Mrs Zas is the only one who can help unscramble my head about Mum being depressed. She told me how she was depressed when her sister got sick. She'll understand.

Returned costumes lie on the backs of chairs, a pile of receipts sits on the counter along with a calculator, Mrs Zas's accounting book, a mug of grey, milky coffee – and her reading glasses. Mrs Zas spends Friday evenings getting everything ready for Saturdays, she never leaves things in a mess like this. It's like she just upped and left. And then I notice an envelope, so jaggedy looking it must have been torn open in a real hurry. It's got a stamp across the top: 'UK Visas and Immigration'. And the letter inside is missing.

There's another envelope too. It's got funny writing on it, which must be Ukrainian. There's a wodge of twenty-pound notes stuffed inside.

I go to the back and call up the stairs. 'Mrs Zas?'

Still no answer.

I climb up to the top landing. All the lights are on but she's definitely not here.

As I come back out of the shop, I notice Rev Cootes by the children's headstones.

I walk across The Green.

'Have you seen Mrs Zas?' I ask him.

Rev Cootes looks up. 'Mrs Zas?'

'She's meant to be in her shop,' I add.

'I believe she drove into town,' he says quickly.

I look at the road and realise he's right, her small Fiat with BEWITCHED painted across the side is missing. But it doesn't make sense; the only time Mrs Zas goes into town is when she goes to Newton Primary to teach her dance classes.

Rev Cootes yanks up a big, jaggedy-looking weed from between the small graves.

'She'd never leave her shop closed on a Friday,' I say, hoping he might give me some more information.

'She was in a hurry. I think something important came up.'

'In Newton?'

'She said she had to get the train to London.' He looks at his watch. 'I imagine she'll be home soon.'

'London? What's she doing in London?'

And why didn't she tell me?

A lorry and a digger make their way through the small road along The Green on their way to the park. The work has started on the Lido.

'Maybe I got it wrong,' Rev Cootes says.

He gets back onto his knees and brushes some moss off the headstone that doesn't have a name on it.

'Thanks anyway.' I look across at the vicarage. Clay's curtains are drawn. 'Say hello to Clay for me.'

Rev Cootes nods and goes back to yanking up weeds.

I tie Houdini back up at home and get the bus to Newton and head straight to the train station. Although Newton's a million times bigger than Willingdon, it's still pretty small, so the station only has two tracks going through it. I go to the side where trains come in from Paddington. The board says that the next train is due in just under an hour.

So I sit on a bench and wait.

And when that trains shows up and Mrs Zas doesn't step off, I wait for the next one.

And the one after that.

As the third train pulls in, I consider jumping on and letting it take me to London. Once I'm in London I could go anywhere. And I wouldn't have to deal with any of the rubbish back home. Kids run away from home all the time, don't they? They make a fresh start. They get jobs. In London, I could be anyone I wanted to be.

Except, as the train doors open, I chicken out. Mum says I'm brave but I'm not really: Willingdon is all I know, I'd be lost in a big city.

By the time the fourth train screeches to a halt, I'm getting hungry and cold and I'm beginning to think that Rev Cootes got it wrong, that Mrs Zas just went back to the shop – we must have crossed each other.

Just as I get up to leave, I get a glimpse of a green head-scarf through the window of the train and a moment later Mrs Zas steps out onto the platform.

'Feather!' Her '*r*' echoes around the station.

Mrs Zas takes my face in her hands and kisses both my cheeks. 'You're freezing. What are you doing here?'

'I've been waiting for you,' I say. 'You were meant to be in the shop.'

She nods. Her eyes look glassy and tired.

'What happened?'

'Why don't we go home,' says Mrs Zas. 'I'll make you some cinnamon milk. And then we can talk.'

As we sit at Mrs Zas's kitchen table, our hands cupped around the special pottery mugs she brought over from the Ukraine, sipping warm, sweet milk, I ask her:

'Why did you have to go to London in such a hurry?'

She takes a puff from her electric cigarette and stares at me for a second as though she's weighing up whether or not she can trust me. But then she says:

'I'm having trouble with my work visa.'

'What does that mean?'

She takes another puff of her cigarette.

'It means I might not be able to stay.'

My throat goes dry. Not be able to stay? Ever since Jake's decided not to talk to me about his life any more and to make Clay his new best friend, and ever since Mum's gone all weird and defensive about everything, and ever since I've worked out that Steph and Dad and just about everyone else in the village has been lying to me for years, I've run out of people to trust – and to talk to. Mrs Zas is the only friend I've got left.

'You're leaving Willingdon?'

She puts down the cigarette and takes a sip of her milk.

'Not if I can help it. But it's going to be quite a fight.'

'But you like it here. And your shop's really popular.'

'I don't think the government will see running a fancy-dress shop as sufficiently important to keep an old woman living and working in England.'

'It's not fair,' I say. 'I want you to stay.'

'Let's not worry about tomorrow before it comes.'

Mrs Zas goes over to her oven, gets the saucepan out and, as she hums her usual song about time and turning and seasons, she pours me some more cinnamon milk and grates some nutmeg on top. She's as particular about her milk as Rev Cootes is about his tea. I really should find a way to get them together. Maybe they could get married, then, perhaps Mrs Zas would be able to stay. But then I remember about

Rosemary, Rev Cootes's wife, being in the nursing home and feel really guilty for having had that thought.

'So, Feather, are you going to tell me what was so urgent that you sat on a train platform for hours waiting for me?'

'It doesn't matter.' Because it doesn't, not next to what she's going through.

'Does it matter to you, Feather?'

I hesitate. 'Yes, but it's not important, not now.'

'If it matters to you, it matters to me.' She holds out her fingers and lifts my chin so that I'm looking right at her. 'My visa problems have got enough attention for one day. Now, are you going to tell me what's on your mind?'

I blink. 'Mum told me why she stopped leaving the house.'

Mrs Zas leans back and lets out a long breath. 'At last.'

'She said it was my fault.'

Mrs Zas's eyes go huge. '*Your* fault?'

'She gave a testimony to the Slim Skills group and said that she got post-natal depression when she had me and that it made her want to stay inside and eat.'

Mrs Zas is quiet. Her eyes go far away like when she talks about her sister and her home back in the Ukraine.

I go on.

'I thought you could help me understand. You said you were depressed when your sister died.'

She focuses her eyes back on me.

'It's. Not. Your. Fault. Feather.' She pauses between each word. I've never heard her sound so stern.

'But if I hadn't been born—'

'It would have been something else. Depression is sneaky. It hides, waiting for something to happen to knock you off your stride and then it pounces. And once it strikes, it swallows you whole.' She gives a big gulp and claps her hands.

Mrs Zas makes depression sound like one of those horrible snakes from the nature documentaries Mum and I watch sometimes. One of those boa constrictors that wind themselves around your body and squeeze you so tight you suffocate. Yeah, depression sounds like a nasty snake.

'So, what you're saying is that Mum would have got depressed anyway?'

'Maybe, maybe not. But that's not the point, Feather. Being depressed isn't about anything in the outside world, it's about what happens in here.' She taps her head. 'And in here.' She presses her palm to her heart.

'I still feel that if I hadn't come along maybe Mum would be okay.'

'A baby doesn't choose to be born, does it, Feather?'

'I suppose not.'

'So, you see, it can't be your fault.'

I feel tired of talking about me. Nothing seems to matter any more, not next to the thought of Mrs Zas leaving.

'If they don't give you a visa, when will you have to go home?' I ask.

'Feather – I told you...'

'I have to know the truth now. I've spent all this time thinking you'll be here running the shop and teaching ballroom dancing forever. I need to know if there are any other secrets you're keeping from me.'

'I don't keep secrets from you.'

'But you didn't tell me.'

'You didn't ask. And, like I said, I don't think it's important. Today is what matters. And today, I'm here. And what's more, I'm going to do all I can to stay.' She smiles. 'And I'm very stubborn.'

I'm not sure I agree with Mrs Zas's distinction between

lying versus not telling. And I'm not sure that being stubborn is going to help her convince the government to let her stay.

'The government shouldn't get to decide who lives here,' I say.

'There are lots of us coming over, Feather. I suppose someone has to do something. And many English people think that it is wrong for foreigners to use their doctors and hospitals and to earn money by taking jobs from English people.'

Mrs Zas talking about money makes me think about the wodge of cash I saw in the envelope addressed to the Ukraine.

'You don't make much money in the shop, though, do you?'

'I make enough.'

'Enough for what?'

She looks at me. Mrs Zas is one of those people who always works out the thoughts you're having.

'I need to support my sister's family back in the Ukraine. They relied on her income as a professional dancer. Now, they don't have anything.'

'Your sister had a family?'

Mrs Zas nods. 'A husband and a little girl.'

'That's an even bigger reason why the government should let you stay then. You should tell them that. If you're willing to work hard and earn money to help people, it shouldn't matter which country you do it in. And then you should get them to come over, too. Jake and me could look after Irinka's little girl.'

Mrs Zas smiles. 'If only you were running the country, Miss Feather.'

I shake my head. 'I'd mess that up – like I mess everything else up.'

'What have you messed up?'

'Helping Mum. Not noticing that you're struggling.'

'You *are* helping your mum. And it wasn't your job to work out anything about me.'

My eyes sting. 'Please promise me you'll stay.'

'I'll do my very best, Feather.'

Which isn't a promise.

She gets up. 'Why don't you go home for a bit?'

'Don't you need help in the shop?'

'I think your mother needs you more.'

I don't want to go and see Mum. Not now. I want to stay here with Mrs Zas and to lose myself in all her costumes and to forget that there's anything out there I need to deal with. But I know she's right. Mum needs me.

I walk to the door of her flat.

'Feather?'

I turn round.

'Yes?'

'You know what the best cure is for depression?'

I shake my head.

'Love.'

'I do love her.'

'I know. But you need to show it to her. Every single day.' She pauses. 'Even when it's hard.'

I think about how angry Mum's made me lately and how I can't get her words from yesterday out of my head, about how she got sick after she had me.

'You must show your mother that you love her no matter what, Feather.'

I nod.

'Promise me?'

'I promise.'

As I walk out, a picture of Bewitched all boarded up with a FOR SALE sign outside flashes in front of my eyes and I get a sinking feeling in my stomach.

28

I stand outside the lounge and, through the door, I see Mum, her face red, her arms flapping.

Dad's scrambling around on the floor, picking up the *Max's Marvellous Adventures* books spread around her feet.

'Are you sure it was here?' Dad asks.

Mum's got sticky patches on her sweatshirt, which can mean only one thing: pineapple syrup. And I can smell prawn cocktail crisps. There's a cardboard box by her feet full of all the rubbish she used to eat. Dad must have stashed away a secret supply and given it to her.

'Mum? Are you okay?'

One of the books she's been holding falls out of her hands.

'It's gone,' Mum says.

'What's gone?' I ask.

Mum points to the shelf. 'The first book.'

'I'm sure there's a logical explanation,' Dad says.

'I'm telling you, it's missing.' She prods the shelf. 'It's always in the same place.'

Clay brought the book back. And Mum placed it on the shelf. I looked through it once to see if the story would give me any clues about Mum and her past but it was just what I thought it was: a silly story about a boy going on boy adventures that girls weren't allowed to be part of. Anyway, the book was definitely on the shelf. And then it comes back to me. Allen standing in the middle of the lounge.

'Maybe you've misplaced it, Josie,' Dad says.

Mum stares at Dad like he's a moron.

I take a breath and put my hand under Mum's elbow.

'Come on, Mum, let's get you back to your seat.' I try to steer her back to the love seat.

Mum stamps her foot. The house shakes.

'Stop treating me like a child,' she says.

She bats away my hand, loses her balance, stumbles against the bookcase and falls to the floor – it's like one of those cool slow-motion sequences in movies, only there's nothing cool about Mum crashing to the floor.

I look at the table where we keep Mum's meds and injections. It doesn't look like she's missed any today.

Mum rolls back to sitting.

I look out through the window and see Jake and Clay jogging back to the vicarage. Jogging is the only thing Clay leaves the house for these days and he's taken to running at night when there's no one else around.

He and Jake wave at Mrs Zas, who's sitting on the front steps of her shop, having an electric cigarette, her eyes fixed on the vicarage.

The diggers that have been working on the Lido rumble out of The Green, their work finished for the day.

I see Rev Cootes open the front door and Steph comes out from behind him. I know she goes to his church services but I've never seen her visiting the vicarage before.

She kisses Jake and Rev Cootes waves his hand towards the door like he wants them all to go back inside.

I turn back to Mum.

'You should have a rest,' I tell her.

But Mum's already already up and heading towards the front door. She yanks it open.

Dad follows after her, saying, 'You're in a state, Josie, please come back in and calm down. Tell me what you want and I'll do it for you.'

Mum steps onto the ramp.

It's the first time since January that she's stepped outside. She shifts her cane to her other hand, grips the handrail and eases her way down the ramp.

'Where are you going, Mum?' I call after her.

But she doesn't turn round. Or stop. She keeps walking, one heavy step after the next as she makes her way across The Green.

Mr Ding comes out of his takeaway van.

'Is everything okay, Jo?' I hear him say.

She ignores him and presses on to St Mary's, trudging past the children's graves and then past the normal, grown-up graves. She keeps going and going, like one of those oil tankers you see on TV: so big that it would take hours to turn it round.

Dad and I follow her.

When Mum gets to Rev Cootes's front door, she puts her hands on her hips, bends forward and takes in some big jaggedy breaths.

I rub her back. 'Come on Mum, let's go home.'

She pushes me away.

'Josephine...' Rev Cootes says. 'How wonderful to see you out and about.'

Mum looks from Rev Cootes to Steph.

'I know what you're doing,' Mum says.

'Boys, why don't you go inside?' Rev Cootes says to Clay and Jake.

They don't move.

'Talking about me, thinking I can't see it,' Mum says.

She's totally paranoid.

'Josie, let's not do this here,' Dad says.

'Do what here?' I ask him.

He acts like he doesn't hear me.

'If you hadn't pushed me,' Mum says to Steph. 'Nag, nag, nag...'

'Let's go to mine,' Jake says to Clay.

'Don't go anywhere,' Mum says. Then she points at Clay. 'You came back for this, didn't you? To dig things up. Was it your mother's idea?' She scans all of our faces. 'Don't you all get it? I don't want to go outside. I don't want to stop eating. And I don't want to talk.' She pauses. 'I want to be left alone.'

'Why don't I help you home, Jo?' Steph says.

And that makes Mum go mental. She moves right up close to Steph, so close I'm worried she's going to flatten her.

'This is all your fault!' Mum yells.

People are beginning to come out of their houses around The Green. I'm worried Allen is hiding out somewhere, waiting to snap a photo of Mum.

'Did you hear what I said?' Mum asks Steph.

Steph blinks.

'I was doing fine. Feather and George and I were doing just fine. And then you stuck your nose in. Just like you stuck your nose in all those years ago.' She turns to face

Rev Cootes. 'And you... I bet you're the one who put Steph up to this, didn't you?'

It's my fault, I want to tell Mum. *I let Allen into the house. He took the book.* Maybe that would put an end to her weird accusations.

But I'm worried that's going to make it worse. And that she'll hate me for having let him in the house.

Then Mum totally loses it. She reaches out and grabs at Rev Cootes's dog collar, pulling the white bit loose and waving it at him. 'You think this gives you the right to have a say in people's lives?'

I don't get it, Rev Cootes hasn't even talked to Mum in God knows how many years.

'I don't want either of you talking to Feather any more,' she says, her voice steady now. Steady and cold.

'Mum...'

Mum's face is red and she's sweating so hard her hair's gone damp. She holds up a shaking finger to Steph and Rev Cootes.

'Stay away from her, do you hear?'

I feel the air shift as she sways. It goes really quiet, like everyone's holding their breath. And then Mum collapses to the ground with a dull thud.

29

Love her no matter what, that's what Mrs Zas said. And I want to try, I really do. But how am I meant to love someone who's just hurt my friends?

No one deserves to be treated like that. Especially the people who care about her.

It's the day after the incident with Rev Cootes and Steph, and I skipped my swim training to be with Mum. She's lying in bed asleep. Nurse Heidi gave her some calming-down pills. As I watch Mum's sleeping face, I wonder whether you're allowed a get-out clause when the person you're supposed to love does something really bad. Because, right now, loving Mum is the last thing I want to do.

Mum was only unconscious for a few minutes last night. When she woke up, Dad went back to the garage to get her wheelchair and we pushed her back home across The Green. I could feel a thousand pairs of eyes staring at us. And I know that, for once, they weren't thinking about her weight: they were thinking about how crazy she was. THE CRAZY, OBESE WOMAN FROM CUCKOO COTTAGE: that would make a good headline for Allen.

Dad had called Nurse Heidi and she stayed most of the

night, checking Mum's pulse and her temperature. She left an hour ago.

I glance out through the crack in the lounge curtains and see Rev Cootes watering the children's graves. He keeps looking over at the house. I was going to talk to him about Mum, to see whether he had any more information about her past, but now Mum's banned me from seeing him, and Steph, and he probably doesn't want to talk to me anyway. Which just makes me want to see him more. He and Steph must know something really bad for Mum to have reacted like that. Much worse than Mum being depressed because of me.

I've never seen Mum be violent before. Everything that's happening at the moment, what she said yesterday, what she did just now, makes me realise that I was just kidding myself about her improving. Maybe Mum's lost seven stone but she's definitely not getting better.

As I look back to Mum, I notice an envelope pushed into her seat; it's wedged in between her thigh and the armrest. I pull it out carefully and notice that there's a Newton Town Council stamp across the front. I turn it over. It looks like it was ripped open in a hurry, the edges are all jaggedy. I pull out the letter and scan down:

> *We thank you for your letter outlining your concerns about the opening of the Lido...*

A stone lodges in my throat. She wrote to the council to protest against the Lido? I don't care how much Mum hates water: she knows how much the swim championships mean to me.

... we would like to ask you to reconsider... to think about the benefits of the new Lido to the community...

So Mum was the one who started the row in the village about the Lido. She's the one who wrote to the council. She's probably the one who wrote to the editor of the *Newton News*.

Mum opens her eyes and looks straight over at me, like she knew I was there.

'My little Feather...' she says.

You have to love her, no matter what... Why did Mrs Zas have to tell me that?

Mum stretches her hand towards me. I shove the letter into the back pocket of my jeans.

I've lost count of the number of times I've helped Mum up. Years and years of looking after her – of *loving her no matter what*. And what good has it done? Only a few months ago, I loved Mum without even thinking about it: it felt as easy and good as floating on my back in the pool. Now, it's like every time she does something to disappoint me, I have to will the love to come back.

I take a breath, go over, and sit on the edge of Mum's bed and take her hand.

'My little Feather...' she says again.

I wonder whether fainting made her brain forget what happened last night.

'If you help me into my chair, we can watch TV,' Mum says.

She wants to watch TV? After everything's that happened?

'I missed my swim practice,' I say.

Mum's eyes cloud over.

'And I can't afford to miss training sessions. The regionals are coming up.'

Mum doesn't say anything.

I hear the diggers rattling along The Green on their way to the Lido. I guess Mum's lost the protest before it even started.

'Do you even care about me?' I ask. 'About the things that matter to me?'

Mum tries to prop herself up in her bed but collapses again. I know I should help her but right now I don't want to.

'I don't understand, Feather.'

'I said, do you even care?'

'Of course I care.'

Mum finally manages to prop her back up against the pillows. Her face looks grey.

'You never ask, Mum.'

'Ask what?'

'How things are going. For me.'

'You *tell* me how things are going.'

'Yeah, but you never *ask*.'

'I don't understand what I've done wrong, Feather.'

I let out a laugh. 'Seriously?' I ball my hands into fists to give me the courage to keep going. 'Proper mums ask questions.'

'What?'

'I train *every* day, Mum. And you never ask me about it. And Steph's my coach and my friend. And Rev Cootes is my friend too.' I gulp. 'I hate the way you spoke to them last night.'

'Darling…'

'We only ever talk about you, Mum. About what you

watch on TV. About what you want to eat or drink. About what you've seen through your stupid window.'

Mum stares at me like a stranger's sitting on her bed rather than the daughter who's loved her since she was born.

'And I don't mind. I like to talk to you about that stuff, because I love you.'

My eyes are welling up.

'You're saying I don't love you?' Mum's voice is flat now, like it's finally sunk in that I'm not okay with what she did last night. Or with what she's been keeping from me.

I ignore her comment and keep going: 'You know what, Mum? I wouldn't even mind if you didn't show any interest in my life outside this house, if you told me about *your* life outside this house.'

Mum's eyes flicker. She takes a breath.

'So tell me, how is your swimming going?' Mum asks in the most unconvincing tone ever.

'That's not the point.'

'You asked me to show an interest – so I'm showing an interest. How's the swimming going?'

'You really want to know, Mum?'

She nods.

'It's not going anywhere. If I don't improve my PB massively, I'm not going to make it through the regionals. Which means I won't even get to swim in the Lido at the nationals this summer.' I gulp. 'And if you'd been able to do anything about it, you would have put a stop to the nationals happening at all, wouldn't you? You'd have made sure that the Lido stayed closed forever.' I whip out the letter from the council and throw it onto her lap.

Mum closes her eyes.

'You see, Mum? Every time I talk about what matters to me, you switch off.'

Mum opens her eyes. 'I'm not switching off.'

'If it were down to you, I wouldn't leave the house at all. I wouldn't swim or have friends or have a job or even go to school. I'd just sit here with you, watching TV, waiting for you to eat yourself to death.'

I notice a tear plop out of Mum's eye. It sits on her cheek. She doesn't wipe it away.

'You weren't always like this, Mum – were you?'

Another tear. And another. Suddenly, they start flowing down her cheeks. My throat seizes up. I hate having to talk to her like this but I can't ignore what happened last night or what I've been finding out about her past.

'You used to care about people, you used to help them,' I say. 'You used to love the village.'

She sniffs. 'Sorry?'

'I saw a picture of you on the Internet. And I found a photo of you at the Lido.'

Mum wipes her brow, props herself up until she's sitting properly and looks towards the open door.

'George…?'

'What? You're calling Dad now because you don't want to talk to me?'

'George!' she yells out, her voice wobbly, her face wet with tears. 'Get in here!'

'Why don't *you* tell me, Mum, why you've been lying to me basically since I've been born?'

'George…' Mum's voice rings maniacally through the room.

'Dad's not here, Mum. It's you and me. And you might have shut Steph up and, for all I know, you might have shut

Rev Cootes up and Clay and Jake and the rest of the village too, but I'm not going to let it go. I need to know.'

Mum wipes away the tears from her cheeks and stares right at me. I recognise the look in her eyes. It's the same one she had last night when she looked at Steph and Rev Cootes.

'It's none of your business, Feather.'

I keep my eyes locked on hers for a beat and then I get up, walk across the lounge, grab the door handle and leave to go to my room, slamming the door so hard the whole house shakes.

30

I run up the stairs, press a chair against my bedroom door and tear down the information wall. The Post-its and bits of string and photographs float to the floor. I sweep them all up in my arms and dump them in my bin.

I'm sick of worrying about other people. I'm going to focus on *my* life for a change and one thing I'm going to make sure of is that I get through to the regionals. No one's going to stop me from swimming in the Lido for the nationals.

I lie back on my bed and stare at the ceiling. My heart thumps and blood rushes through my ears.

Shifting my head to the side, I notice the hole left from where I pulled at the wallpaper the other day.

Behind my thoughts, I hear heavy footsteps plodding up the stairs. I block them out, get onto my knees and peel away more of the wallpaper. And then I keep going, slowly and carefully at first, but then I lose patience and start tearing at the paper, yanking at it. I tear until all the sea animals are floating in front of me: starfish and seahorses and blowfish and sharks. I tear until shades of blue from the sea and the sky shine through. I tear until my fingernails are bloody and my knuckles are raw and my hands are shaking.

The footsteps are on the landing now.

I lie back on the bed and close my eyes, my hands throbbing. The fish and the waves and the sky from the wallpaper flash in front of my eyes.

'Feather?' Mum's voice behind my door, her breathing heavy.

I don't answer.

'Feather, please…'

Under normal circumstances I'd be jumping up and down with excitement at the fact that Mum's made it up the stairs, but right now I don't care. I don't care about her or Dad or Steph or Jake or Rev Cootes or Clay or anyone else.

I hear the rattle of Dad's van pulling up outside. Houdini bleating. And a few moments later, Dad's light footsteps on the stairs.

And then a knock on my door.

'Feather, it's Dad.' A pause. 'Please let us in, my love.'

I swing my legs off the bed, grab my swim bag and throw in my costume, my hat, my goggles and my towel. I stuff my pencil case and all the books that will fit into my school bag. Then I grab an old rucksack and pack some clothes, a few bras and knickers, a set of pyjamas. And after moving the back of the chair out from under the door handle of my bedroom door, I step out onto the landing.

Mum and Dad stand outside my door. They stare at me blankly.

'Feather?' Mum looks at my bags. 'What are you doing?'

'I'm going.'

'Going where?'

I pause. 'None of your business.'

'Feather…' Dad starts. 'Why are you doing this?'

I shake my head and turn to face Mum. 'I'm doing this because I need to get away from her.'

And with that I run down the stairs, my bags bashing the wall beside me, and then I lurch out through the front door.

I stop briefly at Houdini's kennel. It takes all the willpower I have not to untie his lead and take him with me. Because, right now, Houdini feels like the only friend I've got. But taking him would be too complicated.

'Sorry, buddy,' I say. 'Don't take this personally but I can't take you with me.' I kiss the top of his head and rub his horns. 'I'm going to need all the luck I can get.'

I pick my bags up again and run across The Green. I run past Mr Ding's takeaway van and St Mary's church and Bewitched and then I head down Twirl Street, past Steph and Jake's house and to the bus stop by the motorway. If I wait at the stop on The Green, someone will come out and want to talk to me, and I can't face that right now.

As I sit at the bus stop outside the village, I realise that I haven't got a place in the world to go.

'Feather?' A voice sings out across The Green.

Mrs Zas stands there, her hands on her hips, a yellow scarf shining like a beacon from her head. Under her coat she's wearing a *Doctor Who* outfit. I wish I could time-travel right now. Way, way into the future, far away from Willingdon and everyone I know.

She must have followed me to the bus stop.

In a minute she's sitting beside me.

'You planning to go on holiday?' she asks, out of breath, nodding at my bags.

The bus lurches to the kerb and its doors open. I get up off the seat and hitch my bags onto my shoulders.

'I have to get away from *her*...' I say, my voice choking up.

Mrs Zas puts her hand on my arm. 'Why don't you stay a bit and talk, there'll always be another bus, if you still want to go.'

I slowly put down my bags. The bus driver shakes his head and closes the doors again.

'I ran away at your age,' Mrs Zas says.

'You did?'

She nods. 'Though my reasons weren't nearly so noble.'

I don't think my reasons are noble.

'I was jealous of my sister,' she goes on. 'I wanted my parents to notice me too.'

I watch the bus pulling away.

'If you run away, you won't be able to do your swimming training. And your training is what matters. You have to prepare for the regionals now, it has to be your focus.'

I wonder whether Mrs Zas gave pep talks like this to her sister. *You have to train harder, to dance every day...*

I look down at my swim bag. Mrs Zas is right. If I ran away to who knows where, I wouldn't be able to keep up my training, or not in the same way anyway. I must have known that all along, otherwise I wouldn't have packed the bag and taken it with me.

'Why don't you come back to the shop for a bit,' Mrs Zas says, looking in the direction of The Green.

I don't answer but she takes one of my bags anyway and then grabs my hand and we walk over to her Bewitched, breathing in warm spring air.

I look at the daffodils nodding along the edge of the

cemetery and think about how, while the world is coming back to life after a long, cold winter, my life is shutting down.

At the shop, Mrs Zas guides me up the stairs to her flat and opens the door to a box room, which is even smaller than my bedroom back home. She points to the bed.

'There are some fresh towels for you. I've put some warm milk in the Thermos.' She points at the bedside table.

Not for the first time, I think Mrs Zas must be psychic. She must have known that something was wrong and she must have known that she'd persuade me to come back to hers.

I put my bags down and sit on the end of the bed. I like how blank the walls are and that there aren't any decorations or bookshelves or flowery curtains. A blank canvas.

I look up at Mrs Zas. 'How long can I stay?'

She comes over and kisses my forehead. 'For as long as you need.'

Moving across the road isn't exactly running away, but I don't care: sitting in Mrs Zas's small room feels like the only place in the world I want to be right now.

May

31

Most people hate swimming fly because it's the hardest. But that's what I love about it. It stretches every bit of my body. It pushes me so hard that, when I'm in the water, my arms and legs thrashing, my mind driving me to swim faster and harder – everything and everyone falls away. For those fifty metres, all that matters is the water and my body and this moment. And in this moment, the world feels like a good place again.

I'm sitting in the whipping area, waiting for the official to call my name. It's the regional finals. Early this morning, Mrs Zas drove us to Slough, where they're holding the competition this year.

A nasal voice buzzes behind me:

'I'll be so fast, it'll be like a flash of lightning bolting through the water...'

It's Amelia, talking to her mum, who's also her coach. She's speaking loud enough to make sure I hear every word. Amelia and I have been competing against each other since we were seven. If you were to count up all the races we've done since then and which one of us came first each time, you'd probably come out with an even number. I might even have won a few more. But this time, the odds are against me.

Amelia will have been training non-stop since she got through her county competition; whereas, I've been focusing all my energies on Mum and the other crap that's been going on in the village. Plus, Amelia's rich and she goes to a posh school with a posh pool and she has a gym at home and personal trainers who help her with her land work and dieticians who make special menus for her so that she eats right. Amelia likes to tell me these things whenever we meet at a competition; she hopes she can chip away at me so that by the time we dive into the pool, I'm a nervous, wobbly mess. Usually, I don't let it affect me, mainly because I know that having all the posh pools and equipment and trainers in the world still doesn't guarantee you'll be any good. Putting in the work is what matters. That's what Steph's taught me. But things are different now: Amelia will have trained harder than me, and training hard was meant to be my trump card.

'Mummy hired a coach from the Youth Olympics Squad to give me some tips,' Amelia said, earlier on in the changing rooms.

At first, it really got to me. Next year, we'll both be old enough to try out for the Youth Olympics Squad and, now, with her contacts, I bet she gets a place. It makes me even more determined to beat her. The clock doesn't lie: if I swim faster than her, if I win and go through to the nationals, the Olympic coaches will have to take me seriously.

I turn up the volume on Mrs Zas's phone so that it blocks out Amelia's voice. Over the last two weeks, Mrs Zas has been playing me lots of pieces by a man called Tchaikovsky, who wrote ballet music that Mrs Zas's sister danced to. Irinka's favourite piece was the 'Waltz of the Flowers'. They'd listen to it before Irinka's performances and competitions. Mrs Zas said it helped to calm Irinka's nerves and that it focused her mind and her heart. I've never really liked classical music but when I listen to 'Waltz of the Flowers', every muscle in my body both relaxes and feels alive.

And of course the waltz bit of it makes me think of Mum. The other day, Mrs Zas went over to talk to Mum, to explain that I'd be staying with her and that she'd take good care of me. Apparently, Mum didn't respond – she didn't even look away from the TV screen.

I take off my headphones just in time to hear the official's voice: 'Feather Tucker to lane one.'

'Time to go, Miss Feather,' Mrs Zas says.

I slap my thighs to get the blood flowing and circle my arms and shoulders, imitating the fly movement I do in the water. My heart and stomach feel like they're playing ping-pong. And I need the loo, but I've already been three times in the last hour.

I stand up and shake out my legs. Then I close my eyes for a second, trying to get into the zone. Everything draws back: the competitors sitting around me, Mrs Zas, the officials blowing their whistles and making announcements, the supporters cheering.

'You're going to lose…' A hot whisper by my ear.

My focus goes and I'm snapped back into the present.

'Don't listen to her,' Mrs Zas says. Then she shoots Amelia the first mean look I've ever seen her give to anyone.

'Thanks,' I say.

Mrs Zas squeezes my hand and then she looks around the big, echoey room.

'Feather…?' she starts.

'Yes?'

Then she shakes her head.

'Never mind.' Her eyes film over. 'Break a leg.'

I imagine her saying that to her sister and wonder what 'break a leg' is in Ukrainian.

I don't know what I would have done without Mrs Zas. These last few weeks, she's been my mum, my coach and my best friend all rolled into one.

Mrs Zas kisses my cheek.

'Love every moment.' Apparently, she'd say that to her sister too. It is a pretty weird thing to say to someone about to go into a gruelling competition or performance.

You can only win if you love the process, Mrs Zas explained.

And I guess that makes sense.

Mrs Zas goes off to sit with the supporters and I walk to the blocks with the other competitors. Amelia's in lane two, right next to me, which will make it even harder to ignore her.

I spot Allen from the *Newton News*, ambling towards us with his camera. He grins at us with his yellow teeth and snaps some photos. And I wish I had the time to jump off the block and ask him where the hell he gets off stealing a book from someone's house.

I breathe and close my eyes to block him out. *Focus on the race. The race is all that matters right now.*

The official, dressed all in white, blows a long whistle to get everyone quiet. Then two quick whistles followed by a third longer one as a signal to the competitors to get ready.

'Get onto your blocks…'

We step on.

'Take your marks...'

I put my goggles over my eyes, grip my hands under the front of the block, curl my left toes over the edge and pull my body back like a spring, bum up. In under a minute, all this will be over.

I shift my eyes to the left and see the row of competitors on the block. We're all still as statues. No fiddling with goggles. No mumbling. If we breathe too hard we'll be disqualified.

Then I look to the supporters on my right and catch sight of Mrs Zas's sky-blue headscarf. She gives me one of her wide smiles that makes me feel like I'm being lifted off the ground. And then I notice someone standing a little further on, to the side of the supporter benches. A floral dress straining over a massive stomach. Long hair. A red face.

My stomach does a flip.

Mum? Here? Now?

And then Allen notices her too and shifts his camera from us to her and *snap, snap, snaps*. His flash bounces off the tiled room.

I swallow hard.

Part of me feels furious that she's showed up out of the blue like this – she must have known it would throw me off course. But a bigger part of me is so happy to see her that I want to stand up on the block and do star jumps into the water. After all these years, Mum actually came.

Focus, I tell myself again. *Focus*.

The buzzer rings so loud it ricochets in my head and everything else gets drowned out.

I lift my arms and dive in.

Then I become aware of a whistle for the competitor in

lane three, who must have been disqualified for diving past the fifteen-metre mark.

'Never breathe on your first stroke,' Steph taught me. 'You'll waste energy.'

I wonder if she's come too. Mrs Zas has been really great stepping in as my coach and she's good at all the pep talks and all the mind-focusing stuff, but she doesn't know anything about technique. Steph was a total expert and she always worked hard to stay on top of the latest training methods so that she could be the best coach for me. I've felt bad about not getting in touch but I needed to spend the last two weeks focusing on the race – which meant letting go of all the other voices in my head.

I dolphin-kick through the water. A little kick followed by a big kick to get my arms out of the water.

I feel Amelia pushing through the water to my left.

I bet that, right now, there's not a second between us. But she's been training steadily for months with no interruptions.

Mrs Zas's words come back to me: *Love every moment.*

I force myself forward, kick my legs harder and bring my arms out of the water faster.

My legs and shoulders burn, but I keep pushing.

I have to do this for me. And for Mum: to show her it was worth her coming. To make her proud.

Fifty metres. Two laps of the pool. My PB is thirty-six seconds. Amelia's is thirty-four seconds. I need to get to thirty-two seconds if I've got a chance of getting through to the nationals.

Love it, love it, love it, I say to myself over and over as I push through the water.

I sight the wall and make the turn.

I see her surface ahead of me. She always does this – speeds up on the second lap, whereas I'm best in the first lap.

The crowd sounds like white noise: names cheered so loud they all meld into one roar.

Is Mum shouting for me?

I wish I could freeze time and space and look up out of the water at her, to see what she's doing and what her face looks like, what her eyes are saying.

Only a few more metres and the race will be over.

'Go, Meals! Push harder!' Amelia's mum, her voice like a foghorn – it's the only one that never seems to get drowned out by the crowd.

She's going to win. I'm not fit enough to catch up.

And then I close my eyes and for a second the world goes black and I get a few notes from 'Waltz of the Flowers'. It soars through my body and lifts me out of the water.

And then Mrs Zas's voice again:

Focus your heart… focus your mind… love every minute of it…

I take a breath and kick harder. My body shoots through the water. The burning and aching in my muscles melts away. I throw my arms over my head, bring my hands together and then go again. I kick, kick, kick as hard as I can. I'm catching up with Amelia. We're parallel now.

The crowd shouts louder.

And then I hear a voice, clearer and sharper than Amelia's mum – as clear as when Rev Cootes rings the bells of St Mary's and the whole village sings like a tuning fork.

'Go, Feather!'

It's Mum.

I kick and kick and worm my body through the water.

And then, for a moment, I'm going so fast I feel like I'm flying.

The edge of the pool comes towards me. I grab it. A second later, Amelia comes in beside me.

I did it. And Mum saw.

After the race, I want to run straight to Mum but Mrs Zas says I have to go to the swim-down pool or I'll get an injury. When you finish doing a race, especially one as intense as fly, your whole body is as tightly wound as a spring. You have to spend some time in a warm pool, relaxing your muscles, swimming gently, letting all the energy seep out.

I sit on the edge of the pool, my legs shaking.

'Did I do okay?' I ask Mrs Zas.

She grins. 'Okay? You were the best.'

I look down into the water. 'Did you know Mum was here?'

Ever since I finished the race, I haven't been able to stop thinking about Mum standing there by the spectator benches, watching me. It must have taken all the strength and courage she had to get out of the house and to climb into Dad's van and to have him drive her all the way here. Mum's barely stepped out of the front door in over a decade, and when she has, she's gone no further than across The Green. Coming to Slough must have felt like going to the other side of the moon.

'I didn't know she was coming,' Mrs Zas says, 'but, yes, I saw her arrive with your father.'

'Did you talk to her?'

'I said, "Hello" and, "Thank you for coming."'

'And what did she say?'

'She didn't say anything. But it's understandable, Feather.

She doesn't know me and, as far as she's concerned, I've stolen you away.'

'You haven't stolen me... I'm the one who asked you to let me stay.'

'It's easier for your mother to think I've stolen you than to think that you don't want to come home.'

Mrs Zas always makes things clearer – and harder to hear.

'And Jake?' I ask. 'Did he come? And Clay? And Steph?'

She shakes her head. 'I don't think so. But I could be wrong, there were so many people out there.'

Jake's been acting embarrassed whenever I see him, like he's replaying it all in his head: Mum stomping across The Green, shouting all those mean things at Steph and Rev Cootes and grabbing at them like she was having some kind of crazy breakdown. When I asked him if we could meet up, he said that Clay wasn't feeling well and that he needed him. I know Jake's telling the truth: Clay hasn't been to school for over a month and, whenever I catch sight of him, he looks greyer and thinner. But, still, if all this stuff hadn't happened with Mum, I'm sure Jake would still make an effort to see me.

I know that I'm lucky because I've got Mrs Zas, and Clay doesn't have anyone except for Jake, but I still wish I could tell Jake that I need him too. And that I miss him.

Once I've warmed down, I stand up out of the water.

Mrs Zas hands me my towel.

'Is it okay if I go over and see Mum now?'

I feel kind of bad. Mrs Zas has spent two weeks hearing me rant and rave about Mum and now I'm going straight over to her.

She smiles. 'Of course it is,' she says.

I wrap the towel over my shoulders, walk past the whipping area, where the next group of swimmers is waiting for their race, and along the far end of the pool to the benches. I scan the benches, in case Mum decided to sit down, but realise that they're far too narrow for her to fit. As I walk past the spectators and supporters, a few of the mums and dads from Newton clap, and I try to slow down and smile but all I want is to see Mum and to hug her and to thank her for coming and to have her tell me that she's proud of me.

I get to the place where I saw her standing but it's empty. Then I head through the doors to the café, thinking that Dad must have taken her for a snack. But they're not there either. Although I'm still in my swimming costume and towel, with my hair dripping down my back, I walk out into the car park. I stand on tiptoes and scan the rows of cars and buses and vans. And that's when I spot the back of Dad's plumbing van pulling out of the car park and onto the dual carriageway.

32

As Mrs Zas drives us home in her clapped-out red Fiat, I drift in and out of sleep. I realise that, ever since New Year's Eve, I haven't stopped: thinking and worrying and digging things up and training for the next competition. Every cell in my body feels like it's going into shutdown.

My eyelids get heavier and heavier. I could sleep for a zillion years.

When we pull into The Green, I blink open my eyes and get a glimpse of our cottage. If Mum wanted to see me or to speak to me, she'd have stayed around at the pool, wouldn't she? And maybe the reason she left is because she's upset with me or disapproves of the race or is disappointed that I didn't do better, that Amelia nearly beat me. And I can't face that, not right now.

'Give her time...' Mrs Zas's voice sounds like it's coming through a thick fog.

The car rattles to a stop.

My eyelids drop closed and I feel myself drifting into a deep sleep.

At the sound of the bells of St Mary's ringing through the sky, my eyes fly open. I don't remember how I got from Mrs Zas's car to the box room but when I look at my watch I realise I've been sleeping for twelve hours. My head is filled with that squeaky cotton-wool feeling and my throat is dry. But that heavy feeling in my heart that I've woken up with every morning for the last few months, it's lifted.

Kneeling on the bed, I push the curtain to one side. May sunshine streams through the window. The cherry trees along The Green are full of pink and white blossom. Mr Ding is washing his van; the water from his hose splits and sparkles in the sunshine.

Today's going to be a good day, I can feel it.

I look over at our cottage, at how the roses are starting to reach over the door, and I realise that it's time to go home.

Humming the tune from 'Waltz of the Flowers', I pack my three bags: my school bag, my overnight bag, and my swimming bag. I think about wearing the medal I got for coming first in the fifty-metre fly but decide against it – Mum feeling anxious about me swimming can't have just vanished, can it? I stuff it into the side pocket of my swim bag.

I don't know when I made this resolution but it feels like it's been settled in my mind for a while now: I'm going to give Mum the time she needs. I can't force her to be healthy and I can't force her to tell me what went on all those years ago. Mrs Zas is right: my job's to love Mum and, when she's ready, she'll start moving forward. And from the evidence of her showing up at the regionals yesterday, she's already taken a massive leap forward, one that I didn't push her to take, or not directly, anyway. Now it's my turn to take a step towards her.

I clomp downstairs with my three bags.

'Morning, Mrs Zas!' My voice sings through her work-shop and spills out into the store.

I hear the rustle of paper.

I come up behind her. She's got a mug of hot cinnamon milk in her hands and she's shuffling together today's paper. I notice a set of immigration papers on the side too.

'Had a good sleep?' she asks.

'Weird but good, yeah. I don't think I've ever slept that long.'

'You needed it.' She looks at my bags. 'Decided to go home?'

I nod. And then I feel guilty for rushing in when I needed her and then rushing off without talking to her about it first.

'Thank you for letting me stay…'

Mrs Zas puts down her mug of cinnamon milk and misses the edge. It crashes to the floor. She swivels round on her stool and knocks the paper down too. It lands on the puddle of milk.

'Oh!' She throws her hands in the air and then she bunches the paper together.

I put my bags down and kneel beside her. 'Here, let me do this.'

'No!' She takes the paper from my hand.

I stand up, holding my palms out. 'Sorry.'

Her brow is all scrunched up and her eyes have gone dark and serious.

'Oh, Feather, you're going to find out soon enough.'

She shakes out the paper, presses it to her dressing gown to soak up the milk, smooths open the soggy pages on the counter and leans back for me to see. I step forward.

The headline reads:

A BIG SPLASH: GRAND LIDO OPENING TO GO AHEAD
– *by Allen Fisher*

Seeing it, makes my heart skip. I've qualified for the nationals. And now the Lido's going ahead. This day couldn't get any better.

I scan down the article and there's a whole load of stuff about people being for and against the Lido and how the council decided to go ahead. And then I see it, a massive photo of Mum, at the trials yesterday. I read the paragraph under the photo:

> *Josephine Tucker loses her bid to keep the Lido closed... Council says the Lido will make thousands for the village as well as inspiring young people to exercise more.*

Then there's another photo: it's of me in my swimming costume with my goggles and my dimply white arms and legs.

Under my photo, there's a caption: *Josephine's daughter, Feather Tucker, thrilled to be racing at the Lido this summer...*

Under any other circumstances, I'd be chuffed to be in the paper, especially because it's about getting through to the nationals, but I know how much Mum would hate having a photo of her splashed all over the local news. And I don't like how Allen's pitted us against each other like that.

I scan through the rest of the article:

> *Thirteen years after the tragedy that shook the village...*

The tragedy?

Mrs Zas puts her hand on mine. I shake it off and keep reading:

...Josephine Tucker is poolside once again... Her daughter, Feather, Regional Fly Champion, has been kept in the dark for close to thirteen years...

How does he know that Mum's been keeping things from me? And why's he going on about it in the newspaper?

My head spins.

My eyes leave the text and look through the other photos, snapshots from the village: Mum being carried out of the house on New Year's Eve; Mrs Zas standing on the doorstep of her shop, wearing a Superman outfit; Rev Cootes, kneeling in front of a flowerbed by the children's graves, his hands covered in soil; the empty Lido, cracked tiles, leaves and moss gathering in the corners; and then a picture of the diggers with the words: *Will they dig up Jo Tucker's secrets?*

The biggest photo is of me standing in front of our tiny cottage, Houdini next to me, Dad's van parked to the side and, behind me, through a slit in the curtains, Mum's face staring out, white and wide as the moon.

The photo of Mum and me has another caption under it:

Mother and Daughter: Secrets and Lies.

I dig my nails into my palms and go back to the article. Phrases leap out at me.

I feel sick. Aren't local reporters meant to support the community?

I want to tear up all of Allen's stupid, mean lies.

For some reason, there's a picture of a little boy at the bottom of the article. I look at his light blond hair and pale skin and blue eyes and feel a jolt.

I take out the photo I've been carrying in my back pocket

of my jeans all this time, of Mum and me and Clay, and hold it up to the photo in the paper. It's the same boy. Apart from me not being in it, the photo in the paper could be an exact copy of the one I found on the garage floor. But why has Allen printed a picture of Clay?

Then I read the next paragraph, the words wrapped around a dust-jacket picture of *Max's Marvellous Adventures* and I realise that the photo's not of Clay, not even close:

> *On the 1 June, Max Tucker drowned... It was his sister's first birthday...*

33

I run straight to Jake's house and ring the doorbell over and over. I need to know whether he's kept this from me along with everyone else.

Steph opens the door. She's still in her PJs and her hair's all messed up and her eyes are red. I don't know what she's so upset about, it's not like her life has just been blown apart.

'Where's Jake?' I ask, looking past her.

'He took off, Feather.' She looks at the floor. 'He wouldn't talk to me.'

Which only means one thing: Clay.

She reaches out for my hand. 'Feather, why don't you stay and talk?'

Steph's obviously seen the article.

'Not now,' I say and run back to The Green.

When I get to the church I stop dead. Rev Cootes's garden has been vandalised. Rose petals scattered among the graves. Plants upended, their roots sticking up to the sky.

'Feather! Feather!' Mrs Zas calls over from her shop.

I feel bad for ignoring her but I don't need her words of wisdom right now.

Rev Cootes is kneeling by the Fuzzy Deutzia I gave him, a spade in his hands, a stripe of earth on his forehead.

I spin round and look across The Green.

My eyes take in the houses and shops. I think about all the people who were meant to be my friends. I knew they were keeping things from me about Mum's past, but I never thought it would be this big.

I look over to the cottage. Mum's curtains are drawn. And Houdini's lead lies limp outside the kennel. He's gone.

I don't have time to deal with this.

I run up to Rev Cootes.

Behind me, I hear the churchyard gate clink open and shut and then Mrs Zas's heels clip-clopping along the path through the cemetery.

'Feather!' Mrs Zas cries again. 'Feather!'

'I need to talk to Jake,' I say to Rev Cootes.

'I'm afraid he's not here—'

'I know he's here,' I say. 'He's always here.'

Mrs Zas is standing next to me now, catching her breath.

'You should go and see your mother, Feather,' she says.

'No.'

'I'm going inside to look,' I say.

Rev Cootes stands up, wipes his hands on his cassock.

'Feather, you have to calm down.'

'I don't *have* to do anything.'

He holds both my arms.

'Look at me, Feather.'

I pull away from him.

'Feather, please.'

Mrs Zas places her hand on my back. 'Reverend Cootes is right, Feather, it's important to be calm.'

So *now* they decide to team up? Great.

Rev Cootes clears his throat.

'You're right, Feather. Jake and Clay are together, but they're not here. Jake came over and Clay was in a bit of a state, so they went for walk.'

Clay's in a bit of a state? What does any of this have to do with Clay? And I love how Jake didn't come to find me, to see how *I* was.

'Where did they go?' I ask Rev Cootes.

But I don't need him to answer – I know exactly where they went.

The workmen are having a break. The diggers sit on the churned-up earth around the pool, their engines switched off. And then I see them, sitting on the bench a little way off from the Lido. Their heads are bowed so close they're nearly touching. I take a step forward and, as I do, Jake cups Clay's face in his hands and kisses him on the lips.

I stumble backwards.

And then I start running. I run faster than I've ever run before. I want to get out of here. I don't want to see anyone from Willingdon ever again.

The bus is so crowded I have to stand. As I grip the handrail, I notice a family sitting at the far end: a mum, a dad, a boy and his little sister. They're playing cards and eating sandwiches and laughing and nudging each other. That was meant to be us: me and Mum and Dad and Max. A proper family.

I think of Max being dead. And that if it hadn't been for a stupid reporter with nothing better to do than snooping around a tiny village in the middle of nowhere, I would never have found this out.

When we get to Newton, I push down the aisle of the bus and jump out onto the pavement.

'I'm afraid he's busy,' the receptionist says.

I'm standing in the offices of the *Newton News*, a couple of stuffy rooms above the dry cleaner's on the High Street.

The woman looks me up and down. Sweat runs down the small of my back and my cheeks are burning.

I take a crumpled copy of today's newspaper out of my bag and wave it at her.

'This is important,' I say. 'Tell him Feather Tucker's here.'

'Why don't you wait over there?' She points to a bunch of grey, plastic chairs next to a coffee table.

Half an hour goes by and I reckon the receptionist has forgotten about me. I'm about to remind her when Allen comes out of one of the rooms. He's laughing and two of his colleagues are laughing too and patting him on the back.

'Good job,' one of the guys says as they walk past the receptionist.

I stand up.

'Yeah – good job, Allen!' I say, mock-clapping him.

My claps echo off the dirty, beige walls.

Allen looks up. 'Feather…'

The guys with him look at me and whisper to each other and mumble something to Allen.

He leans in to them and says, 'I'll catch up with you later,' then Allen turns to me.

'You didn't have the right to print that stuff… or to take those photos.'

Allen tries to smile but his crooked mouth and his coffee-stained teeth just make him look even more stupid. He holds out his palms.

'Feather, I'm a journalist, it's my job to keep the community informed of important, local decisions.'

'Is it your job to spy on people too? To make them trust you and then take advantage of them? To blurt out people's family secrets to the world?'

I tear the article out of the newspaper, rip it up and throw it at him. It floats to the floor and lands on his stupid, squeaky shoes.

He doesn't move.

'I want the book back.'

'Sorry?'

'You stole it from Mum.'

He lets out a laugh, which makes me want to punch him.

'I could call the police,' I say. 'Tell them how you lied your way into my house and then stole personal property.'

Allen goes quiet. Then he turns and goes back into his office. A moment later, he comes back with the book and hands it to me.

I look at the front cover like I'm seeing it for the first time: a little boy, Max. An adventurer. *My* brother.

I haven't cried yet. About losing a brother. About people keeping his death a secret from me. But now tears push up my throat and into my nose and prick the backs of my eyes.

I gulp back the tears. I don't want Allen to have the satisfaction of seeing me cry.

'Don't ever come near us again,' I say.

And then I run out of the door and down the stairs. I stumble out onto the pavement and stand there, blinking at the bright sunlight and listening to the traffic whooshing past. Every bit of my life that I can remember flashes past my eyes. And it all feels like a lie.

34

I stay in Newton for hours, not knowing where to go or what to do, and then I realise that I've missed the 16.05 back to Willingdon. It's the last bus. And then, knowing I have to face Mum some time, I walk home.

I trudge along the motorway for what feels like hours, my legs and arms aching from the race yesterday, my feet stumbling over the tufts of grass by the side of the road.

It's dark. The stars are out. The village is quiet.

I knock on Mrs Zas's door. A few moments later, a light pings on and I hear the sound of the footsteps on the back stairs.

She opens the door.

'Oh, Feather.' Mrs Zas holds out her arms and folds me into her chest and that's when I let go: I let out big gulps and heaves and sighs and I cry until it's like all the water in my body has dried up.

Then I pull away and look up at her.

'Can I stay with you a bit longer?'

She's wearing a big kimono: a dragon stitched in gold curls up one of the sides. Her blue headscarf is coming loose; she must have put it on in a hurry before answering the door.

'Let's have some hot cinnamon milk,' Mrs Zas says.

I follow her upstairs to her kitchen and, as she's warming the milk, I tell her about how I went to Newton to tell Allen what I thought about him. And how Dad's left a million messages on my phone and I haven't called him back. Because how can I go home? What am I meant to say to Mum?

Mrs Zas hands me my milk and then sits down in front of me. I look down into the mug and feel the steam on my cold face, breathe in the sweet cinnamon.

Mrs Zas cups her mug in her hands. 'What is that saying you have in England? "Today's news is tomorrow's chip paper." It feels like the end of the world now, Feather, but soon that journalist's words will be forgotten.'

'But *what* he wrote about, that won't go away, will it?'

'No, no, it won't.'

I push my cup away. 'You knew, didn't you? About Max?'

She nods. 'I did, Feather.'

'So you all lied to me?' My chest goes tight. 'Everyone lied to me. And I'm not even allowed to be angry, because the lie's about something terrible, something that made Mum sick… But I *am* angry, I can't help it.' I shake my head. 'You must all think I'm a real idiot – walking around the village without a clue about anything.'

Mrs Zas puts her hand over mine and presses down lightly.

'You know all the important things, Feather. You understand people—'

'But I didn't know the most important thing of all, did I?' My eyes are starting to sting again. 'That I had a brother.' I pause. 'And that he died.'

'It was your mother's story to tell. We had to respect her wishes.'

I think about all the strange situations I haven't been able to make sense of these past few months. Steph and Mum falling out at Christmas. How Steph kept going on and on about Mum needing to talk to me. I get it now: Steph wanted me to know about Max. She understood that even if Mum kept it from me, I'd find out about it sooner or later.

I look up at Mrs Zas. Her blue headscarf has shifted to one side. I notice, for the first time, that instead of the long, dark hair I'd always imagined she had underneath, there's a bald patch.

'Do you sleep in your headscarves?' I ask.

She shakes her head. And then, without warning, she whips it off.

I look at her bald head under the kitchen lamp and suck in my breath.

You'd think it would be weird, seeing an old woman with no hair like that, but it brings out her cheekbones and the deep hollows of her eyes and her warm smile. She looks beautiful. And then it hits me. When people don't have any hair, it's because they're sick. It's because they have cancer. I can't breathe.

'You're ill? Like your sister?'

Mrs Zas takes my hand. 'I'm fine, Feather.'

'So why?'

'When my sister had chemotherapy, I shaved my head to keep her company. And now that she's gone, I suppose it's a way of remembering her and what she went through. I suppose it's my secret.'

She puts the headscarf back on and switches on her electric cigarette.

I let out a long breath.

'Is that why you smoke those?' I ask, nodding at the e-cigarette. 'Because of your sister's cancer?'

Mrs Zas nods then smiles. 'If I see Irinka in heaven, I'm going to force her to smoke these.' She smiles again. 'They're disgusting!'

'She smoked?'

'Like a chimney.'

'Even though she was a dancer?'

'She said it helped her. That it expanded her lungs.' Mr Zas takes another puff. 'They were different times. And you know better than anyone that people don't always do what's good for them.'

'You're going to stay, aren't you?' I blurt out.

'I'll do everything I can to make sure that happens.' She squeezes my hand. 'Why don't you go home, Feather? Your mum must be so worried.'

I look out of the window and across The Green. The cottage is dark, all except Mum's room.

'You know how you said I had to love her? That it was only love that would make her better?'

'Yes, I remember.'

'I don't think I can. Not any more.'

'Loving someone isn't just a feeling, Feather. It's a choice. And it's an action. And, yes, it takes all the courage we've got. But if there's one thing I know about you, it's that you have courage.'

'I don't… not for this…'

She looks at me and smiles. 'Yes, you do' Then she gets up and holds out her hand. 'Come on, I'll walk you over.'

Very slowly, I nod. I take my mug and put it in the sink.

'You've had company?'

She blushes.

I didn't think anyone came up here except me.

For the first time today, I feel a smile spread across my face.

'Rev Cootes?'

'Peter looked like he could do with a drink.'

'*Peter?*'

'Isn't that his name?'

'I didn't know he had a name.' I laugh. 'I mean, he never told me he was called Peter...' I look back at the mugs in the sink. 'You made him cinnamon milk?'

She nods. 'He liked it.' She blushes even more. 'He said he would make me a cup of tea next time.'

'You're going on a date?'

'We're going to have a cup of tea together.'

For a second, I forget all the horribleness of today and throw my arms around Mrs Zas and hold her tight.

'What's that for?' Mrs Zas whispers into my hair.

'I'm just happy that you've found each other.'

And then I think about Rev Cootes's wife and how she's sitting on her own in a nursing home and how he still loves her. Why does life have to be such a mess?

'Did you know that Peter can't drive?'

I shake my head. Though I guess it makes sense, I've never seen him in a car.

'Well, I'm going to drive him to visit Rosemary.'

'You are?'

She nods. 'I think Rosemary and I will get on.'

I wish the stupid immigration authorities could be here right now, listening to Mrs Zas. I want them to see how amazing she is: how she shaves her head because she wants to honour her sister; how she's made me feel better on the worst day of my life; how she's going to help a lonely old man visit a wife who doesn't even know who he is any more – and all because she's a good person who wants to make other people's lives better. If England were filled with people like Mrs Zas, it would be a much better place for everyone.

Mrs Zas guides me down the stairs. She puts her coat over her kimono and we walk across The Green together.

When I see Houdini's empty kennel, I remember that he's missing. I should have gone after him this morning – goodness knows what's happened to him.

Mrs Zas puts her arm around my shoulders.

'He's fine,' she says.

'He is?'

She smiles. 'Peter has taken him in.'

My mouth drops open. 'Rev Cootes took in *Houdini*? But he hates Houdini.'

My mind flits to a picture of Houdini sitting at Rev Cootes's kitchen table, sipping tea out of his china cups, and a warm feeling floods through my body; and the first thought I have is that I want to run and tell Mum all about it because she'd find it hilarious. But then I realise that I can't. There's too much rubble between us right now. It will be ages before we can talk about those kinds of things again.

Mrs Zas looks over at Rev Cootes's house. 'Peter thought you and your parents might need a little time to yourselves.'

It comes back to me now, how they both stood in Rev Cootes's garden this morning, trying to get me to calm down. And then I think about what happened next. How I found Jake and Clay together at the park. With everything else that's happened, I'd blocked that out of my head. And I don't have the energy to process it now either. I have to focus on Mum.

At the bottom of the ramp, Mrs Zas kisses my cheek.

'Be brave, Miss Feather,' she says, which makes my body tense up again. I don't know how to be brave, not about this.

Light spills out of the crack in Mum's curtains and I wonder whether she's looking out at us.

I swallow hard and turn back to Mrs Zas.

'What am I meant to say to her?'

'Just listen, Feather. That's all you have to do.' She looks at Mum's window. 'Listen and be kind.'

'How can I be kind – after everything?'

'Because, whatever it is you're feeling, it doesn't come close to what your mum's been through.'

'But—'

'There's nothing so cruel in the whole world as losing a child. No mother ever gets over that.' She holds my shoulders as if she wants to press her words into me. 'So you have to be kind, Feather. There's no other way. You have to listen and you have to be kind and you have to show her that you love her.'

Before I go in, I turn round and watch Mrs Zas striding back across The Green, her headscarf flapping behind her, the hem of her kimono trailing the grass, humming her *turn, turn, turn* song.

It's a clear night. Above her, a fistful of stars shine down on Willingdon.

I look at the shops and cottages around The Green. Even though it's late, there's at least one light on in every home. Maybe Mum's been right all this time, maybe they have been watching. Watching and waiting for Mum to finally tell me her secret.

35

I pause for a moment in the hall and take a breath. Considering everything that's happened today, this is what I expect to find: Mum watching TV, her fist in a packet of crisps, junk-food wrappers everywhere and Dad hiding in his room or out on a pretend job. Basically, everything back to how it was before. Only worse.

I walk up to her door and wait for the smell of prawn cocktail crisps, chocolate and pineapple syrup to hit me. But it doesn't. The window is open, fresh air blows through. I scan the floor: it's clear of rubbish. The TV is off. A bowl of apples sits on Mum's coffee table.

Maybe Mum and Dad have gone, I think. Maybe they've just run away.

And then I hear Dad's snoring, a funny rattly sound like when something's stuck in the Hoover. I take a step in. He's asleep in Mum's chair.

I look over to the bed. Mum's propped against the headboard, her head bent over a copy of *Max's Marvellous Adventures*. Her hair tumbles over her shoulders, casting a shadow over the big white pages. Her fingers, more delicate than I remember them, turn the pages. It's like I'm getting a glimpse of the mum who existed when I was a baby, when Max was still with us.

I take another step forward. The floorboards creak and Mum looks up.

'The books were for him, weren't they?' I stare at the copy in her hand.

Mum nods.

'Did you read them with him?'

She nods again. And then she looks straight at me.

'Eleanor brought them back from America as a gift for both our boys.'

'Max and...' My mind races. Of course. 'Eleanor brought them back for Max and Clay?'

'Yes.'

I sit on the end of her bed and place the first book in the series, the one I got from Allen, on her lap.

Mum strokes the cover.

'Thank you,' she says.

'Why didn't you tell me what happened...?' I start and then I realise how accusing that sounds and how Mrs Zas would be giving me one of her *You're better than that, Feather* looks. 'I mean, please tell me what happened, Mum.'

'You know what happened.' Her voice is small. 'The whole world knows what happened.'

'The article?'

She doesn't move but I know that's what she's talking about.

'The article is a bunch of lies written by a stranger,' I say. 'I want to hear it from you, Mum.' I take her hand. 'I want to hear *your* story.'

Dad stirs in his chair. He rubs his eyes and stands up.

'Feather...' His voice is groggy. He looks from me to Mum. 'I'll leave you.' He heads towards the door.

'No...' Mum starts. 'Please stay, George.'

Dad comes over to Mum and kisses her cheek. 'I think you two need some time to talk.' And then he comes over to me and takes my face in his hands and kisses my forehead. 'I'm glad you came home, Feather.'

And with that, he leaves.

When Dad's gone, Mum closes her eyes. I can feel it in my bones, the sadness and tiredness she's been carrying around with her all these years.

'I don't know where to start,' Mum says, her eyes still closed.

I take her hand again. 'It was my birthday... it was Willingdon Day...'

She nods and then she pulls out a photograph from under her pillow and holds it out to me.

It's one of those 'no clouds in the sky' days. So bright it's hard to keep your eyes open. The Lido's the exact same blue as the sky, like they've bled into each other.

There are more people in Willingdon Park than I've ever seen in the village at any one time. It's like, at this moment, in this photo, our sleepy little village is the most alive place in the world.

In a corner of the Lido, there's a BBQ. I spot Dad with his blue-and-white chef's apron, his cheeks flushed. He's grinning and holding tongs in the air, making crab hands to entertain the children around him.

Bits of the photo are blurry, where kids are jumping and splashing into the Lido. There are toddlers with armbands and older kids with inflatable mattresses and beach balls.

An old lady is doing laps at the far end. A man, about her age, sits on the edge of the Lido with a newspaper on his lap. He's wearing a grey, short-sleeved shirt – and a dog collar. His eyes keep flitting from the newspaper to the woman in the pool, as though he's scared the old woman's going to disappear.

Two small boys, who must be about three, are chasing each other close to the edge. Both blond, the same height, the same build and skin tone. Like twins.

You can't see the sun, it's too high in the sky, but you know it's there because it's touching everything: throwing stars onto the surface of the Lido; lighting up the eyes of the mums and babies in the paddling pool; bouncing off every blade of grass, every flower.

The sun casts a halo around Mum's head: she looks like she's just flown down from the sky.

She's running, wearing a yellow T-shirt over her swimming costume with LIFESAVER printed in red letters across the front. Her body looks strong: her toned arms swing to the rhythm of her running, the muscles in her legs push up against her skin. And she's stretching out her hands, her mouth open.

I follow the trajectory of her gaze.

In a corner of the photo there's a little girl. Not much hair. Wobbly on her feet. Chubby thighs and knees. A pointy party hat sits off centre on her head and she's trailing a balloon behind her. As I look at the little girl, this is all I can think: she's too young to be on her own, too young to be running towards the park gate. That's why Mum's going after her.

I take a breath. Blink. And the photo expands.

All the figures stay frozen, except the two blond boys chasing each other around the Lido.

They're screaming and laughing. And one of them grabs the other's T-shirt, and the other one spins round and pulls away and the first one throws himself forward, his arms outstretched.

A moment later, one little boy pushes the other into the Lido.

No one hears the crack of the little boy's head on the paving stones.

No one sees the little boy's body fall limply into the water.

No one hears him sink through the water.

Not a single person notices.

Not the grown-ups sitting around the park in their picnic baskets.

Not the children splashing in the pool.

Not Dad, pink-cheeked and laughing behind the BBQ.

Not Steph, lying on her towel, sunbathing, chatting away to a woman her age just a few inches from where the boy fell.

And definitely not Mum, who's running and shouting now, her eyes fixed on me.

'So it was my fault,' I say.

Mum's eyes fly open. 'No!'

'If it hadn't been my birthday… if you hadn't been busy looking after me… if—'

'It would have happened anyway.'

'How do you know?'

'Because children don't just die.' She gulps. 'There's a reason Max left us, I have to believe that. And if it was anyone's fault, it was mine. It was my job to look after Max.'

'What about Dad? And Steph? They were there too.'

Mum holds out her hand to make me go quiet. 'It was *my* job, Feather. I was his mum.'

She looks down at the photo and I know she's staring at the two boys, at Max and Clay.

'Clay pushed Max in…' I say.

Mum nods slowly.

'Does he remember that?'

Mum nods again.

'And he blames himself?'

Mum doesn't answer, she just stares out of the window.

I think about what Clay said the first time we spoke, about how there's always a trigger for our behaviour, something which turns us into the people we are today.

If Clay's known all these years that he pushed Max into the pool, and that he died because of it, no wonder he went off the rails.

'Is that why Clay and Eleanor left the village?' I ask.

'I never blamed her,' Mum says. 'But after what happened, Eleanor couldn't look at me in the eye any more. We were such good friends, the boys had grown up together…' Mum's voice chokes up. 'She felt it wasn't fair, that she got to keep her son and that I didn't. That it was her son who'd pushed Max into the water. That she should have been supervising them.'

I take a breath. '*Do* you blame them? Clay and Eleanor?'

I wonder whether that's why Clay's mum went all religious. Maybe it was her way of making sense of it all.

'No. Like I said, I blame myself.'

I lean my head against Mum's shoulder.

'I'm sorry, Mum,' I say. 'For going on about swimming and water all this time. I didn't understand…'

'You didn't understand because I didn't tell you, Feather. There's nothing to be sorry about.'

'And you still came…? Yesterday, at the pool? You came to watch me swim, despite everything?'

·'I should have come earlier, Feather.'

I wait for a beat. 'Did you leave because it made you think about Max?'

'In part. I was tired from the journey, too. And I thought you were still upset with me, that you might not be happy to have me there.'

'So you came even though you knew I might not see you?'

She nods.

'Did you ever like swimming, Mum? I mean, before everything happened with Max?'

She stares out through the crack in the curtains and I'm worried I've said the wrong thing.

'Yes, I loved swimming.'

'So it's true? You ran the Baby Dippers Club? You taught people how to swim…?'

'Yes. And I did the lifesaving training. And I spent my summers telling parents and children to be careful, that water is a beautiful thing but that it can be dangerous too.' She stops and catches her breath. 'And then, when Max fell into the water, there wasn't a single thing I could do to save him.'

There are things in the history of human beings that just don't make sense, that just aren't fair. That's what Miss Pierce, my History teacher, says. Things that feel so wrong they make you want to jump up and down and scream at the sky. Mum must have felt like that.

'It shouldn't have happened, Mum.'

'No, it shouldn't.'

I swing my legs up onto the bed and press my head into her shoulder. I feel her arms folding around me.

'And it wasn't your fault.'

Mum doesn't say anything.

'I'm tired, Feather,' she says. 'So tired.'

'I know.'

I sit up and stroke her hair.

'I'll stay here until you're asleep, Mum.'

She closes her eyes and soon starts to nod off.

I watch the muscles in her face relaxing and listen to her breath going deeper and then I kiss her on the cheek, take the photograph from her hands and slip out of the room.

Dad's sitting at the kitchen table, holding a cup of tea. His hands are all crooked and calloused from his work. There's a scar on his thumb. *Your father's hands tell the story of his life*, Mum once said. I think about Mum's big hulk of a body and how it tells the story of how she's locked herself inside this secret for thirteen years. And I think of Clay's body, all the bones pushing through his skin. And then I think of my body, how small I am, how maybe I'm like that because I lost someone too and didn't want to grow up without him.

I go and grab a mug and use the water from the kettle to make myself a cup of tea too.

'You had a good talk with your mum?' Dad asks.

I nod and sit beside him.

'It's because of Max that Mum stopped leaving the house, isn't it? It's because of him that she started eating so much?'

'She tried so hard at first,' Dad says. 'So hard.'

'Tried hard to do what?'

'To get used to Max no longer being there. To avoid

having to face people from the village, who she felt judged her for what happened.'

'Judged her?' I ask.

'For not looking after her little boy.'

'But no one would have thought that. Everyone understands that you can't watch a kid every second. That horrible accidents happen all the time.'

'You're right, Feather. People didn't judge her. But she believed they did. Guilt isn't a rational thing. It deceives us into thinking all kind of things that aren't true.'

I cup my hands around my mug and let the warmth seep into my fingers.

'But *you* didn't blame her, Dad, did you? You understood.'

'Yes, I understood.'

And that's why he went along with Mum's eating. Because he knew that she blamed herself. And he knew that it was his fault too. And that eating and staying inside was the only way Mum found to cope.

'Is Max the reason Mum hates hospitals?'

Dad nods.

'So he didn't die right away?'

Dad's quiet for a moment and then says, 'He died at the pool. It only took a few seconds. But they took him to the hospital to do tests. Your mother and I spent the night there.'

'Was I with you?'

Dad nods. 'Mum wouldn't let you out of her sight.'

I think back to something Dad said a few moments ago.

'When did Mum stop trying?'

He looks at me and furrows his brow.

'You said that she tried, at first, to get used to things after Max left?'

'We had a meeting with Rev Cootes.'

My mind spins back to a few weeks ago, to Mum standing on Rev Cootes's doorstep, yelling and flapping her hands.

'What kind of meeting?'

'We were planning Max's funeral. Me and Mum – and you, you were there too. You'd just turned one.' Dad looks down into his tea. 'And Steph. Steph was there for moral support.'

'What happened?'

'Mum snapped. Until then she'd been numb, in shock, I suppose. But that day, she got angry. Really angry. She stood up and started yelling—'

'What did she say?'

'She said she didn't want to say goodbye to Max. That she didn't want to put her little boy in the cold ground. And that she didn't want to sit in a church full of strangers blaming her for Max's death.'

I see Mum standing in Rev Cootes's kitchen, me in her arms, her cheeks flushed like they always are when she's angry. And then I see the line of kids' graves in St Mary's Cemetery. And my mind focuses on the one without a name or a photo. It was right in front of me this whole time.

'What happened then?'

'Steph tried to calm Mum down but Mum pushed her away, stormed across The Green, walked into the cottage, to the lounge, drew the curtains and sat down on the sofa. She never left the house again.'

I pull out the photo from the day Max died and place it on the table in front of Dad.

'Mum gave it to me,' I say. 'She wanted me to understand what happened.'

He picks up the photo and stares at it. His hands are shaking.

'Who took the picture?' I ask.

'Allen,' Dad said. 'He was a junior reporter. He gave us a copy as a keepsake.'

'He was already snooping around, all those years ago?'

'He wasn't snooping around, not then. He thought that local news mattered.'

I wonder what it was that changed him, that made him turn on the people he wrote about.

Dad's shoulders start shaking. And then he starts sobbing, big, loud, heaving sobs.

'Dad…?'

He shakes his head. 'I should have taken better care of him… I should have seen it happen.'

His eyes are bloodshot, his face blotchy. He's not even trying to keep the tears in any more.

For a moment, I listen to the quiet cottage and think about how different things would have been if Max was still living with us today. How maybe we'd be sharing a room. How maybe he'd play his music really loud upstairs, like Jake does. How we'd probably squabble over the bathroom in the mornings. How he'd find me annoying because I was his little sister. How we'd fight over loads of stupid things, because that's what brothers and sisters do. But I'd love him, really, and I'd be happy to have a big brother. And Mum would be out saving the world and Dad's business would be going really well and maybe Max would love swimming as much as I do. Maybe we'd go to the pool and swim together.

'It's not your fault, Dad. It's no one's fault.'

He keeps sobbing, his palms pressed into his hands.

'Dad, it's okay…' I rub his back. 'It's going to be okay…'

And I don't know whether what I'm saying is true, whether things are going to be okay, but I know this: I'm going to do everything I can to help Mum and Dad get through this. I'm going to do everything I can to make us a family again.

36

Later that night, when I'm about to go to bed, the doorbell rings. Mum's already asleep, exhausted from the day, and Dad's out on a plumbing job.

I know it's him, like I've known it was him every single time he's stood outside my front door for the last thirteen years of our lives.

'Hi,' Jake says, as I open the door. He gives me a crooked smile.

And without saying anything back, I step forward and put my arms around him and hold him tight.

The Lido is just a big muddy hole surrounded by piles of rubble, so we can't climb in and sit on the tiles, like we usually do. Instead, we go and lie under a tree and look up at the sky. It's a clear, warm night. Thousands of stars and a thin, fingernail moon.

'Did you know?' I ask him. 'About Max?'

He doesn't say anything for a while.

'Jake?'

'Yes... but I've only known for a few weeks.'

Every muscle in my body relaxes. So he hasn't been lying to me all this time.

'Steph told you?' I ask.

'No. It was Clay. Mum didn't think it was fair for me to know before you did. She knew that it would mean me having to lie to you and she didn't want that.'

For a second I feel sorry for Steph, how's she's been caught up in the middle of all this, how she's tried to be a good friend to Mum and to me.

I look over to Jake, lying there beside me, staring at the sky.

'Clay told you what happened on the day Max drowned?'

He nods. 'He thinks his mum blames him. She's never said that out loud but it's his theory for why she's so angry at him.'

I prop my head up on one elbow.

'Do you love him?'

For a second, Jake doesn't move. And then, very slowly, he nods again.

I lie back down, snuggle in closer to him and take his hand.

I realise that I've been so caught up in my own things that I haven't been there for Jake through all of this. I want him to know that nothing's changed, that I'm still his best friend. And that I want to understand.

'You wrote him a Valentine's card?'

It's too dark to see but I can tell from Jake's silence that he's blushing.

'I saw it,' I say. 'In his room.'

'Yeah... that was me.'

'Is that when it all started – between you two?'

'It had been building up for a while, but I guess it made

things concrete. Giving him the card was as much about me admitting my feelings to myself as it was about telling him how I felt.'

'What about Amy?' I ask. 'And the other girls?'

'I liked Amy – a lot. It wasn't love, not even close, but I fancied her. I fancied all of them. And it felt like what was expected of me.'

'What was expected?'

'Kids our age go out with people...'

'I don't.'

'You're special, Feather,' he says, squeezing my hand.

'Hey!'

'In a good way. You don't go along with the crowd, not like the rest of us.'

'Why didn't you end it with her sooner? Once you'd worked out your feelings for Clay?'

'I was scared.'

'Of what?'

'Of how people would react if they found out. And I was scared of my feelings for him, whether I could trust him.' He pauses. 'I was scared about losing you.'

'Me?'

He nods.

'You're my best friend, Jake.' I look right at him. 'You're the brother I was meant to have. And I'll love you no matter what.'

He blinks and I can tell he's trying hard not to cry.

'And at least your taste's improved!' I burst out. 'When you hooked up with Amy, I was starting to get really worried...'

He laughs and looks up and sniffs back the tears.

'So, you're...' I take a breath. 'You're gay – or bi?'

'I don't know.'

'But you feel differently about Clay, right? From how you've felt about anyone else you've been out with?'

'Yeah. But that's because I've never been in love before.'

Jake sits up and leans against the trunk of the tree. I sit cross-legged in front of him.

'I don't really understand what this situation is, where these feelings have come from,' he goes on, 'but there's one thing I've worked out: I love Clay. I love *him*, the core of him. I feel like I've known him my whole life. Like he's part of me. And that has nothing to do with being a guy or a girl or me being gay or straight.'

I nod slowly. 'I get that.' I look over to the bit of the Lido where Clay and I sat that first night. 'What about Clay, has he always fancied guys?'

Jake nods. 'He thinks so. He's been working it out for longer than I have.'

'So he's never fancied girls?'

Jake smiles. 'Afraid not.'

It's actually a relief, to know that I wasn't even in with a chance, that he didn't reject me because there was something wrong with me.

'Does his mum know?' I ask.

'Yeah. Which is another reason they don't get on.'

'Because she's religious?'

He nods.

'He's lucky he's got you,' I say. And, despite having felt left out and jealous about Jake and Clay, I mean it. I guess because I realise that we're not in competition, that Jake's got enough love for the both of us.

Jake's eyes look like pools of water in the night.

'I'm sorry I've been such a rubbish friend these past

months,' Jake says. He blinks and a tear drops down his cheek. 'It's just that Clay's so weak. He's been having heart palpitations at night. He struggles to catch his breath at times. But he doesn't want any help.'

I've thought that about Mum a million times: that she doesn't want my help, that she won't let me make her better. And there's nothing worse in the world than not being able to help the person you love.

I lean forward and take both of Jake's hands in mine.

'You love him,' I say. 'You'll find a way.'

1 June

Willingdon Day

37

I stare up at the wall next to my bed. Dad painted it a sky-blue so that, when I wake up in the morning and go to sleep at night, I can pretend I'm floating in the sky or in the water. He explained how this was Max's room and how he and Mum painted the fish and the boats and the waves onto the walls.

'Where did I sleep?' I asked Mum in one of the splinters of conversation we've had about how things were before Max died.

'With us, in a Moses basket. Then, when you were six months old, we moved you in with Max.'

So I was right, we would have shared a bedroom.

'He must have hated that,' I said. 'Having his little sister invading his space.'

Mum shook her head. 'He loved it. He loved you.'

I asked her too, whether I really made her sad when I was born, and she shook her head and smiled and cried and said, 'You were my angel, my perfect little girl. Nothing about you has ever made me sad.'

I understand then that it was her way of avoiding having to tell me the harder truth, that what really broke her heart, what made her push the world away, was losing her little boy.

Dad said they wallpapered over the seaside scene when I was five. So I guess it took them four years to get their heads round the fact that Max wasn't coming back.

Happy Birthday, Max, I whisper.

Because that's another thing I have to get my head round – we were born two years apart on the exact same day: Willingdon Day.

I close my eyes and imagine him saying it back to me.

Happy Birthday, little sister.

I blink and shift my head and look at what used to be my investigation wall. I'm going to put new photos up – there are two up there already: the one of me and Max we found on the garage floor and another one of Max standing in our front garden in a red jumper, leaning into my pram. Mum's standing behind him, pointing at me and smiling. Max is grinning too and you can see my little hand poking up, reaching for his face. Dad took it.

Soon after the newspaper article came out, Dad gave me the box of photos I found in the garage in January. I'm going to put them up on the wall, one by one, and then I'm going to put other photos up too, from how things are now, starting with pictures of Willingdon Day. Dad's got his old camera out again and he's going to take photos today.

The past is part of our present, wasn't that what Miss Pierce taught us? And she's right, but I also know that we have to allow the past to make our present better, that we can't be locked in by it, like Mum was.

My legs feel heavy and tired. I haven't slept much, probably because I'm too excited about today and because the diggers woke me up early as they left the village. They've been working right up to the last minute to get the Lido ready.

I stuff my towel, my swimming costume and my goggles into my bag. I want to do a few laps before the competition later this afternoon. I want to do a few laps before the competition later this afternoon. I need to float around for a bit and clear my head. Steph's been coaching me again; she's going to join me at the pool.

Dad said he would drive me, so I knock on his bedroom door, but he doesn't answer. When I walk into the room, it's empty.

When I get to the kitchen, I hear a 'shushing' behind the closed door and footsteps, and something clatters to the floor, and then there's another, 'Shush!'

'Dad?' I open the kitchen door.

'Happy Birthday!' Mum and Dad blurt out at the same time.

They're standing in the middle of the kitchen with party hats on. Dad blows through a paper party horn. There are balloons everywhere. And Mum's holding a cake with fifteen candles.

'You made a cake?' I ask.

Mum and Dad nod and grin.

'We made it together,' Dad says.

'From your recipe book,' Mum chips in.

'It's got bananas and avocado in it...' Dad says proudly.

'Blow the candles and make a wish,' Mum says, 'quick, before the wax drips.'

I close my eyes and my mind reels off a list of wishes. And then I think about how I don't need to wish for anything right now, I just need to open my eyes wide and take everything in – that wishing will just make me focus on what's not here yet, and I don't want to do that any more. So I take a breath, fill my cheeks and blow as hard as I can, and I don't make a single wish. Instead, I let myself feel the moment: the glow of candles against my face, the smoke, the smell of chocolate and banana, the sound of Mum and Dad breathing and then clapping when all the candles are out.

'I'll have the cake when I get back from practice,' I say. 'Can you still take me to the pool, Dad?'

I know you're not meant to train too hard just before a race but I need to feel the water on my skin, to tune in.

Mum and Dad exchange a glance. I've tried really hard not to talk about swimming in front of Mum. I get it now, how hard it must be for her, listening to me going on and on about how much I love swimming when all it does is remind her of how Max died.

Dad nods. 'Of course.'

But at just that moment, the doorbell goes.

'Who's that?' I ask.

'Go and see, my love,' Mum says.

I open the door and find Steph and Jake standing at the top of the ramp. They wave balloons and chant, 'Happy Birthday, Feather', and I stretch out my arms and we have a massive group hug.

'We thought we should take you for your last practice,' Steph says. 'Like old times.'

'Thanks, Steph,' I say.

Then I give Jake a massive hug of his own.

As I step out of the house I look across The Green. The whole village got together last night to decorate The Green and the park and the new Lido – balloons and streamers and banners in fire-engine red, Max's favourite colour.

As I get into the car, I notice Jake looking over to the rectory.

'He's coming today, right?' I ask him.

Jake shrugs. 'Maybe.'

Whenever I ask about whether I can come with him to see Clay, Jake says that Clay's not feeling well or that he's too tired to talk. Clay's got worse over the last few weeks. He's basically stopped eating.

As I sit next to Jake in the back seat of Steph's people carrier, I whisper, 'He'll come, you'll see.'

If necessary, I'll march right over to the vicarage and drag Clay out.

By two o'clock, the whole of Willingdon and Newton and, from the looks of it, the rest of the county, are gathered around the Lido. Everyone except Mum. I didn't even ask Mum to come and watch me this time; I know that she doesn't have to be in the middle of the crowd for it to feel like she's with me.

I stand in my swimming costume at one end of the stage they've put up at the far end of the pool, alongside the other competitors. I thought that maybe they'd change the Lido, make it look modern and fancy, but it's exactly the same as in the picture Mum showed me. I feel like I've travelled back in time: whenever I look around the park, I expect to see Max and Clay chasing each other around, too close to the edge.

'Hey.' I hear Jake's voice behind me. 'Just came to wish you luck.' He jumps onto the back of the stage and gives me a hug. 'You're a hero, Feather Tucker, never forget that.'

I watch him run across the park and that's when I see Clay sitting on a bench a little way off from the Lido, a shadow, his head bowed. He's not even paying attention to anything going on around him and he doesn't lift his head when Jake sits down next to him. But at least he came.

The Mayor of Newton taps the microphone. He's standing on a platform they've put up specially for the ceremony, resplendent in his fancy robes and chains, in front of a big blue ribbon that stretches across the pool. In a few moments, the new Lido will be open.

'Good afternoon…' he starts.

A murmur spreads through the crowd. People turn their heads and look around them.

'This is a very special day for our community…' he goes on.

I expect the crowd to shush when the mayor keeps talking but the whispering gets louder. Then someone gasps and people start moving to one side, until a long path opens up from the park gate all the way to the Lido.

I crane my neck to see what's going on.

Someone starts clapping – I turn to see Rev Cootes holding his arms in the air, smacking his hands together. Houdini does pirouettes behind him and Mrs Zas, who's standing next to Rev Cootes, joins in the clapping too. And then the clapping spreads, rippling through the crowd.

People are pressing into each other now and shouting things and elbowing each other to move out of the way.

It's her hair I see first – the sun bounces off it like it did in that photo from fourteen years ago. And then I recognise her walk, wobbly as a toddler. With each step, she presses her palms into her canes. Her eyes are fixed ahead in concentration.

The clapping gets louder, like a wave of thunder rumbling through the park.

By the time Mum gets to the stage, the front of her dress is drenched and her forehead is covered in beads of sweat and her face is so red it looks sunburnt.

She scans the swimmers and then spots me. Our eyes lock and then her face breaks into a smile and she holds up her thumbs.

'You can do it, Feather,' she mouths.

A balloon of light explodes in my chest and every bit of me feels alive.

The mayor, who's been the Mayor of Newton for so long that he was probably there for the opening of the first Lido, gathers up his robes, climbs down the stage steps, goes over to Mum and gives her a kiss on each cheek.

The crowd is still and silent.

The microphone catches his voice.

'It's good to see you back, Josephine,' he says, loud enough for everyone to hear.

He proffers her his oversized ribbon-cutting scissors. And that makes me panic. It's one thing Mum coming to see me swim – opening the Lido where her little boy drowned, that's something else altogether.

But Mum keeps smiling and she puts down her canes and takes the scissors. Then she lifts one of her massive legs onto the stage steps. The mayor offers her a hand but she bats him away and gets up on her own. It should have been embarrassing, watching this big, sweaty woman clambering onto a stage, but no one laughs or smirks, because Mum doesn't look embarrassing: she looks strong and determined and brave. The crowd watches her really quietly, but once she's up there, standing straight in front of the microphone, they clap again, even louder than before.

I run across to Mum and throw my arms around her.

She kisses my cheek and whispers, 'Fly, my little Feather, fly...'

'I love you, Mum,' I say and then go back to the other swimmers.

The Willingdon Marching Band starts up. I notice Mr Ding crashing his cymbals, his eyes fixed on Mum like he's doing it for her.

And Mum takes a deep breath and opens the oversized scissors and slices through the big blue ribbon.

'I declare the Lido officially re-open!' she says, her voice low and rumbling and beautiful.

There's more clapping and Mum climbs down off the stage and goes to sit on one the spectator benches they've put up around the Lido, then the Willingdon Band starts playing one of those jolly, bouncy tunes.

When it's my turn to race, I feel as light as a soap bubble. For once, there's no strain. I just swim. I feel like I did this morning when I blew the candles out on the cake. I don't want to think about what's coming next, about winning, I want to enjoy it. I want to feel the sun and the water, to hear the crowd shouting, to know that the loudest shout of all comes from Mum, standing at the end of the pool, waiting for me to finish:

'Feather! Feather! Feather!' I hear every time my head shoots out of the water.

And, like at the regionals, I do feel I'm flying, flying free this time, flying through water.

I don't come first, or I don't come first on the clock or the competition charts, but as I climb out of the pool, and give Mum a big, soggy hug and feel her chest heaving as she laughs about getting drenched, I know that I've got the only prize I ever wanted: Mum right here with me.

After the races we go and have a massive picnic on The Green. Along with his Chinese food, Mr Ding's selling ice creams out of his van and Dad's manning the BBQ with some help from Rev Cootes, and Mum's pouring drinks.

I grab a tray of noodles and spring rolls and go to sit with Clay and Jake. Jake bites into a burger. Clay pulls at bits of grass. He goes moody whenever we mention food, just like Mum used to when I'd talk about swimming, so we don't even ask him to join us any more. I wonder when he actually last swallowed a proper mouthful of food; I wonder how long his body can keep going on air.

Clay stands up and brushes the bits of grass off his jeans. 'I'm going back to the house for a bit.'

Jake scrunches up his burger in its wrapper and hands it to me.

'I'll come with you,' he says.

I know he has to be there for Clay, but I still feel a pinch.

Clay shakes his head. 'It's okay, I'm just going to sleep.'

These days, Clay spends more time sleeping than awake.

'You'll come out for the waltz though?' I ask him.

He looks at me blankly.

'It's important,' I say. 'For the village. For your grandpa.'

Mrs Zas has decided that this year it's not going to be a competition. She wants everyone in the village to enjoy the dance floor, for it to be a celebration. Mrs Zas has made dresses for all the women in the village, including one for me. Mum probably put me in dresses when I was a baby but this is the first dress I actually remember wearing. It's pale blue, like the sky.

I look over at the boards that make up the dance floor

– they're all set up in the middle of The Green, surrounded by coloured lanterns and loudspeakers.

I can't wait for tonight.

'It'll be fun,' I say to Clay.

Clay shrugs and starts walking back to the rectory. And then, halfway across The Green, he stops dead.

A cab pulls up outside St Mary's. And cabs never come through Willingdon.

I crane my neck to see who it could be.

Clay's body has seized up.

It's the heels I see first: navy, shiny and really high. And then a pair of long legs with those shimmery, flesh-coloured tights. And then the navy suit. And then the blonde hair, tamed into a straight bob.

She looks like a celebrity. Tall and sparkly and nothing like anyone in Willingdon.

The driver takes the woman's small wheelie suitcase out of the boot, shakes her hand and then leaves again.

'Come on.' I grab Jake's hand and yank him towards Clay.

The woman scans The Green and then her eyes settle on Clay.

Out of the corner of my eye, I notice Rev Cootes striding across from the BBQ. When he gets close to Clay, Clay points at him and yells:

'*You called her?*'

And that's when it clicks: it's Clay's mum.

Mum and Dad look across at her from the BBQ.

Steph holds her hand to her throat.

'*You went behind my back?*' Clay yells louder.

Rev Cootes looks from Clay to Eleanor. His eyes are wide and he keeps shaking his head.

Mrs Zas tries to grab his arm but he pulls away from her and walks to Clay.

Jake and I get to Clay at the same time as he does.

'I don't understand,' Rev Cootes says.

Clay gives him a cold laugh. 'Come on, Grandpa...'

Clay's mum strides towards us.

She doesn't hug Clay or kiss him or touch his arm, she just stares at him in shock.

'I warned you,' Jake tells her.

Clay spins round and looks at Jake.

'He needs help,' Jake adds.

'*You* told her?' Clay says.

Jake holds his head high and levels his gaze to Clay.

'I wrote to her.'

For the first time in ages, I feel sorry for Clay. Really sorry. I guess he feels a bit like I felt when I saw Clay and Jake sitting on the bench by the Lido – like my best friend in the whole world had just betrayed me.

'You have to get better,' Jake says. 'And you're not getting better here. There's a special clinic in New York... they can help you...'

'Stop it.' Clay says, holding out his hands in front of him like a barrier. 'Just stop talking.'

Jake's shoulders drop.

Eleanor steps forward. 'Jake did the right thing—'

'You don't get to say *anything*!' Clay shouts her down.

'I understand.' Her voice goes quiet. 'I know you love him. And I know you want to stay here – with Grandpa, with Jake and Feather...'

It feels strange, hearing someone I've never met say my name like they know me. I wonder whether Jake wrote about me in his letter to her.

Clay's cheeks flush pink. He walks up to his mum, stands really close to her face and says, 'You don't get to decide what happens to me. Ever.'

And then he turns round and moves quickly towards to the vicarage. We watch him walk across The Green, more air than flesh and bone, until he disappears in the bright afternoon sun.

I lie on my back, my blue dress floating around me, and look up at the night sky. The stars are clear tonight. The moon nearly full.

I prop myself up and look across at the dance floor. Mum and Dad sway from side to side. Mum's out of rhythm with the music but she's trying: taking small steps, concentrating, willing her body to dance despite the fact that her legs are swollen and that her feet must be killing her.

I look at the others too.

Hemmed in by the loop of coloured lanterns, Rev Cootes dances with Mrs Zas and Steph dances with Mitch and there are a whole load of other people from Willingdon and Newton, too. I wonder whether this was what The Willingdon Waltz was like before Max died.

None of the dancers are talking, they're just lost in the music and their steps and the sway of their bodies. It's nearly midnight. It'll be the last dance soon.

Jake comes over and hands me a glass of champagne he swiped off the adults' table.

I think about Clay being really ill and his mum having just showed up and what that will mean for him and Jake, and how Jake must be really stressed out about it all. And still, he finds the time to make me feel good about today.

'You're awesome, Jake,' I say.

He takes a sip of champagne and looks over to the vicarage.

'I don't think Clay would agree.' He shakes his head. 'He'll never forgive me.'

'It'll take time,' I say, 'but he will. When he's better.'

Clay hasn't left the house since his mum showed up. His mum ran after them into the vicarage and she hasn't come out either.

'Fancy another dance?' I ask Jake.

He shakes his head. 'Not right now.'

We had fun dancing but I know that it just reminded him of the fact that he should have been up there with Clay.

I hand him my glass, get up and brush down the creases in my dress.

'I've got an idea. Stay here, just for a minute.'

Before Jake has the chance to say anything, I hitch up my dress and run over to St Mary's, up the path, through the cemetery to the rectory and round to Clay's room.

I get onto my tiptoes and look in through the window.

Clay's bedside lamp is on. Eleanor is walking around the room, folding clothes into a suitcase. Clay is sitting on the bed. They're talking, which I guess is a good sign. I wonder whether they've talked about the day Max died. How it was Clay who pushed him in. How Eleanor was too busy sunbathing next to Steph to see it happen. How, a few weeks ago, I didn't even know I had a brother.

After a while, Eleanor goes out through his bedroom door into the hall.

I take an intake of breath and knock on the window.

'Clay!' I hiss. 'It's Feather. Open up.'

He comes to the window and looks at me. His face makes me think of the moon: pale and glowing and unknown.

'Please come out,' I hiss through the window. 'Just for one dance.'

Clay opens the window.

We look at each other for a second. And then I just say it, because it's true and it matters and it's the last night they've got together:

'Jake needs you.'

He looks past me across The Green and then he closes the window and draws the curtains.

'Please!' I yell.

He doesn't answer.

I know he's angry at Jake but soon it'll be too late, he'll be gone and then he'll regret wasting these last few hours when he could have been with him.

Dejectedly, I walk back towards The Green and then I hear bleating behind me. And then a voice.

'I like the dress…'

I spin round to see Clay walking towards me with Houdini. He's wearing jeans that hang off his hips and a collared shirt that swallows up his body, but my stomach still does a somersault.

'Thought Cinderella could do with a dance partner,' Clay says, handing me Houdini's lead.

'Hey!' I punch him on the arm. But I'm glad. It's the first time I've heard him crack a joke in ages.

'You saying Houdini isn't your type?' He laughs. 'Poor Houdini.' He pats him on the side.

You're my type, I want to say, but I bite my lip. I wonder if I'll ever stop fancying him.

I want to ask him whether things are okay with his

mum but I'm worried he'll get angry and change his mind about coming out, so I just keep walking alongside him and Houdini.

Mum and Steph are sitting under the chestnut tree. They've kicked off their shoes and they're leaning into each other and looking up into fairy lights twisted around the branches. Things are back to how they should be, only better. This time, Mum and Steph aren't cooped up in the lounge, watching TV and eating crisps – they're out here, on this clear, warm night, laughing and looking up at the stars.

When we get to the dance floor, Jake doesn't notice us, he's too busy tearing around with Mrs Zas, a crazy jive number.

I run over to the DJ and ask him to put on something slow and soppy. And then I push Clay onto the dance floor.

He weaves between the dancers and then taps Jake on the shoulder. Jake turns round and, when he sees Clay, his face lights up.

Clay bows and holds out his hand, like in those old-fashioned films.

Jake smiles, grabs Clay's hand and sweeps him into his arms.

The music switches to a slow song. It's the one Mum and Dad did their wedding dance to: 'Endless Love' by Lionel Richie and Diana Ross. Their voices come over the speakers: *… our lives have just begun…*

All the dancers freeze for a moment as they readjust to the change in tempo. They look around and, one by one, they see Jake and Clay, standing in the middle of the dance floor, their arms folded around each other, so close they could be one person.

*

At five in the morning, Jake and I sit on the pavement outside St Mary's Cemetery. The sun pushes up behind the steeple and makes the whole village glow orange.

We haven't been to sleep. When everyone went home, we sat by the Lido with Clay and talked and laughed and looked up at the stars.

Then he got a call from his mum. They had to get ready for their flight home. He said that he and his mum had a talk. That they're going to try to get on.

I tuck my arm under Jake's and lean my head on his shoulder. The Green is covered in streamers and balloons and plastic champagne flutes. The black dance floor glistens with dew.

Jake sits up and looks at me. 'Feather?'

I blink. 'Yeah?'

'You know what you asked me last year on your birthday?'

I'm so tired it's like the cogs in my brain have stopped moving.

'Last year?'

He places his hand under my chin and lifts it up.

'You're beautiful.'

I laugh and shake my head. 'Hasn't the champagne worn off yet?'

He places a finger on my lips. 'Shush,' he says.

And then he leans in and kisses me, his lips light and gentle and warm. And I know that he doesn't fancy me and I don't fancy him and that we're best friends and brother and sister and everything else that isn't boyfriend and girlfriend, but it feels okay. Better than okay. It makes me feel alive. It makes me feel like there's hope, like maybe, one day, someone will find me beautiful. And someone will kiss me for real.

'Happy birthday, Feather Tucker,' Jake says, our foreheads resting against each other.

Jake leans back against the gate and looks up at the sky. He's been really quiet since Clay went in to pack.

'We can save up,' I say. 'You can go out and visit him – maybe at Christmas…'

Jake shakes his head. 'It's over.'

'Don't say that.'

'It's okay, Feather.' He looks at me and smiles but it's one of those strained smiles people put on when they're in pain but trying to make out they're okay.

'You don't have to say it's okay just to make me feel better, Jake. I understand what you two have.'

Jake points over to Bewitched and says, 'Remember that tune Mrs Zas is always humming?'

I nod and start singing, 'Turn, turn, turn…' My voice bounces on the cold morning air.

Jake joins in, '… there's a time to everything under heaven…'

Jake looks up at the orange clouds and blinks.

'This was our time,' he says. 'Clay's and mine. And now it's time to let go.'

'But you said you love him.'

'Of course I love him.'

'Well, if you love someone, aren't you meant to follow them to the ends of the earth?'

Jake pulls at a tuft of grass growing through a crack in the pavement.

'When did you get so romantic?'

I guess I've always been romantic, I just don't say it out loud that often.

'It's true though, isn't it?'

Jake looks up at the sky. 'He made me find out who I am, who I *really* am. I'll carry that with me for the rest of my life. He has to get better – that means going home.' He leans in and kisses the top of my head. 'And I've got you, Feather Tucker, don't I?'

I hold his hand and uncurl his fingers. Then I take the half-wishbone from my pocket, the one that I snapped with Clay on the day he came to lunch with Mum and Dad, and place it in Jake's palm.

'What's this?' he asks

'Clay's got the other half,' I say. 'I want you to have this, so that you never stop hoping.'

'Hoping for what?'

'That you'll find the other half.'

'I told you that it's over, Feather…'

'Maybe it is, maybe it isn't. But that's not the point. The point is that it will remind you that there's someone out there who's going to love you. And maybe that will be Clay, some time in the future, or maybe it will be someone else altogether but, whatever happens, that love will be real, and it will last forever.'

'Wow, that's quite a big responsibility to place on a chicken bone.'

I punch his arm. 'Just keep it.'

'Of course.' He smiles and puts it in his jacket pocket. 'Thank you, Feather.'

A taxi pulls into The Green, stops a few feet away from us and beeps its horn.

Behind us, the front door of the rectory clicks open.

Clay stumbles out, wheeling the suitcase I saw on Rev Cootes's doorstep in January. That day feels like a million years ago.

Clay's mum and Rev Cootes follow. As does Houdini, who walks along the path to where I'm sitting and rests his head in my lap.

'Hey, buddy,' I say, rubbing his ears.

I miss him not being at home as much but I guess it makes him happy, scooting between our cottage and the vicarage. At least it seems to have stopped him wanting to run away every two seconds.

When Clay's mum is settled in the taxi, Rev Cootes and I step back to give Jake and Clay a moment.

The sun is higher now. The sky a lighter blue. A bird starts singing from the chestnut tree in the middle of The Green.

Jake takes a jumper out of the bag he's been carrying and holds it up to Clay. It must have taken Steph ages. I wonder whether she knew all along, about Jake liking Clay.

Rev Cootes sucks in his breath and says, 'It's beautiful.'

A hummingbird hovering in the air, its wings beating so hard it looks as though it's about to take off into the dark, Willingdon sky.

Jake lifts the jumper over Clay's thin body. And then Clay takes Jake's face in his hands, strokes his cheek and kisses him.

Then, the two of us, Jake and I, stand in the middle of The Green and watch the taxi turn out of the village.

'I'd better get home to Mum,' I say.

Jake nods.

We both look over at the cottage. Mum's curtains are fully open. No blue flashes bouncing against the wall.

We hug one last time and then I walk home.

*

For the first time since I can remember, I go through the front door without a knot in my stomach. I stand outside Mum's room and listen. I recognise her breathing, though it sounds lighter than usual. And there's someone else's breathing too.

As I walk into the room, I'm amazed at how light and warm it is with the early morning sun spilling in through the open curtains. I was right, the TV's off and the controllers are stacked up on the coffee table next to Mum's armchair. And on the bed, Mum and Dad are sleeping, curled up into each other, Dad's hand slipped into Mum's. Shadows from the tree outside the lounge dance over their sleeping faces. They're still dressed in their party outfits, Mum in the emerald-green dress Mrs Zas made for her, the same colour as the one she wore for the ballroom-dancing competition she won all those years ago, and Dad in his tux, his bow tie loose around his neck. Mum's long hair is spread over her pillow. And, wherever they are behind their closed eyelids, I know they're happy.

I go over to Mum, tuck a strand of hair behind her ear and whisper, 'You're going to be okay, aren't you, Mum.'

Her eyes flicker open. She looks up at me and I know she's trying to work out whether this is still part of her dream or whether I'm actually there.

I lean over and kiss her cheek. 'Go back to sleep, Mum.'

She smiles and closes her eyes.

Yes, she's going to be okay.

I tiptoe out of the lounge, head for the stairs and start walking up to my room; my arms and legs ache from swimming and dancing so much yesterday and my eyes are heavy from being open all night. Then I stop walking. I'm tired – really tired – but I'm not ready to sleep, not yet.

I head back downstairs and into the lounge and take Mum's hand out of Dad's.

'Mum,' I whisper.

She shifts her head but doesn't open her eyes.

'Mum…' I say again.

She opens her eyes.

'Come with me,' I say.

It takes me a while to get her fully awake and to help her off the bed and into her shoes.

'Where are we going?' Her voice is thick with sleep.

'You'll see.'

I go to the hall to get her canes but she calls after me:

'I'm fine without them, love.'

I nod and come back to her, slot my arm under hers and walk her to the front door.

We walk across The Green. Fairy lights blink from the trees and glitter sparkles on the dance floor. Streamers and paper cups and plates lie scattered on the grass.

The bird keeps singing from the middle of The Green, light and clear.

We walk past the cemetery and towards the park. We don't talk. We don't need to.

When we get to the Lido, I take off Mum's sandals and then take off my own shoes and help Mum to sit down on the edge of the pool. The lane dividers lie curled up in a jumble of knots on the grass; the competition organisers took them out after the races so that people could just have fun swimming in the Lido. The bunting's still up over the stage they had for the mayor. And there's a single red balloon caught in the branches of the chestnut tree.

Mum and I sit on the edge of the pool, our legs dangling

in the cool water, watching the sun rising, lighting up the world from below.

'Max loved it here,' Mum says.

She's got her eyes closed, her face tilted to the morning sun. She looks as peaceful as she did sleeping next to Dad.

'*I* loved it here,' she says.

I look at the blue sky bouncing off the water and take her hand.

'Happy New Year, Mum,' I say.

Because it is. It's a new year of my life. And a new start, for all of us.

Mum lifts her legs out of the water and lets them fall in again. The water splashes up over us.

'Hey!' I laugh.

Mum splashes her legs again, harder this time.

'Mum!'

And then I start kicking my legs too and then we're both kicking, the water splashing up around us, splitting in the sun. We kick and laugh and sway until we're drenched, until we've laughed so hard that our cheeks hurt, until we know that the new year has started, and that everything's going to be better than okay.

September

This morning, Willingdon is covered in leaves, as though a friendly giant has sighed his warm breath through the trees.

I look out through the window of the lounge.

Rev Cootes kneels on the ground. He's been clearing the graves since dawn. Houdini stands next to him, nudging him every now and then and stamping through the pile of leaves so that Rev Cootes has to pick them up again. But Rev Cootes doesn't mind. He smiles and pulls gently at Houdini's collar. *Mischief* he calls him. *My Little Mischief*. Houdini is spending more and more time with Rev Cootes, which maybe makes up a bit for Clay not being around any more. And Mrs Zas, of course. She goes over to have tea with him at least once a day.

I brush Mum's hair, slow strokes from the crown of her head to the tips, which fall between her shoulder blades. We washed and dried it early this morning.

I put down the brush and kiss her cheek.

'You're beautiful,' I say.

And it's true, she is beautiful. Not skinny or fashionable or glossy-looking but properly, glow-from-the-inside beautiful. Mum still struggles to find clothes to fit her properly and she still has to take injections every day for her diabetes, but she's healthier and happy and, most important of all, she's stepping back out into the world.

And just at that moment, I realise that I was right when I said that no one was as lucky as me. Not in that random way people think of as lucky like winning a Lottery ticket or finding a four-leaf clover. Luck's not about good things happening to me or bad things happening to me. I'm lucky because, no matter what happens in my life, I've got a big family of people who love me and who I can love back. Not jut Mum and Dad but Jake and Steph, too, and Rev Cootes and Houdini and Mrs Zas and Mr Ding and the Slim Skills Gang and Clay, even if he's hundreds of miles away. And all the other people I have yet to meet and love – a whole lot of luck is out there waiting for me.

I sweep a red silk scarf, which Mrs Zas lent her for today, around Mum's neck and shoulders.

Everyone is going to wear something red, for Max.

Red like a fire engine.

Red like a heart.

Red like Max's superhero outfit on the front of *Max's Marvellous Adventures*.

I'm wearing the red Houdini jumper Steph made me for my last birthday. Dad's wearing a red tie. Even Rev Cootes said he'd wear something red.

When Mum's ready, I leave her for a bit and walk across The Green to the cemetery and into Rev Cootes's new greenhouse. Mrs Zas bought it for him so that he has somewhere to keep his more delicate plants. *This year, Peter is going to keep his plants alive through the winter*, she told me. *And it'll keep them out of Houdini's reach, too.*

Mrs Zas is due to hear from the immigration office any

day now. But she has faith that, no matter what the decision, she'll find a way to stay. We're her home now.

I hold the bunch of red roses up to my nose and breathe in. They smell cool and soft. Then I wrap them in a damp newspaper for later.

As I come out of the greenhouse, I see Mrs Zas pull up outside the church in the people carrier she borrowed from Steph. She goes to the back and takes out a wheelchair and then helps an old lady out of the passenger seat.

Rosemary has long limbs and she holds her head straight and although her hair is grey, it's soft and shiny. Mrs Zas has been taking Rev Cootes to visit her at the nursing home, and although Rosemary finds it hard to remember things, she's been doing a little better since the visits. Mrs Zas makes her laugh. And there's one thing Rosemary has never forgotten: the little boy with blond hair, who, thirteen years ago, played with her grandson, Clay. Rosemary said she wanted to be here today.

The service is held outside. Mum said Max would have liked that. *Always running around the village. So much life in that little body.*

The Willingdon Band comes and plays a few pieces as the guests arrive. Mr Ding crashes his cymbals together; they ring out across The Green.

When Rev Cootes has given his talk and when Mum and Dad have said a few words about Max and how he loved swimming and the colour red and going on adventures – and how he loved playing with me, that he couldn't wait to teach me to swim – I hand everyone a red rose.

As they walk past, they place the rose on Max's grave.

Some of them take a moment to bow their heads and to whisper a few words.

And then it's our turn: Mum, Dad and me.

I pull my hand out of theirs and kneel down next to the headstone I've looked at for so many years. I brush my fingers over Max's name, over the dates of his small life. Then I take a photo Dad gave me of Max out of my pocket; I cut around Max's face so that it's a perfect oval. I slot it into the empty glass frame on the tombstone.

I close my eyes and bow my head.

Behind me, the autumn leaves fall over the village.

Dad puts his arm around Mum and she rests her head on his shoulder.

A little further on, Steph and Jake look up at the sky. I know Jake's thinking of Clay, that he wishes he were here, with us.

Further still, Rev Cootes wheels Rosemary out through the churchyard gate and onto The Green. Mrs Zas walks alongside them.

Out on The Green, Mitch and Mr Ding and the Slim Skills group and the people from the village walk in a long, slow line to a big table laid out with tea and coffee and cakes and sandwiches.

And tucked into the hedgerows, perched at the top of the church spire, gripping the branches of the chestnut tree in the middle of The Green, the birds, which have been silent through the whole of July and August, begin to sing again for the first time.

A Word from the Author

When I was seventeen years old, I developed an eating disorder. Within a few months, I'd all but given up food. My periods stopped, my hair thinned, my podgy teenage body became sharp and angular and my days were dictated by working out how few calories I could consume and still stay alive.

There are lots of reasons that led to my anorexia. Some of them were to do with weight: I'd grown up with comments from well-meaning family members about how much better I'd look if I could only shed a few pounds; I was in a girls' school where comparing every aspect of your physical appearance to the most beautiful (or the most fashionably beautiful) girl in the class was part of everyday existence; and like every teenager I was bombarded by unrealistic presentations of the female body in magazines and on TV. But weight loss and body image were only part of it, there were other factors at play, ones that I've only recognised with hindsight.

I had very little control over my life. Few teenagers do. That's why, in adolescence, we work so hard to grab at things that might give us an anchor, even if those things damage us and the people we love. My parents went through a sad and difficult divorce and, like Feather in my novel, I found myself looking after my mum, who was heartbroken. I also had those typical traits associated with people who develop anorexia: I was a perfectionist and a high-achiever, aiming for straight As and a place at Oxford. Making sure my mum was okay and guaranteeing good grades and a place at my dream university felt hopelessly out of my grasp. Counting calories, deciding exactly which bits of food passed my lips, calibrating my eating to ensure a specific outcome on the scales (which I stepped on several times a day), brought enormous comfort. Managing my eating became a hobby and an obsession – even a friend, which, as a lonely teenager, I needed. And of course, as I lost weight, I felt like I was achieving something: every day, I was meeting my goals. I felt successful, a feeling which is hugely addictive, as addictive as eating too much food.

Although I still have a difficult relationship to food, I am back to a healthy weight. I have a lovely husband, a gorgeously bonkers little girl called Tennessee Skye and I get to do the best job in the world: as Tennessee says, *Mummy writes stories*.

I'm one of the lucky ones. Some battle with anorexia their whole lives. Some get so ill that their bodies give up altogether.

When I started my first teaching job in a boarding school and taught, cared for and lived with teenagers, I came to understand the forces that are at play in making young people undertake harmful behaviour. For my teenage self and many of the girls and boys I taught, it was an eating disorder; for others it was smoking, drinking, taking drugs or having damaging sexual relationships. All these behaviours were driven by the same needs: to find a sense of self, to get some kind of grip on our lives.

It was also in my first teaching post that I came across male anorexia. I observed a boy I taught growing thinner and thinner. I remember him mentioning to me, proudly, how he'd spent a whole week surviving on nothing but a box of cereal: he could recite exactly how many calories there were in that 500g box of cornflakes.

We have a long way to go in understanding and supporting boys and men who suffer from anorexia: many people still associate eating disorders with girls and women, and men often find it hard to talk about their eating problems and harder still to ask for help. That is what inspired me to write the character of Clay. In my research I found a wonderful charity, which offers information and support, called Men Get Eating Disorders Too: http://mengetedstoo. co.uk. There's also a great book by Jenny Langley called, *Boys Get Anorexia Too* with an associated website: www. boyanorexia.com.

In 2008, I took a group of girls from my boarding house to work in primary schools along the Lamu Coast in Kenya. I'll always remember the chat I had with the headmaster of one of these schools. He asked me to tell him about the problems that young people face in English schools and I told him about anorexia. He threw his arms up and shook his head: 'In Kenya, if you are thin, it means you are either sick or poor.' He could not see the appeal of being thin: being curvy and carrying some weight was a sign of attractiveness, wealth and success. It taught me about how differently cultures perceive beauty. We could learn a great deal from how Kenyans see and appreciate the female form.

For the last twelve years, I have continued to observe and

be fascinated by the psychology of eating: of how we starve ourselves and also overeat to get some kind of comfort and control. At the same time, through the news and simply by watching the world around me, I've noticed that obesity has become a huge health concern for children, teenagers and adults. Both extremes can have devastating consequences.

In the UK, anorexia nervosa has the highest mortality rate of any psychiatric disorder in adolescence. At the other end of the spectrum, around one in every eleven deaths in the UK is now linked to carrying excess fat. Around half of British adults are overweight, and 17 per cent of men and 21 per cent of women are obese. The National Institute of Health and Clinical Excellence (NICE) guidelines on eating disorders showed that 1.6 million people in the UK were affected by eating disorders in 2004 and 180,000 (11 per cent) of them were men. In 2007, the NHS Information Centre carried out a snapshot survey of people in England over the age of sixteen. It found that an alarming 6.4 per cent of adults had a problem with food, a figure much higher than previously thought. A quarter of this figure was men, suggesting a possible increase in the number of males affected. Recent reports from the Royal College of Practitioners has indicated a 66 per cent rise in male hospital admissions. It's clear that weight issues are a serious concern for the health of the men and women in our country and in the West as a whole.

It's my belief that only when we work to understand the psychological factors behind eating disorders will we be able to help people to lead healthier, happier lives and to develop a positive relationship to food.

In my presentation of both Clay and Jo, I hope to give readers a rich and complex picture of individuals who struggle with their weight, their sense of themselves and their relationship to food – and that although one character refuses to eat and the other can't stop eating, they are not so very different: they have suffered loss and rejection and feel that they have very little grip on their lives.

I also wanted to show how challenging life can be for those who love and care for people with eating disorders, as is the case for Feather.

But more than all this, I want my readers to see beyond Clay and Jo's weight issues to the interesting, wonderful people they are. Through them, I hope to widen our understanding and appreciation of true beauty.

I believe that novels have a special role to play in building compassion: for others and for ourselves. I hope that *Wishbones* will allow us to develop a deeper and richer appreciation for all the glorious differences there are between us as human beings.

Acknowledgements

With each novel I write I become increasingly aware of how many people are involved in getting my stories into readers' hands.

Thank you, Bryony, for believing in *Wishbones* from the very start and for helping me find the best home for it at HQ, HarperCollins. You are a dream agent.

Thank you, Anna, for falling in love with my story: I am so excited to be sharing my YA adventure with you.

Thank you to the whole team at HQ for making *Wishbones* sparkle and for getting it out into the world.

Thank you to my faithful writing buddies: Helen Dahlke, Jane Cooper, Joanna Seldon and Patricia Lee-Lewis.

Thank you to the friends who have encouraged me on my writing journey: Linda Gibson, Pam and John Owles, Laurence and Beryl Hobbs and Richard George.

A big thank you to the lovely Emily Pittick who sat with me over many a hot chocolate, teaching me all about what it means to be a competitive swimmer, in particular the joys and challenges of swimming butterfly.

Thank you to all the wonderful people who have looked

after my beloved Tennessee Skye while I wrote this book: Dionne, Juliet and the most awesome godmother and nanny in the world, Charlie.

Thank you to Mama, my first reader and the most courageous person I know.

Thank you to my faithful, bonkers cats, Vi and Seb, who keep me company during long hours of writing and inspire me to include animals in my stories. Thank you especially to dear Vi, who passed away as I was editing *Wishbones*.

Thank you to my darling Tennessee Skye: every day, you teach me a little more about the world. I love you so much.

Thank you, Hugh, my soul mate and the love of my life, for never, ever, doubting that I can do this. And for putting up with my lack of housework!

And thank you to you, dear readers. Thank you especially to my young readers, for taking the time to read my story when life offers you so many other tempting distractions. I love writing for you and I hope that we'll share many stories.